Thomas H. Cook is the author of fifteen novels, including the Edgar Award-winning *The Chatham School Affair*. *Sacrificial Ground*, *Blood Innocents*, *Early Graves* and *Blood Echoes* (the last two both true-crime works) were all Edgar Award-nominated. His latest novel is *Interrogation*. He lives in New York City and Cape Cod.

'A gifted novelist, intelligent and compassionate'
New York Review of Books

'Displays an impressive narrative simplicity and a therapist's insight – finely crafted psychological crime fare' *Kirkus Reviews*

'Lyrical, poetical, focused with minute precision upon the human experience. There are only a very few writers who can evoke such feelings through the printed word' *Mystery News*

'His strength is his ability to shine a high-watt bulb on the sinister parts of humanity, combined with an acute sense of place and a true feeling for the ugliness and squalor of urban chaos' *People Magazine*

'A writer of poetic gifts, constantly pushing against the limits of crime fiction . . . Unforgettable'
Los Angeles Times

'A climax so astounding and unexpected that you'll be stunned . . . Compulsive' *New Woman*

By Thomas H. Cook

PLACES IN THE DARK

Thomas H. Cook

ORION

An Orion paperback

First published in Great Britain by Victor Gollancz in 2000.
Reprinted by arrangement with Bantam Books, an imprint of
The Bantam Dell Publishing Group, a division of Random House,
Inc., New York, New York 10036, USA. All rights reserved.

This paperback edition published in 2001 by Orion Books Ltd,
Orion House, 5 Upper St Martin's Lane, London WC2H 9EA

A CIP catalogue record for this book
is available from the British Library.

ISBN 0 75284 386 9

Typeset at The Spartan Press Ltd,
Lymington, Hants

Printed and bound in Great Britain by
Clays Ltd, St Ives plc

This book is dedicated to
Irvin and Lucille Harris
Vena and T. L. Gilley
Duard and Violet Harper
Emory and Ruth Harper
Nell and Starling Davis
Mickie and Virgil Cook
Lillian and Julian Ritter
Noma and Leon Townsel
Jetta and Rayford Carson
Salt of the Earth

and to
Brian Furman
Back at you on paper

It is so well known in every village,
how many have either died for love,
or voluntarily made away themselves,
that I need not much labour to prove it;
Death is the common Catastrophe of
such persons.

ROBERT BURTON
The Anatomy of Melancholy

PART ONE
Port Alma, Maine 1937

Chapter One

More than anyone I ever knew, my brother Billy felt the rapid wings of summer, how it darted like a bird through the trees of Maine, skittered along streams and ponds, then soared away, bright and gleaming, leaving us behind, shivering in coats and scarves.

It was on one of those fleeting summer days that he saved Jenny Grover's life. He'd built a wooden raft out of planks discarded by a local sawmill, packed the space between the boards with rags and mud, then asked me to help him carry it to the spot where Fox Creek widened and deepened, its current growing turbulent again just beyond the bend, where it made its headlong rush toward Linder Falls.

'I'm going to make it all the way across,' he declared. He was twelve years old, shirtless, barefoot, dressed only in a pair of cut-off trousers.

'It's going to sink, Billy,' I warned him. 'Believe me, it's going to sink like a stone.'

He laughed. 'If it sinks, we'll swim.'

'We? I'm not going out on that thing.'

'Oh, come on, Cal.'

'No,' I said. 'Look at me.'

Unlike Billy, I was fully dressed, having made no compromise with summer beyond a pair of sandals.

'Okay then,' he said. 'You can go back home.'

'No, I'll wait.'

'Why?'

'Because someone has to pull you out of the water,' I told him. 'That's why I came along. To save your life.'

This was not entirely a joke. Five years older, I had long ago assumed the part of the vigilant, protective brother, certain that throughout our lives I would be there to protect him. I'd already caught him as he tumbled from chairs and staircases, tugged him away from blazing hearths, snatched his fingers from closing doors. Once I'd even managed to drag him off a rearing pony, lower him safely to the ground. My mother had scolded me for that. 'He can't avoid getting hurt, Cal,' she said. 'Next time let him fall.'

It was the sort of statement I'd come to expect from my mother, the great value she put on experience, especially painful experience.

It was not the sort of advice I cared to take, however. Nor, following it, did I in the least intend to let my brother sink into Fox Pond.

'Be careful, Billy,' I cautioned as he stepped onto the raft, plunged his wooden paddle into the water, and pushed out into the current. 'It's white water just around the bend.'

His eyes sparkled. 'You'll be sorry you didn't come with me.'

'No, I won't.'

'You miss all the good stuff, Cal.'

I pointed to the trickle of water already seeping into his raft. 'Like drowning?'

His smile was a light aimed at the world. 'Like *almost* drowning,' he replied. 'See you on the other side, Cal.'

With that, he shoved the handle against the rocky bottom again, this time with all his might, so that the raft shot forward with such force, it left a rippling wake behind it.

I watched as he floated out into the stream, then sprinted for the rickety wooden bridge that spanned it.

Billy had already made it a third of the way across the water by the time I reached the bridge. He was paddling furiously now, trying to reach the opposite bank before his inadequate make-shift raft sank beneath him. At midstream he grinned and waved to me.

'Will it make it?' I called, growing anxious now.

'Sure,' he returned breathlessly, the raft still afloat but riding low in the water.

I bounded off the bridge, then along the edge of the water. Billy was two thirds across by then, grinning, triumphant that the raft was still afloat.

'Land ho,' I yelled.

He laughed for an instant, then stopped, his eyes suddenly concentrated on some point in the distance.

It was at that moment that Jenny Grover swept out from under the bridge, clinging, terror-stricken, to a black rubber tube. She was moving swiftly on currents that had not yet tamed, and which would inevitably propel her across the still-turbulent surface that lay between the bridge and the lethal, churning waters that waited just beyond the bend, water that would, within minutes, carry her over Linder Falls.

The horrible truth hit me instantly. Jenny Grover, five years old, was going to die. It was an irrefutable fact. I might dive into the water, try to intercept her, but she would have long swept past any point I might reach along her path. There was nothing between Jenny and the falls, nothing that might grasp the rubber tube or direct it toward shore.

Nothing, that is, but my brother.

I spun around and saw that he stood in place, the paddle motionless in his hands, the raft sinking beneath him, his gaze fixed on Jenny Grover. Instantly, I knew what he was thinking.

'No!' I shouted. 'Don't!'

He looked at me, sunlight glistening in his wet hair, then turned and dove headlong into the water, a gleaming, graceful, fleeting thing, the white bird of summer.

I felt my heart quake, all my passion surge in a silent, shining prayer, *Live!*

Then I rushed into the stream myself, swimming madly toward Billy even as he swam away from me, his arms shooting in and out of the turbulent water, plowing with all his might toward Jenny Grover.

I had made it to the raft by the time he reached her, saw him grasp the black tube, then, with a fierce backward stroke, pull it toward him.

'Got her,' he called. There was a strange, exultant happiness in his voice.

I swam out to him, grasped the tube, and together we hauled it back to shore.

Once on land, Jenny wept softly, wrapped tightly in my brother's arms.

'You're a hero, Billy,' I said.

He looked at me, blue eyes sparkling.

'A real hero,' I repeated.

My father, however, had a different view of what Billy did, one he made the mistake of declaring that same evening as we came to the end of dinner. I'd just finished telling the whole tale, Billy's raft, his sail out onto Fox Creek, how he'd leaped into the water, pulled Jenny Grover from death's way.

As I finished, Billy glanced at our mother, confirmed that she was unmistakably proud of what he'd done, then looked at our father, no doubt expecting the same admiring response.

Instead, he encountered a solemn face, stern, dark eyes.

'Don't you think that was rather foolhardy, William?' my father asked.

Billy stared at him quizzically.

I sensed trouble on the wing, set down my knife and fork, and waited expectantly.

'You have to think before you act,' my father said. 'That's what the mind is for.' He tapped his forehead to emphasize the point. 'It reins in our impulses. And if you don't pay heed to it, then . . .'

'What are you telling him, Walter?'

It was my mother's voice, firm, determined, a sword flourished in the air between them.

I knew that the old battle was about to erupt again, my father in command of reason's stolid force, my mother the determined general of passion's fiery legions. It had been going on for years, though the end seemed already settled, the spoils divided, I the sturdy coin claimed by my father, Billy my mother's golden treasure.

'What's that, my dear?' my father replied, his tone not so much condescending as already seeking to dampen the fuse he'd unintentionally lit. It was a tone I'd come to expect on such occasions. For although my father could appear impressive, a man of strong opinions who peppered his talk with learned citations, I'd early recognized that he was, in fact, curiously weak. When faced with confrontation, he was always quick to retreat, particularly before the formidable and unbending figure of my mother.

She faced him from the opposite end of our dining table, blue eyes leveled with resolve. 'Do you think Billy should have let Jenny drown? Is that what *you* would have done, Walter?'

'Of course not.'

'But why not? Wouldn't you have controlled any impulse to save her?'

'I'm not twelve years old, Mary,' my father replied. He glanced at me, his usual ally at such moments, but I offered nothing. 'William could have drowned. That's the long and the short of it. He could have died. Would *you* have wanted that?'

True to her nature, my mother chose not to answer a question she recognized as purely rhetorical. 'The real issue is not whether Billy might have drowned,' she replied. 'It's how he should live his life.'

'And how is that?' my father asked, folding his napkin now, placing it tidily on the table beside his plate.

'Certainly not by "controlling his impulses,"' my mother said.

'Mary, I was only making the point that—'

'I know precisely the point you were making.'

'I'm not sure you do.'

'That Billy should live as a coward.'

'That was not my point at all.'

'You can dress it up any way you like, Walter, but it amounts to the same thing.'

My father adjusted his fork, spoon, water glass. He said softly, 'What do you think he should have done?'

'Exactly what he did,' my mother answered.

'Risk his life?'

'Follow his passion.' Her gaze fell proudly on my brother. 'We're not always directed by our minds.'

'Follow his passion,' my father repeated, allowing only the slightest skepticism in his voice. 'Without rules of any kind.' A small, faintly timid smile fluttered onto his lips. 'The voice of the apostate, my dear.'

It was a reference to the fact that my mother had been raised a Catholic but had long ago rejected that faith, substituting the romantic poets for the Holy Father, their wild verse for the harsh injunctions of Mother Church.

'Call it whatever you wish,' my mother snapped.

'Do you really believe, Mary, that passion can guide a life?' my father added, his voice barely above a whisper.

My mother stared at him unflinchingly. 'Yes. Absolutely.'

'So the heart is the only reference one should consult?' my father asked, now assuming a professional manner, as if trying to neutralize the confrontation he'd unwittingly started and now wished only to defuse.

'Yes.'

My father pretended to consider my mother's idea. 'And so, for William, that would mean following his heart regardless of the consequences?'

'Regardless of "thinking" about the consequences,' my mother answered stiffly.

'Passion,' my father mused. 'William should let passion be his guide. It's a noble idea, Mary. No one can argue with that.' Nodding sagely, he offered my mother a conciliatory smile. 'I'm glad you have such ideas, my dear. Romantic ideas.' As he ticked them off, he tried to look as if he actually took them seriously. 'That we should listen to our hearts.'

'What else should we listen to?' my mother countered.

He did not answer her question, but continued with 'That good triumphs over evil.'

'It does when it stands its ground.'

'That love is eternal.'

'Some love is,' my mother said, glancing toward her favorite son.

'That there is but one true love for each of us,' my father concluded.

'Do you doubt that too, Walter?' my mother demanded, now exasperated with the lightness of his tone. 'Do you dismiss that too?'

'Not at all.' Peace was my father's only goal now, truth and candor merely obstacles on the way to it. He got to his feet, a creature in full retreat, placed his hand on Billy's shoulder. 'I'm sure there's just one true love for William.'

I looked at my brother with mock seriousness. 'Just one, Billy,' I said.

He smiled his boyish smile.

I raised a finger and pointed it toward the window, the world of night that lay beyond it. 'She's out there somewhere,' I teased, grinning widely now, no more believing that such a one existed for my brother than I believed in the glittering mermaids the old salts spoke of when they were in their cups.

And yet, as I've since calculated, she had just turned eight years old that summer, a little girl with deep green eyes, already so real, so terribly in the world, that had my finger extended infinitely westward, it might have touched her long, blond hair.

Chapter Two

I often think now of the darkest moment of her life, of how much it shaped her, and in shaping her shaped Billy and me, shaped all that happened after that.

I watch children as they skate heedlessly across a frozen pond, slicing circles in the ice, laughing as they go, never imagining the lethal depths beneath them, nor that buried within themselves there are places in the dark, deep and hidden, from which their fates uncoil. Then suddenly, I think of Dora, and see a little girl running through an unlighted house, stalked by a man with shaggy hair gone white before its time, and a teenager in ragged, bloody jeans. The girl finds the stairs, slips up them as silently as she can, then huddles, terrified, at the top. Below, the man stops. The beam from his flashlight sweeps about the ground floor rooms of the house, then settles at the bottom of the stairs. The teenager stands at his side, watching mutely, the beam now nosing hungrily up the stairs, as if the light itself has caught the scent of a living thing.

The child watches the light inch toward her, squeezes her eyes shut, draws her knees tight against her chest, makes herself as small as possible, a little ball of life.

There she is, the man says.

Footsteps pound up the stairs. A pungent odor sweeps over her. She opens her eyes. The teenager hangs, a ragged scarecrow, above her, staring down, now joined by the man, his voice cold, matter-of-fact, strangely ceremonial.

Turn over.

The child turns obediently onto her stomach, her cheek pressed against the dusty hardwood floor. Skinny fingers close over her mouth. A filthy hand chokes off her whimper.

Lay flat.

With one eye, she watches as the shadow of a knife crawls up the wall.

A hand yanks her blouse up to her shoulders.

The blade descends. A second voice whispers in her ear.

It won't hurt.

Then the blade rakes the pale skin of her back in swift slicing motions, like someone carving hugs and kisses in the soft bark of a tree.

I'm sure Dora relived this moment many times as she made her way over the Rockies and across the Great Plains, taking the same roads I later took, following the last slim lead I had.

She reached the East Coast, lingered for a time, then fled northward, no doubt winding through New England along Route 1. Finally, in late October, the leaves in their autumnal glory, she reached Port Alma, a town fixed to a rocky coast, bordered by a seawall, graced with a long stone jetty and a jeweled island in the bay.

Local legend had it that Port Alma had been named for a sea captain's wife. It was Billy who set the record straight in a little talk he gave two days before his sixteenth birthday, the town historical society gathered in the front room of the old lending library to hear him speak.

'Alma was the captain's lover, not his wife,' Billy explained. 'She was a beautiful young woman who lived in Seville.'

According to Billy, Captain Brennan had sailed up the Guadalquivir River, master of an eighteenth-century merchant ship in search of olive oil and Spanish sherry. The captain had been graciously entertained by the local Spanish aristocracy, invited to their dances, shown their fabled gardens, where flowers hung in perfumed abundance from brightly painted walls. It was during one of those long, scented evenings that Brennan had met Maria Alma Sanchez. Seventeen. Olive-skinned. Raven-haired. They'd walked along the narrow streets of Santa Cruz, kissed at the Torre del Oro, alongside the same river down which Columbus had set sail.

Then the story darkened. The couple was forced to part. Worse things after that. Alma's suicide. Captain Brennan set wandering again. He'd finally settled on a remote beach in Maine, where he'd built a small trading post. He christened it Port Alma. 'It was the perfect place for Captain Brennan,' Billy concluded, relishing the high romance of his tale, glancing at our mother, who watched him approvingly from the front row, 'because every other place served only to remind him that he had sacrificed the one true love of his life.'

That was the last line of Billy's talk. And I remember how Mrs Tolliver dabbed her eyes at the end of it. How strangely Mr Tolliver gazed at her, as if some long suspicion about his wife had been suddenly proved true. I don't know if my brother noticed their reaction, but had he noticed it, I know he would have been pleased.

For all his life Billy loved the idea that people had secrets they held within themselves like gemstones in a velvet pouch, precious, dazzling, rare. Perhaps that was what initially drew him to Dora. Not her beauty, but how grotesquely it had been marred. Not what she let him see, but what she *hid*.

'It was a beautiful talk, Billy,' my mother said as the three of us stood together on the steps of the building, the main street of Port Alma crowded with its usual weekend throng. Her eyes were like soft blue lights. 'Very beautiful.'

'Thank you,' Billy said. He smiled happily. 'Cal's giving a talk next month.'

She turned to me. 'Really? What about, Cal?'

'Civil disobedience,' I answered.

She laughed. 'Against it, I suppose?'

'Adamantly.'

She pressed her hand to my cheek. 'Your father's son,' she said with a bright, indulgent smile. She turned back to Billy. 'Well, congratulations. It was a lovely talk.' With that she strode down the stairs, turned to the left, and grandly sailed down Main Street like a great ship through a tangle of lesser vessels.

'She's so sure of herself,' I said once she was out of earshot. 'So sure that she's right about her view of things.'

With an insight that even then struck me as older than his years, Billy said, 'If she weren't, she wouldn't be able to live. She would die, Cal. She would just curl up and die.'

We went for a walk after that, more or less following our mother's route through a town bustling with activity, people coming in and out of shops, then along a beach strewn with families, children darting in all directions.

The crowd had thinned by the time we reached the jetty. We stopped at its edge, peered out over its huge gray stones.

'It looks like the backbone of a dragon,' Billy said.

I studied the jetty, decided he was right. 'Yes, it does.'

He climbed onto it, then said, 'What do you think it was like between our parents? In the beginning, I mean. Before they got married.'

'I have no idea.'

'They couldn't have known each other very well.'

'Probably not.'

'Maybe that's the way it should be, Cal, when you fall in love.'

'It's the way it has to be. Or you won't.'

He offered me a hand, pulled me up beside him. 'You're just like Dad.'

'In what way?'

'The way you think everything through.'

'What's wrong with that?'

'Nothing, except that in the end, you pick everything apart. Bit by bit. Until there's nothing left.'

'And you're like Mother.' I peered down the length of the jetty, where white water surged and retired around the stones. 'You trust everything.' I glanced up at the sky. All afternoon a storm had been bearing down from the north. Now it hovered overhead, its clouds thick and billowing, like a poisonous gray smoke.

'We'd better be getting back,' I said. 'The rain could hit any second.'

Billy paid me no mind, turned, and strode out toward the end of the jetty, where he stood, facing the bay, his coat flung over his shoulders, hanging from them like a cape.

I lifted my collar against the wind and followed after him.

He turned suddenly as I drew in upon him. The wind tossed his hair.

'She's out there somewhere,' he said, nodding inland.

I held my eyes upon the bay, where a rusty trawler slogged wearily toward the open sea, its wake flowing behind her, white and ragged, like an old woman's hair.

'Who is?'

'The one,' Billy answered.

I looked at him quizzically.

'Don't you remember what you said?' he asked. 'That night, after Jenny Grover? You said that she was "out there somewhere." My one true love.'

'I was joking,' I told him.

'Of course you were,' Billy said. 'But what if you were right, Cal? What if she really is out there?'

I could see that my brother had actually come to believe that there might be such a person, a one love for whom he was destined.

'Well?' he asked.

I knew that during the years I'd been away at college he had been pursued by a host of village girls, earthy, willing, destined to work the canneries or marry those who did. According to my father, he'd shown no interest in returning the attentions of such girls no matter how blatantly they'd expressed them. Now I knew why. Romance had become his sword and shield, made of him a true romantic. Simply put, he could not lust for one he did not love, and had come to believe, with all his heart, that he would love but once.

'If she's out there, I hope you find her,' I said, though with no expectation that he might.

'What about you?'

'Me?'

'Do you ever think that there's this girl out there who's . . .'

'No,' I said firmly. Which was true enough. Such vaporous notions had never had any power over me. As for the last few years, I'd concentrated exclusively on my studies at Columbia Law, torts and the rules of civil litigation, broken contracts, and unsupported claims.

'Mother believes that for every person there is . . .'

'I'm sure she does,' I said, abruptly weary of such talk. 'She's probably as sure of that as she is about everything else.'

Billy grew quite serious. 'The thing is, I believe too, Cal.'

'Really?'

'Yes.'

I could see no harm in going along with my brother's romantic suppositions. 'Well, perhaps you're both right.'

But I didn't in the least believe that either of them was right. In fact, the possibility that my brother's one true love might actually appear never occurred to me at all. Nor that within eight months of her arrival in Port Alma, she would vanish no less mysteriously, leave blood-spattered roses in her wake, and in me the merciless resolve to track her down.

Chapter Three

Luther Cobb was the first person I talked to on the day I began my search for Dora. Cobb had managed the bus station in Port Alma for thirty years, seen scores of sinister figures arrive, linger, then depart. And yet he looked at me warily as I approached him, as if I were a stranger. It was a wariness I'd gotten used to by then. I knew that in the time since Billy's death I'd taken on a thin, starved look, that I cast, in every light, the shadow of a predator.

My brother had been dead for thirty-seven days before I began to look for Dora. Terrible days during which I'd felt the worms wriggling within me as surely as they wriggled within him, felt a ruthless and insatiable devouring. I'd slept only fitfully, ate only enough to keep my body going, continually replayed the story in my mind.

And so, on the thirty-seventh day after Billy's death I decided that there had to be an end to it, that I couldn't let her escape. The order had seemed to come from the crisp cold air around me, *Find her.*

Luther Cobb was my first stop on the road to Dora March.

''Morning, Cal,' he said as I stepped up to his counter.

Without preamble, I told him what I wanted, whom I

was looking for. 'Dora March,' I said, and in that instant saw her standing there in Port Alma's dusty bus station, a spectral figure, clothed in shadow, her face without expression, dead green eyes.

'Dora March.' Luther peered at me intently. 'What a strange one she turned out to be.'

'What do you remember about her?' I asked. 'The day she came to town, I mean.'

'Came at night. Got off alone. 'Round midnight, as I recall. Can't tell you much more. Just that nobody met her.'

Luther had a smooth face, round as a coin, with sunken, curiously stricken eyes. His son Larry had drowned in 1911, his boat sunk and never recovered from what, by all accounts, had been a tranquil sea. The mystery of that lost boy hung like a veil over Luther's features. I had no doubt that he'd spent the long years since his son's death in a fruitless conjuring of possibilities: murder, suicide, a serpent rising from the placid depths. Studying him that morning, I knew that if Dora got away, I'd be locked in the same dark prison all my days.

'That time of night, you'd expect someone to meet a woman alone,' Luther said. 'Nobody did though.'

A rider stepped up to the counter, middle-aged, a ragged hat pulled low across his brow. He asked for a ticket to Rockport.

'Be right with you, Cal,' Luther told me, then went about the business of selling the man a ticket.

I stepped aside and waited.

A loudspeaker called the passengers to board the Portland bus. People began getting up, gathering their bundles. Young and old, they heaved duffel bags or struggled with suitcases, trunks, battered cardboard boxes wrapped with twine. Only in the narrowest sense, it seemed to me, could they know where they were going.

'She came up to the window,' Luther said once he'd given the man his ticket and his change. 'Wanted to know where the nearest hotel was. "Out the front," I told her, like I always tell anybody that asks that question. "Then turn left."'

I watched as she drifted past the old red Coca-Cola machine, then beneath the station clock. The sound of her footsteps beat softly in my mind.

'Didn't say another word,' Luther added. 'Just headed for the door.'

A breeze rushed forward across the station's speckled linoleum floor, swept over her plain black shoes, then curled up the opposite wall to finger the tattered pages of an old drugstore calendar.

'Thick fog that night.' Luther shook his head. 'Doubt she could have seen the lights at the hotel. But she headed for it anyway.'

I saw her step resolutely into the fog, saw her as Luther had that first evening in Port Alma, a woman briefly glimpsed, then instantly enshrouded.

'Never saw her again,' Luther added.

Each time I closed my eyes, I saw her.

'Didn't make a lasting impression.'

For a moment she stood motionless at the curb. Then, without warning, she spun around to face me, her eyes flaring, pronouncing their grim warning, *Go back*.

It was all I could do not to answer her aloud, *I can't*.

And so I followed Dora's route down Main Street to the

Port Alma Hotel. A light snow had begun to fall. It reminded me of something my father had once said, that if life worked like the weather, we'd get some warning of the storm ahead. True enough, perhaps, but at the same time it struck me that my brother had wanted no such predictability. Billy had always preferred, no matter what the cost, a life of wonder or surprise. 'I'd rather each day hit me like a stone,' he'd once said. At that moment, I'd draped my arm over his shoulders, hugged him close, muttering 'William the Lion-Hearted,' and with those words felt the one sure thing I knew in life: that even if I lived alone forever, wifeless, childless, there would always be at least one person I truly loved.

The snow had just begun to gather on my coat by the time I reached the Port Alma Hotel. Back in what the old men called 'whaling times,' the building had served as the county courthouse. The stairs that led to its second floor were wide, with hand-carved mahogany banisters that Preston Forbes, the current owner, polished every day. It was the only part of the hotel that offered an aura of elegance. The rest of the building had been left to languish, its carpets frayed at the edges, its velvet curtains faded. There was a dustiness in the air. It gave the place a dispirited and exhausted look, like a man who'd been passed over again and again, abandoned at altars and in moonlit gardens, the one he wanted rushing forever into someone else's arms.

But for all its forlorn appearance, the Port Alma was the only hotel we had. On the night of her arrival, Dora had had no choice but to come here.

According to Preston Forbes, the front door was locked when she arrived. Most of the people who stayed at the hotel were full-time residents rather than transients. That was why Preston had been so surprised to see her that night, a woman alone, arriving so late, lugging a battered leather suitcase.

'She was just standing there with her suitcase in her hand,' he told me. 'Nothing I hadn't seen before, of course. A woman with a suitcase.'

He watched with undisguised curiosity as I took the notebook from the pocket of my overcoat, flipped open the cover, and began to write. 'So I guess you're looking into this yourself, then, Cal?'

I nodded silently, a man of few words now.

Preston wore a faded brown suit, shiny in the pants, the jacket speckled with curls of cigarette ash. His eyes were small and slightly popped, his nose sharp and pointed, with practically no chin, a fact that seemed to take small bits of whatever it gazed upon.

'I heard you resigned from the district attorney's office, Cal. Don't blame you at all. For going after her, I mean. A stranger wouldn't care as much.'

I couldn't imagine what a stranger might feel, staring down at my brother in his bloody ruin. What stranger would know of his goodness, his courage, the fierce hope that had flooded his final hours, or of how fully, in his last breath, he'd pledged himself to her?

'Is it pretty clear she did it, Cal?' Preston asked.

My mind presented the evidence Sheriff T. R. Pritchart had been able to accumulate: Dora's notations in the *Sentinel*'s ledger books, providing by their fraudulent entries the sole motive he could find. He'd learned of the angry words that had come from Dora's cottage near the bay, seen the bloody kitchen knife on the floor beside my brother's corpse, the gold ring and red roses, also splattered with his blood. As for Dora, she'd been seen sitting rigidly at the rear of a departing bus that same afternoon, her brown suitcase in the rack above, her green eyes shining in the shadows.

'T. R. thinks so,' I said.

Preston shrugged. 'Well, I wish I could help you, Cal. But the fact is, I just didn't have much to do with her. Just checked her in that night. That's about it.'

He'd heard the buzzer used to signal him on those rare occasions when someone arrived after midnight, he told me. His first thought was that the woman had come to visit one of the old people who lived at the hotel, Mrs Kenny or Mr Washburn. 'I figured maybe she was somebody's long-lost relative.' He fished around for the right words to describe her. 'She had a look. Not exactly spooky. But, well, like nothing good had ever happened to her.' He grabbed a shoe box from beneath the counter and began to flip through the cards he'd stuffed inside. 'She would have come about when?'

'Around the middle of November,' I said.

He worked the cards, then plucked one from the rest. 'Here it is. I remember now. I gave her Room Seventeen.' He handed the card to me. 'Probably not much help, Cal, but it's all I can tell you.'

She'd signed the register but left the rest of the card blank. Her signature was quite small and oddly fractured, the name broken into fragments, like something smashed with a hammer, a script so different from any other I'd ever seen that when Henry Mason had looked up, shocked and amazed, asked his question, *Could it be Dora?*, my mind had instantly given an answer I could not bring myself to say, *Yes*.

'I offered to take her bag,' Preston said, 'but she didn't want that. Looked real skittish. Like she thought I might do something to her.'

'Do what?'

'Maybe touch her in the wrong way, you know. Skittish like that.'

I wondered if that thought had actually occurred to Preston. His wife, Mabel, had been dying for weeks by then, and terrible odors were said to come from the room where she lay. Maybe the sight of a young woman, fresh, beautiful, perhaps even vulnerable, had summoned something from its dank cave, Dora once again the object of a grim, relentless need.

'Anyway, I kept my distance after that.' Preston added. 'Didn't say another word. Just gave her the key. She went up to Room Seventeen, and that was that.'

I glanced toward the stairs. A woman was making her way up them. She was dressed in a dark blue coat, drab and inelegant. The hotel's red plastic key holder dangled from her left hand.

I turned back to Preston. 'Did Dora come down again that evening?'

'Not that I noticed,' Preston replied. 'But Claire Pendergast might be able to help you. She was making up the rooms back then. And she's nosy. It's one of the reasons I let her go. Couldn't keep her mouth shut about the guests, you know. She works at the shoe factory now.' He hit the plunger of a small chromed bell and Sammy Hokenberry stepped up. He was wearing a navy blue jacket, military style, with frayed gold epaulets. It was at least a size too big for him, so that Sammy looked like a battlefield scavenger, the jacket something he'd stripped off the corpse of a braver man.

Preston handed him a package wrapped in plain brown paper. 'Take this to Mr Stimson.'

Sammy took the package and sailed across the lobby to where Mr Stimson sat playing checkers with himself, twisting the board around with each new move.

'And nobody came to visit her that night?' I asked Preston.

He shook his head. 'Nobody could have gotten in without me knowing it.'

'How about later? Did anyone ever come around asking for her?'

'Just Ruth Potter. With that note she left. About the job she was offering. Someone to take care of Ed Dillard. You know about that, I guess.'

I nodded, saw Dora's fingers open the note, imagined what Ruth had written inside: *Elderly gentleman needs housekeeper. 210 Maple Lane.*

'Yes,' I said.

'Don't know anything else about her,' Preston said.

'Did she get any mail while she was here?'

'Never noticed any. She just came and went, you know.' He shrugged. 'I wish I had more to offer you, Cal.'

I thanked him and walked out of the hotel, swung to the right and made my way to the bay. The sidewalk was slippery with snow, people grabbing anything they could find to steady themselves, the old ones locked in a dreadful fear of falling, children laughing heedlessly at the same icy peril. A cold front was sweeping down from Canada, bringing with it a blinding wall of white. Everything seemed to be waiting for it. The bay lay flat, like someone under fire. The seabirds hunkered down in their stone aeries. At the far end of the pier an old gull preened itself silently, raking its long beak across raised wings, while just below my feet cold water swirled at the wooden pylons with little gulping sounds, desperate and gasping, like a drowning child.

I thought of all the times Billy and I had raced along this pier, then saw him lying faceup on the floor, the roses he'd brought her scattered all around him, their petals sticky with his blood. A wave of loathing swept over me, deep and pure, carried on her name, the way it had fallen, soft and needful, from my brother's lips, *Dora*.

If the love he'd dreamed of came to me now, I thought, it would hit like water on a granite slab.

The great timbers of the north woods rose all around me as I drove along Bluefish Road. Several miles outside town, I passed the Hooverville that had sprung up near the rail lines and now spread almost to the road. It was a shantytown of clapboard structures, unsteady lean-tos plugged with cardboard and newspaper, roofs slapped together using scraps of rusty tin and jagged strips of discarded asphalt shingles. A thick smoke hung over it, dense and acrid, as if blown in from some vast pit that smoldered eternally at the heart of things. Lean, hungry men shambled beneath the smoke or gathered beside large metal drums, feeding slats into a crackling fire. They had the baffled look of the dispossessed, like people after a storm, shocked that such destruction could have swept down upon them so abruptly, taken them unawares, left them with nothing.

I imagined Dora crouched among them, passing as a man, with soot on her face and dust in her hair, careful to keep herself apart, give no sense of her true identity, a figure fixed forever in a web of grim deceit.

The shoe factory sat on a muddy lot scraped out of the surrounding hillside. A rutted gravel road curved into a parking lot where a few cars huddled together, rusty and dilapidated, like old mules in a broken-down corral. I recognized Claire Pendergast's Ford from two years before, when I'd prosecuted her on a bad-check charge. She'd made restitution and apologized to all concerned, but I'd always expected her to do it again. Claire was like a lot of the people who'd recently drifted down to Port Alma from the hills, not so much malicious as simply unable to think things through.

She didn't seem apprehensive when I spotted her on the factory floor and motioned her over to me. She asked a fellow worker to take her place stamping shoe soles out of wide red sheets of rubber, then led me to the room where the workers took their breaks. It had whitewashed cinder-block walls and a cold cement floor. A few tables with spindly legs and wooden tops carved with initials were scattered here and there. In one corner, a battered tin coffeepot rested on a black potbellied stove, a broken wicker basket on an unpainted stool beside it. A hand-lettered sign had been taped to the wall above the basket: *We trust you. Coffee 5 Cents.* No pictures adorned the walls except for a photograph of the factory hung in a plastic frame, its original workers, grinning young men in flannel pants and checkered shirts, grinning girls in floral dresses. The date said October 17, 1922.

'The Polasky sisters are still working here.' Claire pointed to two of the girls in the photograph, both with bobbed hair, smiling brightly at the camera, relieved to be employed. 'Can you imagine that? Stuck in this crummy place for fifteen years.'

'I'm trying to find Dora March,' I said.

She dropped a nickel into the wicker basket and poured a cup of coffee. Black. 'I guess Mr Forbes mentioned me.' She took the coffee and led me to a table in the corner. 'So, what'd he have to say?'

'That you might remember Dora better than he did.'

She sipped her coffee. Steam rose from it and fogged the bottom third of her glasses. 'That's possible,' she said. She yanked a pack of cigarettes from her blouse, thumped one out, seized it with her lips, then offered the pack to me.

I shook my head.

'You don't say much, do you?' Claire asked. 'Tall, silent type, I guess.' She took a long draw and eased back in her chair. 'Well, that's probably better. The ones that talk don't end up saying much.'

She was probably in her early forties but looked older. Her hair was brown with curling wisps of gray, her skin as parched and dry as the tobacco in her cigarette. Bony shoulders poked from her dress like sticks in a pillowcase.

'When I went into her room, I noticed it right away,' she began. 'At first I thought Preston must have given me the wrong room number, that no one had been in this one. Then I noticed that the chair was pulled up to the window. I always put the chair at the other side of the room. So I knew that whoever had stayed in the room that night had brought it over to the window.' She brushed a wrinkle from her dress, leaving two equally unsightly ones untouched. 'That was the only thing she did, far as I could tell. Just move that one chair. Didn't use the bed at all. The bedspread was just like I'd left it the day before. Tucked under the way I tuck it. So I knew the bed hadn't been slept in and made up by whoever took the room. It just plain hadn't been slept it. Pretty strange, don't you think?'

'Did you see anything in the room?' I asked. 'Mail. A newspaper.'

Claire used her little finger to scrape a speck of tobacco from the corner of her mouth. 'It's been over a year, Mr Chase. Even if I'd seen something like that, I would have forgotten it by now.'

'Anything at all.'

She worked her mind a few seconds. I pictured it as a stamping machine, unoiled and poorly maintained, the cogs grinding slowly, producing very little.

'Fact is,' she said finally, shaking her head. 'Fact is, in that job, if you don't find something disgusting in a room, you don't much notice what you find.'

'Did you ever talk to her?'

'Twice, I think it was,' Claire answered. She took a hard drag on the cigarette. A patchy burst of smoke once more exploded from her lips. I could tell her mind had caught the groove, was now spinning more smoothly. 'She come down the stairs and over to the desk. She says, "Should I pay now?" You know, like a person who'd never stayed in a hotel before, didn't know how the bill was paid, or when. I told her there was two ways to do it. Weekly or daily. A little was knocked off on the weekly, but you had to pay it in advance. I think she took the weekly, but I can't be sure.'

'And the second time?'

'The second time was a day or two later,' Claire

replied. 'Preston wanted me to get some fresh eggs over at Madison's. On the way, I passed the park and there she was, sitting on a bench. She had glasses on, reading the paper. She took them off when she saw me coming over to her.'

I imagined Dora facing Main Street, the granite Revoluntionary War Monument to her left, the old band shell to her right, her coat wrapped tightly around her. A copy of the *Sentinel* rested in her lap, two hands placed on top, her fingers delicately wrapped around a pair of gold-rimmed glasses.

It struck me that had my brother glimpsed Dora in such a pose, he would have felt an instant allure. Even seen briefly, Dora would have made an impression on him.

'She sort of drew back when I came toward her,' Claire said. 'Like a cat that don't know you. So I just says, "Looks like it's going to be a pretty day." She didn't look like she knew how to answer me. She says, "I'm looking for work." Just like that. Real fast.'

Claire had immediately supposed that Dora was the sort of woman who'd always been supported. And yet, she did not appear so much sheltered as deserted, so that Claire had suddenly entertained the idea that Dora had been recently abandoned, perhaps widowed. In any event, abruptly left to fend for herself.

'So I told her, well, you could just go around town introducing yourself. But I could see that idea didn't appeal to her. So I told her she should just go over to the *Sentinel* and put in a notice. That was the last thing I said to her.'

'The times you talked to her, did she ever mention anybody else? A friend or acquaintance?'

Claire shook her head. 'Not that I recall. She wasn't much of a talker.' She smiled. 'Like you.' She plucked the cigarette from her lips, drained the last of the coffee. 'I wish she'd just kept on going.' She crushed the cigarette in the bottom of the cup. 'Of course, I wish that for everybody that ever come to this town. God knows Port Alma's fit for nothing.'

She gazed into the cup a few seconds, rolling it between her rough factory-worker's hands. Then she looked up, stared at me quite blatantly. 'You got a nice face,' she said.

I glimpsed my ravaged features in the window glass, how well they mirrored my wolfish core.

'Nice eyes too.'

The better to see you with, I thought.

Chapter Four

On the drive back into town, I thought of my brother, of how different we'd always been, two answers to the same riddle, as my father had once said, I the heir to all my father's ways, Billy the golden scion of our mother.

And so it hadn't in the least surprised me when it was decided that I would be sent to Columbia Law, while Billy would inherit the *Sentinel*.

'Your mother believes that William is best suited to run the paper,' my father told me the night I was informed of their decision. 'As you know, he's always enjoyed being around the office. The printing machines. And your mother tells me that recently he's taken to composing little essays.'

We were in my father's study, a room hung with faded engravings of classic scenes, Cincinnatus behind the plow and Cicero in the Senate. It was the room in which we'd read the ancients together while Billy tumbled playfully in the snow beyond the window or went flying past with a baseball bat or a fishing pole. My father sat in a highback leather chair, his gray hair shimmering in the firelight, my mother a few feet away, tucked into a floral window seat, a book in her lap.

'As for your own future, Cal,' he added, 'I've often thought that you might be quite well suited for the law.'

'The law?' I asked.

'Everything is cut-and-dried in a legal practice,' he explained. 'There's no need for . . .' He searched for the word. 'Sentiment.'

'Unless there's something else, Cal,' my mother said abruptly, her eyes upon me searchingly. 'Some other direction you'd prefer. Or something you have a particular feeling for.' She waited for me to point out such a direction, then suggested it herself when I remained silent. 'Your drawing, for example.'

She meant the sketches I'd made over the years, mostly local scenes, stone walls, wooden fences.

'There are schools where you could study drawing,' she added.

I'd never considered such a thing, but its disadvantage was obvious. 'I couldn't make a living drawing.'

'Exactly,' my father said. He seemed impatient that such a course had even been broached. 'I was thinking of Columbia Law. It's a fine school. What would you think of studying there?'

'Fine,' I said. 'I need a profession. The law is a good profession.'

'Yes, it is,' my father agreed. 'It requires a fine mind. And you certainly have a fine mind, Cal.' He glanced toward my mother. 'And Billy has the right requirement for running a newspaper,' he added.

'What requirement is that?' I asked.

My mother's answer came softly. 'A heart,' she said.

The kind of heart Billy had already demonstrated, fierce and impulsive, disinclined to calculate the odds before diving into turbulent water, swimming out to a drowning child.

'So we're all in agreement, then?' my father asked,

getting to his feet now, visibly relieved that so much had been decided without argument.

'Yes,' I said. 'All in agreement.'

I left for Columbia Law the following year, leaving Billy behind in Port Alma, writing to him often but seeing him rarely, save for the all-too-brief summers when I returned to Maine.

Over the next few years, while I continued my studies in New York, his interest in the *Sentinel* steadily deepened. He went there almost every day after school, staying as long as my father would let him, writing imaginary columns, covering imaginary stories. It didn't surprise me that after graduating from high school he chose not to go to college, but went to work at the paper instead.

Several years later, my father retired, and Billy took over. By then he'd become 'William' to everyone but me, no longer a boy, but a man poised to take his place as a pillar of the community.

We celebrated his ascension with a dinner in Royston. It was the last time we ate together as a family. My mother moved into a cottage on Fox Creek a month later, leaving my father alone in the big house outside of town. She'd planned the move for a long time, Billy told me later. She'd waited only for her sons to grow up, to establish lives of their own.

We'd done just that by the time she left our father. Billy was fully in charge of the *Sentinel* by then. He'd moved into a small house not far from the newspaper's office, filled it with his usual array of books, magazines, and the bric-a-brac he'd gathered over the years. I got a job in the district attorney's office, routinely prosecuting whatever cases Hap Ferguson tossed onto my desk, and finally took a somewhat larger house only a few blocks down the same street as my brother.

And so our lives went forward. When the water mill burned down, we walked its charred remains together, Billy in order to describe the destruction, I to make sure it had happened by accident rather than design. Still later, when the county's one remaining covered bridge collapsed, we surveyed the ruins side by side. I made sure no harm had been intended, while Billy searched for some small symbol of the vanished humanity the old bridge had served, the wagons and buggies that had rattled through its dark tunnel, as he later wrote, 'carrying wood chips, coffins, brides.'

Over the years, I read scores of his articles and news stories, never in the least imagining that his fate might be coiled invisibly within the folds of a few plain lines: *Single woman seeks employment. Any offer will be considered. Inquiries should be forwarded to the Port Alma Hotel. Attention: Dora March.*

She'd been in Port Alma over a month before I saw her. Then, on one of those December days when chill winds whip cruelly around corners and snap at cloth awnings, I spotted her coming out of Madison's General Store. She was wearing the long cloth coat I would see so often in the coming months, and carried a bag of groceries and supplies. She didn't so much as glance in the window of Ollie's Barber Shop as she swept by.

'That's Ed Dillard's new girl,' Ollie said when he saw that she'd caught my eye. 'Took over from Ruth Potter. Does whatever needs doing around the house.' His eyes followed Dora as she strode beneath the fluttering awning of Bolton's Drug Store, head bent against the wind. 'She's a pretty thing, that's for sure. Can't blame Ed for hiring her.'

Ed Dillard was a retired businessman who'd once been the town's mayor. He'd been a widower for as long as anyone could remember, and there'd never been any children, a fact that had generated a certain level of speculation as to whom his considerable fortune would go to when he died. He'd suffered a heart attack some six years before, and since then a series of local women, mostly widows from surrounding farms, had come and gone from the great house he'd built on Ocean Street three decades earlier. Some of the women had been fired, but most had quit, the common complaint being Ed's irascible and demanding nature, along with the sheer amount of work necessary to see after such a large house, clean its many rooms, dust the scores of porcelain figurines Ed had collected over the years.

'You could never satisfy him, or even get all the work done,' Ruth Potter told me when I came by her house, the Canadian storm bearing down upon us with its weight of snow, so that I'd had to stomp my shoes outside the door. 'That's why I was so glad to see Dora show up that day. I didn't know a thing about her, of course. Didn't much care either. She was willing to take the job. That was enough for me.'

We were in the front parlor of Ruth's house when she spoke of these things, a room crowded with overstuffed chairs and a lace-covered table cluttered with framed pictures of her son, Toby, a lanky, somewhat lazy boy who'd been blown to bits in the Great War. I remembered him as dull and slow-witted, with little to recommend him but a toothy grin. Glancing at the little mausoleum Ruth had created to his memory, it struck me how ordinary and inconsequential a person might be and yet inspire a deep and deathless love, the joy of Barabas's mother that Christ would die instead.

'Mr Chase?'

I tried to focus once again on the reason I'd come. 'Yes, go on.'

'Well, I'd seen that little notice she put in the paper,' Ruth continued. She was wearing a brown dress with large lemon-colored flowers and a tattered wool sweater, frayed at the cuffs. A musty smell came from her, sweet and pungent, like overripe fruit. Outside, I could hear her husband chopping firewood, grunting slightly with each blow.

'So you contacted Dora?' I asked.

'Left a note at the hotel, saying that I'd seen her notice in the paper and might have employment for her.' She glanced toward the window. 'Say it's gonna be a bad one. The storm. Hope we don't get snowed in too long.'

'Did you mention what the employment was?'

'No, I didn't say anything about it. I was afraid that if she knew it had to do with Old Man Dillard, she might not give it a chance. He had a reputation, you know. For being hard to deal with.'

'What did you tell her in your note?'

'I just wrote my name and the address. I figured if she was interested, she'd come by.'

Which she'd done later that same afternoon.

'I was working upstairs when I seen her come up the walk,' Ruth told me. 'Mr Dillard was in a fury over something. I kept trying to calm him down. Good heavens, I remember thinking, if he keeps carrying on like this, nobody'll ever take this job.' She drew a weary breath. 'Then I looked out and this young woman was coming up the walkway. Selling something, I figured. Bibles. Something like that. It didn't strike me that she was the one who'd put the notice in the paper.'

'Why not?'

Ruth thought for a moment before she answered. 'Because she didn't look like the type who'd be looking for that kind of work. Young, I mean. And pretty. Didn't look the type who'd be interested in seeing after a crotchety old man.'

'What else do you remember about her?'

'Mostly that she was real ill at ease. Like she'd never been invited into a house, didn't know how to act in one.' She glanced toward the window again, to where Mr Potter could be seen slumped on a heap of wood, breathing heavily, snow swirling around him like a horde of white-winged moths. 'He's going to kill himself, chopping that stuff.' She continued to watch her husband for a moment, then returned her attention to me. 'Tense, like I said. Figured she was that way because she really needed a job, and that was making her jumpy.'

There'd been a kind of desperation in Dora's eyes, Ruth said, like someone who'd reached the end of her rope, exhausted the last of her resources.

'But even if she really needed work, I made it plain that this was no picnic. I was real honest. Told her all there was to it. All she'd have on her shoulders. Sweeping. Cleaning. Doing dishes. Laundry.'

Dora hadn't flinched at the amount of work.

'That's when I got to the hard part,' Ruth said. 'Tending to Mr Dillard. The way he was. That he could get real snippy when things didn't go his way. Stubborn, too, always wanting to do things for himself, even when he couldn't do them. Told her all that, but she didn't seem to mind that she might get treated a little rough.'

Suddenly, I felt that I was in the dark again, spying on the yellow light that seeped from Dora's window, the red robe dropping from her shoulders, revealing all the evidence I would ever need of how 'rough' she had been treated.

'Maybe she was used to it,' I said.

'Being treated bad, you mean?' Ruth asked. 'Could be.' She shrugged. 'But I told her that the worst thing was the reading. How Mr Dillard liked being read to. Hour after hour. Enough to drive you crazy. She said that wouldn't bother her. So I said, "Well, okay, then. The job is yours." She came to the house the very next day.'

An impulse overtook me. 'Any way I could see it?' I asked. 'Her room.'

Ruth was clearly surprised by the question. 'What for? Dora ain't been in that room since Ed Dillard died.'

'I'd just like to take a look at it.'

'We could get stuck in all this snow.'

'We won't,' I assured her.

'Well, okay, then.' She pulled herself to her feet, wincing slightly. 'I still got a key to the place. But we'll have to take your car. Ours ain't running.'

A few minutes later we arrived at Ed Dillard's rambling house, walked up the snow-covered walkway and into the front room. Everything was silent, motionless, the furniture covered with sheets.

'Can't find a living relative, that's what the lawyers say,' Ruth told me as she peered into the ghostly parlor.

'That's why everything just sets here. 'Cause they can't find nobody to give it to.'

The white sheets sent a shiver through me. Billy had lain under one with the same stillness, a lifeless arm dangling toward the floor until I'd finally placed it on his chest, then drawn the sheet back over him again.

'I guess Dora covered everything up,' Ruth said. Then she led me up the stairs to the room Dora had occupied during the few weeks she'd worked for Mr Dillard.

It was plain but tidy, its single window overlooking the broad front lawn of the house, a chair drawn up beside it. Lace curtains hung over the window, and there was a beige paper shade with a string pull that jumped slightly, like the pendulum of an edgy, disordered clock, each time I took a step.

While Ruth watched, I looked in the closet where Dora had hung her dresses, then went through the drawers of the bureau beside the bed that had been hers. I even searched behind it for some clue to where she might have gone. Finally, I sat down in the chair by the window.

'She didn't seem to care what the room looked like,' Ruth said. 'I don't think it mattered to her. The accommodations, I mean. Probably glad to get a room of her own. She'd been living at the hotel, you know.'

She'd come early the very next morning, Ruth told me.

I imagined it as a typical autumn day in Port Alma, brilliantly clear and windy, with gusts sweeping waves of crimson leaves across the lawn.

'She come on foot,' Ruth said. 'Nobody brought her. She was toting a suitcase. All she had, I guess.'

I parted the curtains and peered at the grounds below.

'I was getting this room ready when she came back to take the job,' Ruth added. 'Mr Dillard was sleeping in his wheelchair. He always took a nap in the afternoon.'

The snow now obscured the lawn, but as I continued to peer out the window, the seasons reversed themselves. Fall returned, blustery and windswept.

'I just looked out that window, and there she was.'

I imagined a woman striding resolutely toward the house.

'That's when Mr Dillard woke up all of a sudden.'

Wearing a long cloth coat, her emerald eyes fixed straight ahead.

'And started squirming around, all upset and panicky.'

Dora sailing toward me.

'Like he did when the pain hit him.'

On a river of red leaves.

Chapter Five

I looked in on my mother the next morning, something my brother had done each day on his way to his desk at the *Sentinel*. His loyalty to her had been heartfelt, an ardent affection she had in every way returned. I was a poor substitute for Billy, of course, merely the surviving son, as she no doubt regarded me, tied to obligations she assumed I did not feel.

She no longer lived in her beloved cottage by Fox Creek. The stroke had made that impossible. And so Billy and I had moved her into a house not far from Main Street. We'd done most of the work, getting the house ready for her ourselves, enlarging rooms and putting in windows so that she would get the light that brightened both the space around her and her spirits. We'd hung bird feeders outside each window as well, hoping to occupy her eyes, the one part of her body, other than her mind, that the stroke had not damaged.

Her daily needs were taken care of by Emma Fields, an old woman who'd recently lost her husband, and with him, her rented home and livelihood. Emma was a short, round woman with white hair and watery blue eyes.

'Snow's gone, looks like,' she said when she opened the door.

'Not for long,' I told her. 'Another storm's coming in.'

Emma looked at me, alarmed. 'Soon? I need to get to Madison's.'

'You have a couple of hours,' I assured her. 'But you can go now if you want. I'll look after Mother.'

'Guess I better do that,' Emma said. She snatched her coat and scarf. 'I'll try and be quick about it.'

My mother lay in her bed, propped up against the headboard, her eyes bright, fully aware, her speech remarkably clear despite the fact that the left side of her face was drawn down sharply. It was a miracle, Doc Bradshaw had told Billy and me, that she could talk at all.

If so, it was the only miracle. For in every other way, she was dreadfully weakened. Her hands trembled uncontrollably, making it impossible for her to hold a cup or a book, and she could not walk at all.

But for all her physical suffering. I knew that her inner anguish was now deeper still, knew too well that she lived within a cloud of grief, continually remembering Billy at every stage of life, the gleaming boy, the sterling man. For that grief, there was no relief. Long ago, she had abandoned the consolations of her Catholic faith with the same commanding resolve and self-confidence with which she'd replaced it with ideas of social improvement, deism, and the high romance she had bequeathed to her now-dead son.

I'd known Billy was her favorite long before he was given the *Sentinel*. It had been clear from the time he was a little boy. She loved his energy and his unruliness. The great mess in which he kept his room filled her heart with hope. During the long New England winters, when my father and I hunkered in his study, gravely discussing the works of ancient Greece and Rome, Billy and my mother would curl beside the fire, chatting quietly or playing board games, while outside, Maine slowly sank beneath its yearly pall of snow.

She believed that Billy illuminated everything, and in doing that, illuminated her, offered living proof of the ideas she had in her own youth so fiercely embraced and never since abandoned. Passion. Freedom. Love. The fact that he took no academic prizes, graduated without honors, chose not to go to college, a circumstance that deeply aggrieved my father, did not in the least disturb her. 'I'm sure Billy's a disappointment to you, Mrs Chase,' I once heard a teacher say to my mother. I'd never forgotten the force of her swift reply: 'I would be disappointed in my son,' she answered, 'only if he did not know his heart.'

Now she had only me.

'How are you?' I asked as I drew my chair up to her bed.

She dipped her head, then glanced toward the window, bright sunlight on the glistening untouched snow. Since Billy's death, she'd sunk into a grave silence, rarely initiating conversation, replying to questions in short, clipped sentences, hardly ever asking any of her own. It was as if the inner light that had glowed from her had been rudely snuffed out, leaving her in shadows.

'The weather's cleared up a little,' I said.

Her eyes followed a flock of Canada geese as they glided across her glimpse of sky, smooth and sure, like skaters on an ice-blue pond.

'Dad seems to be doing all right,' I told her.

In fact, of course, he was not doing well at all, drink his only consolation. The few times I'd suggested that he visit my mother, he'd waved his hand in abrupt refusal, adding only, 'She's got trouble enough without seeing me.'

'He's eating well,' I added.

She watched me silently for a moment, then, 'And you, Cal?'

'I'm getting along,' I assured her.

Her head trembled as she drew her attention to the nightstand beside her bed, the gold ring that lay in a velvet box beside the lamp, resting on a month-old edition of the *Sentinel*. Her eyes returned to me.

'Dora?'

'There's still no sign of her.'

She released a defeated breath, her body shriveling before my eyes, life seeping from her inexorably, like air from a punctured tire.

In her present state, it was hard to think of her as the woman she'd once been, the beautiful, lively, infinitely rebellious daughter of a prominent Catholic family. She'd been taught music and manners in the hope of making her ever more desirable to the many quite suitable young men who'd waited for her in the curtained drawing room of her father's gracious house. Various finishing schools had been offered, but she'd turned any such 'finishing' aside, and had enrolled in a nursing school instead, a lowly profession her father had regarded as only a small step removed from domestic service. Upon graduation, she'd taken a job with a Dr Benjamin Putnam, a Port Alma physician whose modest small-town practice catered mostly to the hardscrabble farmers, trappers, and cannery workers, the wretched of the earth to which she had intended to devote her life. She'd been twenty-four when she met my father, an established newspaper editor twelve years her senior. In a world of loggers and fishermen, where people ate clams from brine-soaked newspaper, washed down with a frothy ale, he'd no doubt shone like a comet. 'He'd read a lot,' my mother always answered crisply when Billy pestered her about what had attracted her to a man so clearly different from herself. Then, with a peal of laughter, she'd added, 'But only the old stuff. Greeks and Romans. Nothing A.D.'

They'd met when my father turned up at Dr Putnam's clinic. He'd gotten his hand caught in a printing press. Dr Putnam had been injured in a hunting accident two days before, however, so it was my mother who treated my father's wounded hand. 'There were younger men, of course,' she'd tell Billy, 'but I preferred the bread to the yeast.' They were married eight months later, lived together for the next twenty-five years.

I'd been at work in the district attorney's office for four years when she left my father in order to 'be with her thoughts,' as she put it.

She'd chosen to live in a tiny cottage on Fox Creek, only a stone's throw from the old bridge that spanned it, and from which I'd watched my brother guide his raft across the water. She'd furnished the cottage sparsely. A bed, a few chairs, books, almost nothing else. She wanted to 'pare things down,' she said, the only explanation she ever gave. But the little cottage, spare as it seemed, was always flooded with light and music, the quick step of my mother's feet when suddenly, in the middle of a sentence, some bit of verse struck her and she rushed to her books, searching for the reference.

In the years before her stroke I'd visited her often at Fox Creek, usually in company with Billy. On occasion we'd find her inside the cabin, humming as she swept the floor or washed the dishes. At other times she'd be sitting along the bank of Fox Creek, an old cane fishing pole stuck in the ground beside her, her eyes fixed on the little red bob that floated idly in the stream, a book of poetry always in her lap.

My brother worshiped her, of course, referred to her teasingly as 'The Great Example,' as in, 'The Great Example came by the paper this morning.' Or 'I had a talk with The Great Example last night.' He adored her for her joy and energy, the way her laughter rang like bells, but more than anything for the one great lesson he said she'd taught him, that you're alive only when you feel you're alive, all else 'a breathing death.'

We'd last been together at Fox Creek on a bright day in early summer. Billy brought a blanket for Mother and spread it on the ground beside the creek. After picking a cluster of mountain laurel, she lowered herself gracefully onto the blanket and sat Indian-style, her back propped against a tree. She had been living at Fox Creek for four years by then, and during that time her hair had turned completely white, though her skin remained remarkably smooth, with only a few telltale wrinkles at the corners of her eyes and mouth. She seemed to know that something was coming for her, something she could only wait for, see like a dark horse in the distance. Her own mother had died at forty-three, her father at forty-six, both, she said, of poor hearts. Even so, she wanted to continue as The Great Example. And so she worked at being cheerful, discussed her gardening with me, bantered merrily with Billy. But after a time, her mood seemed to alter. She looked out over the creek, the lush green meadows beyond it. 'How perfect it all is,' she murmured.

'You've never regretted it?' I asked. 'Leaving Dad? Moving here? Living alone? No doubts that . . .'

Billy touched her hand. 'Mother has never doubted anything,' he said.

She looked at me as if I'd challenged her. 'Not anything basic, Cal,' she said.

I could see how certain she remained, how convinced of her wisdom, assured that she'd never deluded herself nor misled anyone, that by following her heart she had arrived at the small paradise she now occupied along the banks of Fox Creek.

The stroke came three days later.

I found her. Lying faceup beside her bed, her eyes open, staring, her mouth pulled down on the left side, fixing her face in a terrible scowl. She'd soiled herself, and a dull yellow stain spread across her nightdress. That she had lain for many hours in such indignity sent a fire through my brain.

'She shouldn't have been out there by herself,' I told Billy as we paced the hospital corridor the following night. 'She could have lived with me. Or with you. Maybe even moved back in with Dad. At least, that way, she wouldn't have laid there, all alone, helpless . . .'

A nurse swept past, pushing a metal cart.

'She wanted to be alone,' Billy said, defending her to the last, no less convinced than she'd always been of the decision she'd made, the path she'd followed. 'That's why she moved out there in the first place.'

I shook my head at how extreme her action had been, how unnecessary that our mother had so isolated herself.

'She wanted freedom, Cal,' Billy said emphatically.

'Freedom?' I mocked. 'And what did she hope to get from that?'

'Wisdom,' Billy answered.

He clearly admired her for it. And since his death, I've often wondered if, had he lived, my brother might have done the same.

It was a thought that occurred to me again as I sat with my mother that morning – months later – doing the best I could to show her that she still had one son left, though the one who'd most believed in her was gone. I thought of all my brother might have learned. All he might have given. And in that instant, I saw him as an elderly man, sitting beside Fox Creek, feeling the sun's warmth, letting it all fall into place, his eyes beginning to sparkle as he closed in upon a final wisdom. I saw a smile form on his lips, heard his voice in the air around me, *Now I know, Cal. Now I know.*

'Cal?'

My mother's voice drew me back to the present. 'Yes?'

'Cal . . . I?'

A dreadful unease seized her eyes, as if she'd glimpsed something terrible in her own mind, something she couldn't say but which I took to be yet another expression of her loss, her grief, the fact that the one who'd most nearly shared her vision of the world, taken most to heart her wild instruction, believed in her as much as she'd believed in herself, her one true son, was dead.

I took her hand and squeezed it gently. 'I know' was all I said.

The snow had begun to fall again when I left her an

hour later. It lay in a crisp white layer over the sidewalk and outlined the bare limbs of each tree and shrub. I remembered how often Billy had taken his sled up the high hill behind our house, then hurtled down it, colliding with the huge drifts that lay at its bottom, then leaping to his feet, rapturous, covered in snow, laughing, dared me to join him on his next plunge. I heard his voice again, *You miss all the good stuff, Cal.*

It was only a short walk from the house to Fisherman's Bank. Joe Fletcher, the bank president, sat behind his desk, a few papers neatly arranged on his blotter, others impaled on a thin metal stake.

I took the chair in front of his desk, asked my first question.

'Miss March came in every Monday morning, as I recall,' Fletcher answered. 'She'd make a cash withdrawal of twenty dollars.' He was a broad-chested man, dressed in a dark double-breasted suit. Overall he had the look of a man long used to holding others in suspension, dashing or fulfilling thousands of small dreams. I could tell that he was treating my request for information about Dora as if it were a loan, trying to determine how I might use whatever he gave me, gauge its profit or its loss.

'Did you ever learn much about her?' I asked him.

'Not really, no.'

'Did she open an account of her own?'

'You're thinking she may have tried to pull one over on Ed Dillard?' The suggestion amused Fletcher. 'Old men are easily taken in, of course. And Miss March was quite lovely, as you know, but . . .'

The phone rang.

'Excuse me,' Fletcher said as he picked up the receiver.

While he spoke, I looked out the window into the narrow street that ran through Port Alma, shops on either side, a piece of the bay snagged between the hardware store and the bakery, frozen and opaque, dull as a dead man's eye. The snow was falling relentlessly now, lacing the power lines in white, gathering windswept mounds along the curb. Those few people who were still on the street trudged through it determinedly, the snow merely something added to their burden.

Fletcher had put down the phone when I looked back at him. He was watching me worriedly, observing my wintry features, I thought, the leafless tree I had become.

'You took it hard, didn't you, Cal? What happened to William, I mean.' He leaned forward, an older man, offering advice. 'It's a shame, a real tragedy. But a man has to go on, don't you think?'

It wasn't a question I could answer.

'As to what I might know about Miss March,' he said when I gave no response, 'I saw her only once. Outside the bank, I mean.'

'When was that?'

'About two weeks before Ed died,' Fletcher replied. 'He was sitting in that little room off his parlor. Miss March brought him in there when I told her I had some papers for him to sign.'

I remembered the room. I'd seen it when Ruth Potter had taken me to the house. It had a polished wooden floor and there were terracotta pots hanging here and there. The pots were empty when I saw them, and according to Ruth they'd remained empty during the time she'd worked at the house. It was Dora, she said, who'd 'spruced the room up' with flowers and greenery, then removed it all after Mr Dillard's death.

'Ed was fully dressed,' Fletcher continued. 'Not in pajamas and that old bathrobe he'd been wearing when I'd dropped by at other times. But pants and a shirt. And his hair was combed too. Looking at him, you'd have thought he was back to normal.'

'The papers you brought. What were they?'

'Business papers. Evaluations of what his real estate holdings were worth, that sort of thing. Ed had asked me to gather it all together. He wanted to look over it all. Check out the books, you might say.'

In my mind, I saw my brother's eyes drift up from the ledger book, heard his stricken, unbelieving voice, afraid to admit what he knew she'd done, *Something's wrong*.

'Did Dora look at the papers?'

Everything Joe Fletcher had ever learned of human venality during his forty-three years as a banker in Port Alma flickered behind his eyes. 'I usually know when something like that's going on, Cal. Some kind of fraud, I mean.'

'Why would Ed Dillard have wanted all this financial information about himself?'

'He was intending to make a will.'

'He'd never made one before?'

'He'd never had anyone he wanted to name before. As a beneficiary, that is.'

'But suddenly he did have someone?'

'Yes.'

'Who?'

I could see a dark wind blow through Fletcher's mind. 'I don't know,' he answered, then stared at me silently, so I said the name myself.

'Dora March?'

'I wouldn't know that, Cal.'

'Who would?'

'Art Brady was Ed's attorney.'

I realized that something in my eyes, or in the tone of my voice, had suddenly warned Fletcher not to tell me anything else about Dora or Mr Dillard. 'If you found Miss March, you'd turn her over to the authorities, wouldn't you, Cal?' he asked.

By then my heart had told so many lies, my mouth had no trouble with another.

'Yes.'

The snow was ankle-high as I left the bank. The wind howled through the trees, whipped along the seawall, rattled signs and awnings, fierce and snarling, like a cornered dog.

Art Brady was in his office, standing before a wall of books, all with uniformly black spines. They towered above him, a dark obelisk, the grave, unbending laws of unimpassioned Maine.

'What can I do for you, Cal?' he asked as he turned toward me. He was a short man, wiry as a jockey, with gleaming white hair swept back over his head and parted in the middle. He had a close-cropped beard, also white, which made him look like a figure from a distant century, someone who'd put his ornate signature on a famous document no one read anymore.

'I talked to Joe Fletcher down at the bank. About Ed Dillard.'

Brady shoved a book into its assigned place on the shelf. 'What about Ed?'

'Joe said Mr Dillard intended to make out a will.'

'And?'

'Well, you were Ed's lawyer.'

Brady sat down at his desk. He didn't invite me to take the chair opposite it. 'This is about Dora March, isn't it? You've decided that Miss March had a bad character. You suspect her of being involved in William's death. You think she may have had a reason to murder Ed Dillard too.' He didn't wait for a reply. 'Well, you couldn't be more wrong, Cal.'

He rose, walked to a file cabinet on the far side of the room, rifled through a line of folders, and returned to his seat carrying a single sheet of paper. 'This is the "will" Ed made,' he said as he handed it to me.

I took the paper and read the five words written on it. The letters were thick and awkwardly formed, but I could easily make out what it said: *Draw will. Everything to Dora.*

'As you know, as a legal document it won't hold up,' Brady told me. 'For one thing, there's no last name. For all I know, "Dora" might be one of Ed's long-lost cousins.'

'Except that a woman named Dora happened to be living with him.'

'But as you, of all people, should understand, knowing something and giving it legal force are two different things.' Brady drew the page from my hand, eyed me coolly. 'Look, Cal, if I hadn't seen Miss March with Ed, then I might have had the same suspicions you do.' He smiled, but not lasciviously. It seemed rather the smile of one who'd come to accept our frailties, the pitfall of desire. 'It's happened to old men before. But it didn't happen to Ed Dillard. And I can prove it.'

He'd gone to Ed Dillard's house the day following the old man's death, Brady told me. It was two days before Christmas. Dillard lay in an open coffin in the front room, his face rouged and powdered. Dora sat stiffly in a chair a few feet away while other people, mostly aging business acquaintances, milled about, talking quietly.

'I waited until everyone had left, then I showed that to Miss March.' Brady gestured toward the paper he'd set on his desk. 'She read it and handed it back to me. "No," she said. "I don't want anything." Simple as that. I told her she could make a claim based on the note. She said she had no interest in Ed's money. So I said, "Well, why don't you take some small thing from the house. Ed would want you to do that."' He fell silent, looking down at the page Dillard had written.

'Did she?' I asked. 'Take something from his house?'

'Yes,' Brady said. 'A little porcelain figure. Ed had scores of them. She took one of a little girl with long, blond hair.'

It rose into my mind exactly as I'd seen it, illuminated by a single candle. 'Naked. Sitting on a rock,' I said. 'With her legs drawn up.'

'So you've seen it?'

'Yes.'

'It wasn't much of anything. Just a little china figure. Cheap, not worth much. But that's the one she chose.'

It had rested on the bureau in her bedroom, and other than her clothes and the leather suitcase she'd packed them in, she'd taken nothing else from the cottage on the day she fled.

'She never asked for anything else?'

'Nothing,' Brady said. 'I always got the feeling that Dora didn't want very much from life.'

In my mind, I saw her on the bank of Fox Creek, bending over to dip her fingers in the swirling water, a strange delight in her eyes, small and fierce and frail, like something lifted on the tiniest wings.

'And I certainly never thought she was the sort of woman who'd take advantage of an old man.' Brady considered his next words carefully. 'I have some evidence of that.'

'Evidence of what?'

'That she cared for Ed. That it wasn't just some sort of act.' He leaned back in his chair. 'One evening, I dropped by Ed's house just after work. This was a few days before he died. He was sitting in the front parlor, in his wheelchair, dressed up, like he was going to church or a wedding. He even had a tie on. Looked handsome.' He'd chosen the wrong word, and corrected himself. 'Well, not handsome. You couldn't look handsome in Ed's condition. But he looked calm. Not mad at the world, the way he usually did.'

When he arrived, Brady told me, Dora had been seated on a chair beside Mr Dillard, a book open in her lap.

'After a while, she went to the kitchen and brought out a cake she'd made. She'd cut Ed's piece into small squares.' He studied me closely, seemingly determined to prove his point. 'And she got down on her knees, Cal. She got down on her knees and fed cake to that pitiful old man.' He waited for the image to sink in, then added, 'She was good to Ed. That's my point, of course. Very good to him. Because she cared about him. Not to get something for herself. And she read to him hour upon hour.'

I remembered her in my study, her face in the firelight, the way her hands caressed the book she'd taken from the shelf, then later, in her cottage, the book I'd found open on the small table by the window, the stark lines she'd underscored.

Brady gave his final word on the subject. 'Dora was good to Ed, Cal. From the moment she started working for him until the night he died.'

The night he died.

I remembered that night well, the sound of a Christmas bell somewhere as I knocked at the door and waited, then a hand parting the white lace curtains, after that a woman's face, beautiful and still, her green eyes peering catlike from the darkened house.

Chapter Six

Ed Dillard's house was set far back from Maple Street. It was the only one that bore no sign of the Christmas holidays, no candles in the windows, no gleaming tree, nor any obvious sign that the house was occupied at all.

Then I saw a woman in a second-floor window, her arms held stiffly at her sides so that she looked as if she'd been placed there, like one of those stone figures that the ancients used to guard the portals of their souls.

She'd come downstairs by the time I reached the door. When she parted the curtains, I saw only her face, white and luminous, a cameo pinned to black velvet. Then she opened the door and a slant of light fell over her, slicing her in two, casting her eyes in deep shadow but bathing everything else in a treacherous yellow light.

'Sheriff Pritchart said you called,' I explained. 'He's got a pretty bad cold, and his deputy's gone to Portland. So he asked me to come over.' I took off my hat. 'Cal Chase. I work in the district attorney's office.'

She stepped back. 'Please come in,' she said.

I had seen Dora before, on that morning as she passed by Ollie's Barber Shop. But I'd never seen her close up. Now I noticed that she'd cut her hair short and without regard to style. I noticed other things as well. That her skirt fell to her ankles, her sleeves to her wrists, as if her body were a thing she sought utterly to conceal.

'Mr Dillard is upstairs,' she said.

He lay in his bed, eyes closed, a blanket drawn over him and tucked just beneath his chin. The pillow his head rested upon looked newly fluffed, the case crisp and white. A water glass rested in a silver tray on a table beside his bed, along with a blue china cup, half filled with tea. A white candle burned fitfully in a crystal holder; a single red rose, fresh and impossibly fragrant, had been placed in the small vase that stood beside it.

I glanced at the rocking chair on the other side of the bed. A book lay upturned on its seat, a pair of gold-rimmed glasses beside it. *The House of the Seven Gables*. I'd read it in high school, remembered well how the old man had died, his eyes wide, frantic, glaring, his mouth spitting blood.

By all appearances Ed Dillard had died the way people wanted to, peacefully in his sleep. I doubted that he'd actually gone that way, of course. I'd had enough experience with death by then to know that people died like old cars, shaking and clattering, spewing fluids, gases. I suddenly remembered my mother as I'd found her in the cottage, alive but barely, sprawled across the floor, her nightgown sticky with sweat and urine. My old anger leaped up in me again, like a cat in wait. When I glanced toward Dora, I saw something move across her features, swift as a shadow. I felt that she'd seen the very image that had darted through my mind, had sensed how quickly grief turned to rage in me.

'Mr Dillard seems to have gone peacefully,' I said as I pulled out my notebook. 'I just have to ask a few questions,' I explained.

She gave a quick nod.

'Were you with Mr Dillard when he died?'

'Yes.'

'Do you remember about what time he passed away?'

'Shortly after nine o'clock.'

'And he died right here? In his bed?'

'Yes.'

'Has anybody been in the room since then?'

'No.'

'Has he been moved?'

'I washed him and changed his clothes. Should I not have done that?'

'No, no, that's fine,' I assured her. 'Nothing to worry about.' I glanced at my notebook, writing nothing. 'Just for the record, what was your relationship to Mr Dillard?'

'I was his housekeeper.'

'Live-in?'

'Yes.'

'Do you know if he had any relatives? People who should be contacted?'

'He never mentioned anyone.'

'And your name is?'

Her arms drew upward protectively, as if against invisible fingers unbuttoning her blouse. 'Dora March,' she replied evenly.

I closed the notebook. 'Well, that's all I need to know at the moment. I'll have to send Dr Bradshaw over. He's the county coroner. Do you want me to call him now?'

'Yes,' she said.

I used the phone downstairs, a wooden one that hung on the wall. Dora stood a few feet away, beside a lamp with a bloodred shade, listening silently as I made the arrangements.

63

'The doctor will be by in just a few minutes,' I told her as I hung up the phone.

She nodded.

'I'm sorry about Mr Dillard,' I added.

'Thank you.'

She walked me to the door.

I stepped out onto the porch. 'Well, good night, Miss March.'

'Good night, Mr Chase.'

I was back in my office, sleeplessly toiling at some nondescript prosecution, when Doc Bradshaw came by an hour later. He was an old man, careless in his dress, with a rumpled hat, and a day or two's growth of gray stubble. One leg was shorter than the other, so that when he walked his left shoulder rode a good two inches higher than the right. It gave him a mangled appearance, like a bicycle that had been run over then crudely hammered back into shape.

'Here's the death certificate,' he said. He slid a single sheet of paper onto my desk.

I picked it up and began to glance over it. 'Anything I need to tell Hap?'

Doc Bradshaw lowered himself with a sigh into the chair opposite my desk. He didn't answer my question. Instead, he asked, 'You wouldn't happen to have a shot of whiskey, would you, Cal?'

'I don't keep it in my office.'

'Because it's against the rules?'

'Because it's too tempting.' I glanced at the bottom of the page. 'Natural causes. You have any reason to doubt that?'

Doc Bradshaw chuckled. 'You looking for trouble, Cal? Not enough felonious activity in Port Alma for you?' He laughed again. 'No, I didn't see anything out of the ordinary. Old men die, that's the long and short of it.' He bent forward, massaged his knees, then sat back with a soft groan. 'Poor old Ed. Not a person in the world to shed a tear for him.'

'Except that woman,' I said, surprising myself as I said it.

'Think they were close?' Doc Bradshaw asked.

'She seemed to care about him.'

Bradshaw glanced toward the window. 'I guess she'll be leaving Port Alma.'

'Why's that?'

His eyes returned to me. 'Probably have to. I don't know of any other old man who could afford to hire a live-in housekeeper. Not in times like these.'

I put the report in a folder and shoved it in my desk. 'She'll find something else to do.'

'Maybe so,' Doc Bradshaw said. He grabbed his knees and drew himself to his feet. 'You ought to give her a call, Cal.'

'Give who a call?'

'That young woman who was taking care of Ed. You know, there's not that many single women left in Port Alma.' He smiled slyly. 'He who hesitates is lost.'

Doc Bradshaw was right, of course, but I hesitated nonetheless. The following morning new cases were on my desk, people mistreating each other in the customary ways, mostly by breaching contracts involving money or the heart. Sheriff Pritchart came by to pick up Doc Bradshaw's report. He asked if everything had appeared 'normal' at Ed Dillard's house. I told him that it had, and gave the whole incident no further thought.

Then, two days later, the day after Christmas, I

noticed a brief piece about Ed Dillard in the *Sentinel*. I knew Billy had written it, for it bore the mark of my brother's style, the distinctive romantic wistfulness that also marked his mind. He wrote of the old man's struggle against poverty, all he'd had to overcome, the devotion he'd shown during his wife's long sickness, the fortitude with which he'd later borne his own ill fortune. 'The grace of Ed Dillard's life came to resemble the roses he tended in the garden beside his house,' my brother wrote, 'all the more beautiful for thorns.'

I visited my brother the following afternoon. For the last few years we'd made it our business to have lunch with our father each Sunday. After my mother left him, moved into the cottage on Fox Creek, he'd gone through a period of pronounced withdrawal. He'd briefly considered returning to the paper, then just as abruptly dropped the idea, deciding to act only as an 'adviser.' This had meant little more than his depending upon his old friend, Sheriff Pritchart, to alert him about any newsworthy events in the county. For the rest, my father pretty much remained secluded in the house on Union Road, reading his cherished books and picking out the melody lines of the few pieces of sheet music my mother had left with the piano.

On that particular Sunday, he'd seemed somewhat more animated, telling stories from his early days at the *Sentinel*, the past, as always, considerably more alive than the present, while the future seemed hardly to exist for him at all, a land across the river, still and windless, already locked in death.

After lunch, we settled in my father's parlor. It was a blustery day, with dark clouds rolling in from the north.

Beyond the rattling windows, winds gusted suddenly, then settled no less abruptly, like horses whipped then brought to heel.

My father handed out cigars, then took his place in the rocker beside the door. Billy leaned against the brick mantel, restless as ever, while I took my usual place on the leather sofa.

My father took a quick draw on his cigar. 'Anything new at the paper, William?'

Billy shook his head, then slumped into the chair opposite me and folded one long leg over the other, bouncing his foot rhythmically, like someone keeping time to a song no one else could hear.

'Well, there must be some news,' I said.

'Not really. Things are pretty quiet.'

My father turned to me. 'And in the legal profession, what news?'

'Not much there either.'

'All right, then,' my father said. He drew a piece of paper from his back pocket. 'Let's begin Four Lines.'

Four Lines was an idea my mother had come up with years before, when Billy and I were boys. After Sunday lunch, each member of the family had to recite four lines from some work of literature. Each recitation was to be carefully chosen for its beauty or its wisdom. Ideally it would reflect either our current mood or some problem that had arisen in our lives, one for which we were seeking a solution. In continuing the activity after my mother deserted him, my father no doubt hoped that it would encourage my brother and me to discuss our deepest hopes and fears with him. Four Lines had not achieved that end, but he'd continued to believe that one day it might.

We went in order of seniority that afternoon, as always. I don't remember what my father recited, but he was inclined toward aphorisms, particularly when neatly housed in heroic couplets, so it was more than likely something from Pope or Dryden. For my part, I'd quickly thumbed through *Bartlett's Quotations* an hour or so before and located a few lines about the law. I recited them without enthusiasm, then nodded to Billy for the last recitation of the day.

'Your turn,' I said.

My father drew in a somewhat impatient breath, already suspecting that he would not much care for Billy's choice. 'Your brother had rather cut grass with a mustache trimmer than read anything other than that romantic drivel his mother pushes on him,' he'd grumbled years before as the two of us sat in his study, gravely pondering Euripides, while Billy frolicked in the yard, tumbling madly, hand over hand. It was a judgment he'd never changed, although I think my mother's departure had greatly challenged it, suggested that he might have learned something from the poets she'd cherished, their ardent songs of love.

'So, William, what do you have for us?' he asked now.

The rhythmic motion of my brother's feet stopped suddenly. He smiled softly, fiddled unnecessarily with the right cuff of his shirt, then rose, his eyes quite still, his voice very nearly solemn as he recited.

> *The desire of the moth for the star.*
> *Of the day for the morrow.*
> *The yearning for something afar*
> *From the sphere of our sorrow.*

When he finished, he sat down and fixed his gaze on the hearth. A soft golden light danced in his face, an effect that gave him an exposed and vulnerable look, something I'd never seen before.

'Who's the poet?' my father asked.

'Shelley.'

'Your mother's favorite,' my father said. 'No wonder. She was always looking for something afar.'

Billy nodded. 'Still is, I suppose,' he said softly.

I looked at him intently. 'Are you?' I asked.

His eyes drifted over to me. 'Maybe,' he said with a quiet, strangely somber smile.

Two weeks would pass before I put it together, the quotation he'd chosen, the pensive mood with which he'd offered it. Two weeks before I learned that in fact he had found that afar thing he'd spoken of that afternoon.

And that her name was Dora March.

PART TWO

Chapter Seven

In the days immediately following my brother's murder, Sheriff T. R. Pritchart made every effort to find Dora March. He traced every lead, talked to everyone who might have known anything about where she'd gone. From me he learned that the ring we'd found beside Billy's body was my mother's. From Betty Gaines he discovered that a car had been parked on the road behind Dora's house not long before Billy's death. She'd also heard a voice coming from Dora's house, a male voice, Betty insisted, though she could not be sure it was Billy's. Rushing through the rain, skirting along the edge of the lawn, she'd been able to make out only a little of what she'd heard.

Four lines:

> *I don't believe it.*
> *It's not true.*
> *It can't be true.*
> *It's you!*

As to Dora's whereabouts, Henry Mason, an employee at the *Sentinel*, turned out to be the best witness. He'd seen Dora that day walking on the road that led to Royston, he told T. R. She'd been carrying a suitcase and headed toward the concrete pillar that marked the stopping place of the Portland bus. It had been raining, he said, and so he'd stopped, picked her up, and driven her to the bus station in Port Alma. She'd looked very tense, according to Henry, but she'd given no explanation as to why she was leaving town. From the look on her face, he'd gotten the idea that something had happened, the sudden illness of a relative, perhaps, or some other distressing news that had abruptly called her away. He'd asked her where she was going. She'd replied only, 'Away for a while,' so that Henry had fully expected her to return to Port Alma in a few days, had not in the least guessed that she was 'on the run.' He'd dropped her off at the bus station at 'somewhere around three' in the afternoon, he told Pritchart, and had then driven directly home.

According to Sheila Beacham, who'd sold her the ticket, Dora had looked nervous and upset when she bought her ticket to Portland. She'd gone directly to her bus, then taken a seat at the very rear.

After that, she had simply vanished.

And so, during the next few days, I'd searched Dora's house again and again, gone through closets, the small attic, even dug through the ashes in her fireplace and peered up its blackened chimney, looking everywhere for some sign of where she'd fled. I'd found only the battered anthology of English verse she'd left behind. The label inside read *Ex Libris, Lorenzo Clay, Carmel, California*, a clue, perhaps, to where she'd once been, but not to where she'd gone.

'I know you want her caught fast, Cal,' Sheriff Pritchart said the afternoon he summoned me to his office.

He'd found out that I was conducting my own investigation and wanted to stop me, he said, before I 'got into trouble.'

'It's up to other people to find Dora March,' T. R. told me. 'Not you, Cal. That's not your job at all.'

He leaned against the gun cabinet in his office, a row of rifles propped on their stocks behind the glass door. A steel chain was threaded through each trigger guard, then locked to an eyebolt in the wooden frame.

'You understand?'

When I gave no answer, he watched me silently, then said, 'You look like hell, Cal.' He noticed me studying the lock on the gun case, the ravaged look in my eyes. 'I wish William had just steered completely clear of Dora,' he added.

An earlier judgment reared its head, *Death follows her.*

'But he just couldn't keep away from her, I guess,' T. R. said wearily.

'He loved her,' I told him in a matter-of-fact tone that gave no hint of the boiling wave I rode.

'It cost him his life.'

That seemed the most bitter of all conclusions, that Billy had died for love. I recalled the joy and peace that had come over him during the last hours of his life. It was as if he'd finally solved the great riddle of his existence, found in Dora the one key that unlocked him.

'Some money too, I guess.'

T. R. was referring to the embezzlement, paltry sums stolen from petty cash, fraudulent notes made in Dora's hand.

'He didn't care about that,' I said.

'William didn't care that Dora was a thief?' T. R. shook his head. 'He was just going to forget about that?'

'He would have done anything for her,' I said quietly.

75

'There was something about her that—' I stopped, recalling the touch of her hand.

T. R. looked at me cautiously, like a hunter who'd just spotted bear prints in the snow. 'Something about her that what?'

'That made my brother want to live.'

T. R. shook his head, again unwilling to be diverted by such notions, and returned to the reason he'd called me to his office. 'I know you've been talking to people, Cal. Joe Fletcher. Art Brady. Others.'

I could feel the noose tightening. T. R. would soon go the rounds, instruct the good citizens of Port Alma to keep their mouths shut if I should happen by, asking questions about Dora March.

'What would you do if you found her?' he asked.

I gave him the minimum, a shrug.

'That's not a good enough answer, Cal.'

'It's the only one I have, T. R.'

'Well, before you burst through Dora's door, you ought to give one thing some pretty serious thought. If that woman killed William, she'd sure as hell kill you. So, where does that leave us, Cal?'

He wanted me to tell him that I'd give it up, stop searching for Dora, let what was left of his investigation run its course through the remaining official channels. But that was a pledge I could not make, knowing I would never keep it.

'If the money didn't matter to William, then maybe what we're dealing with here is a lover's quarrel,' T. R. said. 'I've seen it quite a few times. Spats that get out of hand, and somebody ends up dead.'

'He loved her,' I repeated.

'But did she love him?'

I saw her eyes lift toward mine, *I can't.*

'Yes, she did.'

'I've seen love make people do good things,' T. R. said. 'But at the same time, I've never seen it stop a person from doing something bad.'

T. R. was nearly seventy. In him, the illusions of romance had died long ago. He saw love's passionate certainties as little more than fleeting claims, eternal love a thing that would endure no longer than a season.

'Maybe she said no, that's what I'm getting at, Cal. Maybe that's what started it. He offered her the ring, and she said no. And as to why she said no. Well, that could be the oldest story there is, son. Maybe she had another man. You wouldn't know about anything like that, would you?'

'No.'

'William never mentioned some other fellow Dora might have fancied instead of him?'

Truth rose like a bloody gorge into my throat, but I choked it down again.

At my silence, T. R. shook his head despairingly. 'Who was she, I wonder.'

I saw the dingy trawler turn toward the sea, heard my brother's voice in all its youthful ardor, *She's out there somewhere.*

'She was the one he'd hoped for all his life,' I said.

'You ask me, he'd been better off picking a name out of a hat.'

I glanced toward the window, snow falling thickly beyond the clouded glass. 'He couldn't do that. He loved Dora. Only Dora.'

'Yeah, that was William, all right,' T. R. said in a tone of undisguised pity. 'He never grew out of it, did he?

That kid way of looking at things.' He squinted at me knowingly. 'It's better to be like you, Cal.'

'Like me?'

'The type that never gets swept away.'

I felt my hand on her white throat, quickly got to my feet. 'I'd better be on my way,' I said.

'Remember what I told you,' T. R. warned.

'I will,' I said, then left him to his paperwork and his guns and trudged back to my house.

Once there, I stripped off my coat and hung it in the front closet, pulled off my winter boots and placed them on the mat. A storm was raging now, angry gusts rattling my windows, sending frigid bursts of air across the cold wooden floor. I made a fire in the hearth and huddled close beside the flames. As children, Billy and I had often done the same, wrapping our arms around each other, amazed by the heat our bodies generated. Thinking of those times, I felt my brother's death sink deeper and deeper into me, thick as a black dye, staining everything, past, present, future, leaving its mark on everything I touched.

One by one, I returned to the events of the past year – Billy's Four Lines, my first sight of Dora as she'd swept past Ollie's Barber Shop, meetings, conversations, the words that had passed between us, moments when we'd touched. And yet, as the evening wore on, my mind returned more and more determinedly to a particular night, a man, a child, a burning house, Billy in the distance, Dora beside me, her eyes upon the fire, staring at it so intently, her gaze seemed almost to feed the flames.

The fire had started just after nightfall. A Friday night,

January 17, to be exact. Snow had been falling steadily since nine o'clock that morning, blocking roads, slowing traffic, so that by the time the town's volunteer firemen reached Carl Hendricks's house on Pine Road, the ramshackle building was already a lost cause.

By the time I arrived, flames had spiraled up the front stairs and blown out the single dormer window on the second floor. They now clawed at the roof with fiery red fingers.

There'd been nothing anyone could do to save the building. But a few of us, rather than merely milling around while it burned, had formed a line and dutifully relayed water buckets from a nearby creek to douse the little shed behind the house.

Carl Hendricks had joined the relay for a time, then slouched away to stand a few yards from his home, wrapped in a tattered blanket, his daughter Molly standing silently at his side. He was a large man, with a fleshy face and a crooked, flattened nose. His ears were small and curled, and from the side they appeared apish. Molly looked like someone else's child. She was eight years old, with golden hair that fell to her waist and skin so smooth and luminous it looked like polished porcelain.

Billy arrived a few minutes before the house finally groaned its last, shuddered briefly, then collapsed, his battered old Ford sedan clattering through the snow until it ground to a wheezy halt beside my own car. He wore his brown overcoat, frayed at the lapels, the expensive red scarf I'd given him for his last birthday wrapped around his neck, and a felt hat tugged far down, so that he resembled some melodrama detective.

What I noticed most, however, was that he was not alone.

She stepped out briskly, closing the door behind her, her eyes leveled upon the fire, studying it intently, as if its thick smoke and red flames were a riddle she was determined to solve.

I recognized her instantly, of course. She was the young woman I'd seen first through the window of the barbershop, then later at Ed Dillard's house on the night of his death.

'I believe you've met Dora,' Billy said when they came up to me.

In the shadows carved by the fire, my brother looked older, more experienced, and I suppose I should have guessed that she was already beginning to deepen and enrich him, bestow upon him that sense of 'something to lose' that lies at the heart of all maturity.

'Yes I have,' I said. I touched the brim of my hat. 'Good evening, Miss March.'

'Mr Chase.' She dipped her head slightly.

'Dora's working at the *Sentinel* now,' Billy told me. 'We were there when the call came in.' His eyes swept toward the house. 'Looks like a goner.' He pulled a notebook from his coat pocket and glanced at Dora. 'Well, let's look around.'

I watched them as they made their way toward the house, snow swirling thickly, cloaking the ruin in a robe of white. Billy stopped to point something out to Dora, scribbling a note into his pad as he spoke. She listened to him with the greatest attention, then, at his signal, moved forward again.

'Who's the woman with your brother?'

I turned and saw Hap Ferguson standing next to me.

He was my boss, the district attorney of Jefferson County, a plump, gray-haired man nearing fifty, cheerful, sometimes bawdy, with a Highland flush to his cheeks.

'Dora March.'

'Name rings a bell,' Hap said.

'She was Ed Dillard's housekeeper. You probably read her name in my report. She was living with him when he died last month.'

Hap grinned slyly. 'Lucky Ed.'

I kept my eyes on Dora for a while. When I finally returned my attention to Hap, I saw that he was peering at me thoughtfully.

'You seem a little moonstruck, Cal.'

I waved my hand, dismissing the comment. 'I don't get moonstruck.'

'Already too old and world-weary for that, are you?'

'What's on your mind, Hap?' I asked bluntly.

Instead of answering, he yanked something from his coat pocket. 'This may not be the best moment, but take a look at this, will you? Her name's Rachel. Rachel Bass. She's a cousin of mine.'

In the leaping firelight, the photograph showed a lanky woman with broad shoulders and a frank expression, her face the type I'd seen as a boy, usually on women-in-war posters, the nurse who braves the fire and shrapnel, bears the wounded soldier home.

'Rachel's about your age,' Hap said. 'Her husband's been dead a couple years now. She's got a five-year-old named Sarah.'

Rachel Bass wore a cheap dress dotted with flowers, the sort that hung on metal racks in general stores. Her hair fell just above her shoulders, full and wavy, parted in the middle. In the photo, she stood on the porch of a wood-framed house, a tin thermometer nailed to the post she leaned against. A white cloth dangled from her hand, and the apron she wore seemed slightly soiled. A little girl stood beside her, the right side of her face pressed against her mother's left leg, one small hand clutching her stained apron. More than anything, Rachel Bass looked like a woman who'd put in a full day, cooked and cleaned and washed, explained to the grocer that she'd have the money by the end of the week. She needed rest, I thought, not a man like me.

'She taught English at Royston High School for a few years,' Hap went on. 'Now she rents rooms to keep things going.'

I brushed the snow from the photograph and offered it back to him. 'Not my type, Hap.'

'And what might that be?'

I dared not tell him, since I knew that for all the blue stories he told at work, my weekend visits to a water-front bordello in Royston would not be welcome news from a prosecutor in his employ.

'I guess I'll know it when I see it. But it's not her.'

'Hell, I know she's no spring chicken. But she's still a handsome woman. And she's got a pretty good education. Reads anything she can get her hands on. I figure you might like her.' He faced the house, leaving the photograph still dangling from my fingers. 'So just hold on to that, Cal. Give it some thought.'

Before I could offer any further protest, he turned his attention to Carl Hendricks. 'Poor bastard. His second wife died two months ago, you know. My God, what will he do now?' He shook his head at the multitude of misfortune that can befall a single life. 'Well, let's go over and extend our sympathies.'

We walked over to where Carl Hendricks stood with his daughter. The heat from the fire had sufficiently warmed the air immediately around it so that Hendricks had let the blanket drop from his shoulders. It now lay wet and crumpled at his feet, while he stood in shirt-sleeves, one large hand gripping tightly to Molly's shoulder.

'Terrible thing, Carl,' Hap said, gazing at the fire. 'Anything I can do?'

'Didn't have no insurance on it,' Hendricks muttered. 'Couldn't afford none.' Hendricks seemed dazed by his misfortune, stricken and befuddled. I suspected that even in the best of times, Carl Hendricks was a man of starkly limited resources, the sort who forever finds himself pushed, battered, backed finally into a corner, his life like a bar brawl he didn't start or know how to finish. 'Sprung up in the kitchen,' he muttered. 'Spread all over.' He snapped his fingers. 'Just like that.'

The house was little more than a scorched outline on a field of flame. Billy and Dora were walking back toward us.

'Fastest thing I ever saw, that fire,' Hendricks said as they came up. He nodded to Billy, his eyes glancing briefly toward Dora, then skittering away. He pointed to the blanket that lay curled at his feet. 'Tried to beat it out. Nearly caught fire myself. Seems like everything caught fire at once.'

As for Molly, she'd been upstairs when it started, Hendricks told us. The fire had moved so swiftly, she'd very nearly gotten trapped. But at the last moment, she'd managed to open a window, crawl out onto the roof, then jump into a saving bank of snow.

I saw Dora's eyes fix on the little girl. She started to touch her hair, then drew back and dropped her hands into the pockets of her coat.

'Everything I got.' Hendricks's fingers squeezed his daughter's shoulder. 'All caught fire at once.'

With a groan, the roof gave way. A geyser of glowing cinders exploded into the air, mingled briefly with the falling snow, then mutely fell to earth. Molly glanced up at Dora. It seemed to me that their eyes locked, Dora's suddenly agitated, as if she'd glimpsed something grave and alarming in Molly Hendricks's pretty, young face. With a quick backward step, she turned and walked to an isolated area some twenty feet away.

It attracted me, the way she stood so silent and solitary while others milled around her, and so after a time I also drew out of the circle and headed toward her, all but following the very tracks she'd left in the snow.

'You'll have to get used to seeing this sort of thing,' I said as I neared her. 'Since you're working at the *Sentinel* now, I mean.'

'Yes, I will.'

'And worse,' I added. 'Port Alma's a small community, of course. But even so, things happen. Fires like this one. Logging accidents. Drowning. We have a crime or two once in a while. We even had a mass murder about twenty years back. A whole family carved up. Man and his wife. A little girl.'

Her eyes shot over to me, then swiftly away, her gaze now fixed on the smoldering timbers.

I decided to pursue a less disturbing subject. 'You're going to need a more substantial coat if you stay here in Port Alma.'

'William said the same thing.'

'I'll bet Billy offered you his own coat,' I said, lightly mocking my brother's old-fashioned chivalry. 'He's a knight in shining armor.'

Something in her face softened. 'Yes, he is.'

'Stray dogs. Stray cats. He was the one they were always following home,' I added.

She looked at me quite frankly. 'And what followed *you* home?'

I felt my answer like a subtle weight added to my soul. 'Nothing followed me.'

She faced the fire again, making no further comment, but in some sense I felt that she was still watching me. Judging me. My first and only impulse was to get away.

'Well, it doesn't look like there's much more I can do around here. So I'll just say good night, Miss March.'

I left her and made the rounds, told Hap and Billy I was leaving, offered my sympathies to Carl Hendricks, then walked to my car and got in. As I pulled away, I glanced back at the scene, struck by the glowing mound of embers and boiling gray smoke, the shadowy figures huddled among stripped and icy trees, silhouettes against the snow. If hell were a wintry landscape, I thought, it would look like Maine. Then I caught sight of Dora again, standing alone, my brother now striding toward her, eager and responsive, as if he alone had heard her silent call.

Chapter Eight

During the days following the Hendricks fire, I passed the *Sentinel* on my way to and from work, I sometimes took note of Dora as she sat at the little metal desk my brother had assigned to her, but I had no occasion to speak with her again. She was usually bent over her desk, hard at work by all appearances, intent upon whatever paper lay before her. She never looked up, never noticed me, certainly never saw my eyes latch on to her as I passed, linger briefly, drawn to her perhaps, but coolly, like an animal drinking at an icy stream.

A week after the fire Hap called me into his office.

'Your brother thinks there's something fishy about that blaze at the Hendricks place. Has he mentioned anything to you about it?'

'No.'

'I happened to be in the probate office yesterday afternoon, and William came up and started talking about it. I got the feeling he had a funny feeling about it.'

'Funny feeling?'

'Like he thought maybe something was amiss, you know?'

'Did he say that?'

'Not in so many words, but I think you should go out

there anyway, poke around a little, see if anything looks fishy.'

'What am I looking for, Hap? The place burned to the ground.'

'Just show the flag, that's all I'm saying, Cal. Cover us. Anything comes up, we can say we've been looking into it.'

It was the sort of political task I disliked but could not avoid, and as I drove out to the Hendricks house an hour later, I found myself mildly annoyed that it was Billy's chance remark that made my trip necessary. I could not imagine where his notion that there was something 'fishy' about the fire had come from. After all, I'd gotten there quite some time before he'd arrived, helped the other volunteers douse the shed behind the house. At no point during that time had I seen anything to make me doubt that the fire had begun and spread exactly as Carl Hendricks had described it.

I was still wondering where my brother's sinister idea had come from when I pulled my car into the slushy driveway of what had only recently been Carl Hendricks's home.

Then I knew.

She was standing with her back to the road, facing the charred rubble of the house. She turned when she heard the car, and I saw that her shoes were soiled and wet, as was the bottom of her coat. She held what appeared to be a charred piece of paper.

'Good morning,' I called as I got out of the car.

She nodded as I approached, drew off her glasses with one hand, sank the paper into the pocket of her coat with the other.

'I didn't expect to find you out here.'

I noticed that her fingers were dotted with soot, took a handkerchief from my pocket and handed it to her.

She wiped her hands, then gave the handkerchief back to me. 'Thank you.'

The blackened skeleton of the small house was laced with melting snow. An acrid smell tainted the air.

'I hear my brother has some suspicions. He mentioned them to my boss. Hap Ferguson. The district attorney. I wonder if Billy can seriously believe that in times like these a man would burn down his own house.' I took out a cheroot and lit it, dropped the match into the dirty snow at my feet. 'An uninsured house, by the way.'

Her gaze touched on the soggy blanket that lay half buried in the snow a few yards away. It was the one that had dropped from Hendricks's shoulders the night of the fire. She said nothing.

'How'd you happen to get out here?' I asked her.

'William dropped me off. I told him I'd walk back.'

'Well, I can take you back into town if you want. This "investigation" won't take long.'

With that I stepped away and headed over to the sodden rubble of Carl Hendricks's house. While Dora waited, I walked among the charred timbers, kicking at them or prying among them with a stick. I even bent down from time to time, plucked something from the ruin, and sniffed it for gasoline or heating oil.

I wasn't sure what I was looking for. Something out of place or stupidly left behind, a kerosene can in the scorched remains of what had once been a bedroom. I'd long ago discovered that a criminal mind was usually a dull one, woolly and unskilled, capable of quite comic idiocies. As a type, our local criminals were guileless, crippled by poor memory and limited concentration.

They tripped themselves up more often than the authorities tripped them. If Carl Hendricks had set his house on fire, I had no doubt but that he'd probably left some sign of it.

But I found no indication of arson, nor any attempt to conceal it. The rubble was exactly that, heaps of burnt wood, naked mattress springs amid soggy piles of scorched bedding, a kitchen stove, blackened but otherwise intact, save for the collapsed pipe that lay in broken pieces around it.

I tossed my cigar into the snow and trudged back toward Dora. 'Okay, we can head back to town now,' I said when I reached her.

In the car, Dora sat quite still. But in that stillness I thought I could detect some fierce movement in her mind, a strange, inner darting, like a bird flitting right and left, forever alert and on guard.

About halfway back to the main road, I steered clear of a fallen branch, then made a hard right around the road's final curve. Perhaps a hundred yards ahead, two figures lurched toward us. It wasn't until I drew near that I recognized Carl Hendricks and his daughter.

He'd halted abruptly when he caught sight of the car and placed a restraining hand on the little girl's shoulder. She stopped in her tracks, then waited as her father continued forward, a tattered wool scarf wrapped loosely around his mouth and nose, a knit cap pulled over his ears, his eyes leveled on us as if he were taking aim.

' 'Morning, Carl,' I said as I pulled up beside him.

He jerked the scarf below his chin and tucked it there. His lips were blue and trembling, his cheeks shadowed with stubble. ' 'Morning.'

'Where you headed?'

'To the shed.' His head slumped forward, massive as a stone. 'Me and my girl's living there. It's got a wood stove in it.'

'I could take you to it.'

Hendricks looked past me to where Dora sat, staring straight ahead. 'No,' he said as he looked at me again. 'I guess I'll be on my way.' He nodded once, then stepped back from the car and began to trudge down the road again, motioning Molly to follow along.

I pressed the accelerator. Molly had begun walking again, but she stopped as we drew near. Her eyes were fixed on Dora imploringly, reaching for her like two small hands.

Within an instant, I'd swept by, but in the rearview mirror I could see Carl Hendricks as he trudged down the road, ponderous, hunched. Molly trailed behind him, head down, leaving small gray footprints in the snow.

When I turned back to Dora, I saw, to my surprise, that she was deeply shaken, like a child who'd seen something terrible but knew no way to describe it.

'Could you stop the car,' she said. 'Let me out please.'

We'd turned another bend in the road. Neither Hendricks nor Molly was visible behind us. I pulled over, then watched silently as Dora left the car and walked a few paces up the road. She'd dropped her hands deep into her pockets, and I could see her fingers twitching inside them, quick and frantic, like someone grasping for a line.

After a time, those same desperate motions diminished, then finally stopped. She took a long breath, turned, and walked back to the car, stamping snow from her shoes before she got in.

'Thank you,' she said.

'Carsick?' I asked, though I suspected that it was nothing of the kind.

Dora nodded briskly but said nothing.

I dropped her off at the *Sentinel* a few minutes later, then returned to my office. Hap Ferguson was standing in the corridor, munching a sugar cookie from the bag of them his wife made each week.

'Find anything over at Carl's place?'

'Nothing,' I told him.

'Wonder why'd William got the idea that . . .'

'I think maybe someone else at the paper had some suspicions.'

'Who?'

I gave the only answer possible. 'The woman who came with him to the fire.'

There was nothing more to say. It seemed to me that the matter had ended, that there'd be no more talk either of the fire or of my brother's unfounded suspicions. And yet, I noticed that as I turned to leave, Hap drew a pen and notepad from his pocket and wrote down Dora's name.

I met Billy for lunch at the Bluebird Café that same afternoon, but I told him nothing about Dora, the way Hendricks had stared at her, nor the agitation that had followed. I had no wish to talk about her, nor any woman like her, the type it was impossible to get a fix on. I preferred my woman on the waterfront, the one I called Jane or Celia or any name that occurred to me at the moment, who smoked my cheroots and drank my

whiskey and led me to her bed with a clear under-
standing of what I was to give and get. She was broad in
the hips and thick in the ankles, and she took me into
the safe harbor of her arms without expecting me to lose
my senses over her, or ever promise more than a single
night's attention.

And so it was my brother who brought Dora up that
afternoon. In fact, he seemed more or less unable to
think of anything else.

'Dora said you met Carl Hendricks on the way back
from his house this morning.'

I nodded, forked a bite of meat loaf into my mouth.
'We ran into him.'

'What do you think, Cal? Could he have done it?'

'I haven't seen any evidence of any crime at all, Billy,'
I said sternly. 'In my profession, I need that. As a matter
of fact, I think you're supposed to require a little of it in
yours too.'

He looked at me as if I'd slapped his face. 'What's the
matter, Cal?'

I decided to be blunt. 'Well, for one thing, because of
you, of what you said to Hap, I got sent on a wild-goose
chase this morning. Had to go out to Hendricks's place,
poke around like I had the foggiest notion of what I was
looking for. And for all that, I didn't find a damn thing
to suggest that Carl Hendricks torched his house.' I
shoved my plate aside. 'Let me ask you something, Billy.
Was it Dora March who put the idea in your head that
there was something odd about the Hendricks fire?'

He was clearly stricken by my question. Instead of
answering it, however, he said, 'Dora senses things,
Cal.'

'Senses things?'

'Yes,' Billy said. 'I think she . . . experienced something that made her—'

'Wait,' I interrupted. 'Just wait a second. First, what do you actually know about her? Details, I mean. Like, where she was living before she came to Port Alma?'

'New York City,' Billy replied. 'At a residence hall there. For women. As a matter of fact, I even know the address, Eighty-fifth and Broadway.'

'What was she doing in New York?'

'Like I said, living there.'

He added nothing else, and so I suspected that he'd already pretty much exhausted his information.

But rather than release him, I closed in. 'Does she talk about her past?'

'Not much.'

'So as far as you know, she just popped up here in Port Alma?'

'Yes.'

'Why here, I wonder. I mean, it's a long way from New York. And very different.'

'Cal, what are you getting at?'

'I'm trying to make a point.'

'What point?'

'Just that you don't know much about her.'

'What would I need to know?'

'A lot before you start giving her . . . powers.'

Billy grinned and leaned back in his seat. 'That's the difference between you and me, Cal.'

I laughed. 'You don't *want* to know about her. That's the real difference between you and me, Billy. You don't want to know about her. You might find out she's pretty ordinary. Probably just some shopgirl from Macy's who climbed onto a northbound bus one afternoon, ended up here because her money ran out.'

My brother's expression turned grave. 'Something happened to her, Cal.'

I wasn't buying it. 'She was born. She lived. More than likely, that's all that ever "happened" to her.'

'No.' Billy said it firmly. 'Something happened to Dora.'

'Something tragic, no doubt.'

'Yes.'

I'd had enough. 'Why do you want to believe that something "tragic" happened to Dora? Is it because it would make her different from other women? Why can't you just face the fact that nobody's really that different from anybody else? We're just people. Plain. Ordinary. Nothing great about us. Nothing splendid. We come out of the dirt and we go back to it.'

'I know you believe that,' Billy said. 'Dad does too. But I don't.' For the first time in his life, my brother regarded me with pity. 'I don't want to live like you, Cal. Spend my life like you.' He searched for the right words, then said them: 'Like someone waiting for a change in the weather.'

He'd never drawn the line more clearly, never delineated more precisely what distinguished us as brothers and as men. For me, the prospects of life, and certainly of love, would remain innately limited. Human life was lost in folly. No human was truly worthy of devotion, and so I would not offer it. What one could not worship, it seemed fitting to despise. These were my true beliefs, and I didn't in the least feel compelled to deny them. And so I said, 'You were born to be disillusioned, Billy. Born to have some woman kick

your heart out. Because you want something impossible.'

He stared at me steadily. 'What do *you* want from a
woman, Cal?'

'What I always get. A little pleasure, then a good
night's sleep.'

'So it's only sex, then? You've never in your life
wanted more than that?'

He was alluding to the Saturday nights I spent on the
waterfront in Royston, of course. I'd never kept that
aspect of my life from him. But neither had I ever
expected him to bring it up in this way, as an accusation.

'Don't you want more from a woman than that?' he
demanded. 'Something . . . beautiful? Something that
lasts forever?'

I felt under attack, and struck back.

'Dad did, didn't he?' I asked hotly. 'Dad wanted a lot
more from our mother. Something perfect. That would
last forever. Someone to share his life with, his soul
with. What good did it do him? Or her, for that matter.
She'll die alone. And so will he.' I felt the air harden
around me, the walls of the Bluebird Café squeeze in. I
reached into my pocket, flung a few coins on the table.
'Let's get out of here.'

The sun glittered on the snow as we made our way
down Main Street. We walked all the way to the front
door of the *Sentinel* without exchanging a single word.
Then, as he was about to go inside, my brother took my
arm and turned me toward him. 'What I said at the café,
I didn't mean it, Cal. That you're just a . . . whore-
monger.'

'But, I am, Billy,' I said without apology. 'That's
exactly what I am. That's my dirty little secret.' I stared

at him emphatically, driving home an earlier point. 'Everybody has one. Something weak about them. Something grimy.' I gave the nail a final bang. 'Even this new woman of yours. Dora. This woman who "senses" things.'

Billy stared at me silently. I knew I'd reached that place where the next word mattered so much, it would be best not to say it.

I glanced down at his worn overcoat and found a joke to save us. 'Well, one thing's for sure, she couldn't be after your money.'

He seemed relieved that I'd found a way past our harsh words, that for all our differences, we were still brothers. He grinned and clapped me on the shoulder. 'I'll give you that, Cal. Dora couldn't be after my money.'

He turned and headed into the building. I watched him hang his coat on the peg by the door, then stride deliberately toward his desk, rolling his sleeves up as he walked. Henry Mason was scribbling classifieds at the front counter. Wally Blankenship was setting type, his body swathed in a stained leather apron, his face half hidden beneath a green eyeshade. But it was Dora March I found myself watching. She was sitting at her metal desk in a far corner, her back to the row of wooden filing cabinets where back issues of the *Sentinel* were kept. A newspaper was spread before her on the desk. She was peering at it intently, a single finger moving back and forth along the gold band of her glasses. As I watched, she read a moment longer, then closed the paper and looked up. Her lips remained tightly sealed, but somehow in that silence, I thought I heard a scream.

Chapter Nine

That was why I did it. The look on Dora's face, along with my brother's certainty that 'something' had happened to her. I didn't doubt that she might have suffered some loss in her past. Most people had. And for those who hadn't, it was only a matter of time. No life went forward without bereavement. No human being had ever, in the end, outrun regret. What I feared was that this wound had scooped something from the core of Dora March, dug a pit within her, and that my brother now walked perilously along its ever-crumbling rim.

It happened three hours later, when Jack Stout came into my office. He was wearing baggy pants, as always, black except for the places where cigarette ash left small dusty stains. He plopped down in the chair opposite my desk, unfastened his jacket, and let his belly flop over a cracked leather belt. 'Headin' for New York, Mr Chase,' he said. 'To pick up Charlie Younger.' He thumped a cigarette from a crumpled pack and offered it to me.

'No, thanks.'

Jack plucked the cigarette from the pack, lit it with a match raked across the side of his boot. 'They got him in a place called—' He stopped, yanked a piece of paper from his pocket, and squinted. 'Tombs.'

'That's the city jail.'

'It's on an island, Mr Ferguson told me.'

'Rikers Island. It's in the middle of a river. The one that runs along the east side of Manhattan.'

Jack crammed the address back into his shirt pocket. 'It's just me, you know. Nobody else going with me.'

'You don't need anybody else.'

Jack grinned, his bottom teeth rising like a jagged yellow wall. 'Figure Charlie'll go peaceful, do you?'

'He'll be wearing everything but a muzzle,' I said. 'Feet and hands, both shackled. A chain running under his crotch. You won't need help, believe me. Not to bring Charlie Younger home.'

'Well, he sure scared the shit out of Lou Powers.'

'The gun wasn't loaded. Charlie was desperate, that's all. He never had a problem before that. He won't give you any trouble.'

Jack Stout grinned again. 'Famous last words, Mr Chase.'

'When are you leaving?'

' 'Bout an hour. Just gonna grab a clam roll at the Bluebird, then head out.' He crossed one leg over the other. A huge brown boot wagged in the air, the heel worn flat. 'Hoping I won't hit too much weather.' He stroked his chin. 'Think I need a shave? Mr Ferguson says I need to look professional.'

I didn't see how Jack Stout could ever look professional. Shave, haircut, even dressed in a neat blue ready-made suit, none of it would have mattered much. Jack bore the mark of what he was, one of six brothers from a family of scavenges and poachers, the type who lived in shacks at the end of winding mountain roads. As a group, the Stouts had always preferred, as if by nature, things that were unhinged and collapsible, could be broken into pieces and dragged through the piney woods or hauled up rocky trails. Jack was the only one who'd made a life within the law, usually as a laborer, but sometimes running errands for Hap and Sheriff Pritchart, fetching prisoners back to Port Alma from the places they'd fled to, and from which they surrendered, penniless and hungry. Charlie Younger was just the latest in a growing line of such men, driven by harsh times to harsh acts, then tracked down in flophouses from Portland to Baltimore, and brought back to face consequences no less harsh. I pitied them briefly, prosecuted them energetically, and sent them, dazed, to jail.

'You look fine,' I told him.

Jack pinched off the lighted end of his cigarette, blew a speck of ash from what remained, and dropped the rest into his pocket to smoke another time. It was the sort of small economy the poor practiced in those days, and I couldn't help admiring it, not so much for the savings as for the sheer frankness of the gesture, a raw admission of want, offered with neither apology nor resentment.

Jack slapped his knees and rose. 'Well, can I bring you anything from the big city? Besides Charlie, I mean?'

At that instant, I saw Dora's face as she'd looked up from her desk a few hours before. An idea came to me. It was one of those impulses we either act upon casually or casually deny, then live forever in the wake of a fatal choice.

'As a matter of fact, you *could* do something for me, Jack.'

'What's that?'

'There's a place in New York. A residence hall for

women. I'd like for you to drop by, check something out.' I took a piece of paper and wrote the address and name, *85th and Broadway, Dora March*. 'Find out what you can about this woman,' I said as I handed him the paper.

Jack glanced at the note. 'Dora March.'

'She works at the *Sentinel*. It's always good to have a little extra information.' I smiled. 'I'll pay you for this, of course.'

Jack's bulb burned dully, but not without illuminating a small patch of ground. 'Looking out for your kid brother, are you?'

'You could call it that.'

'You bet, Mr Chase,' Jack said. He stuck the note in his shirt pocket. 'I'll be back in four or five days.'

'We can settle up then.'

'You bet,' he repeated as he left my office.

A few minutes later I saw Jack trudging through the slush toward the Bluebird Café, his red jacket open, his belly pressing against his plaid shirt. He'd pulled on his cap, and the earflaps dangled haphazardly, like furry black legs. He was by no means a crack investigator, of course, so I expected to learn relatively little about Dora, perhaps no more than a few scant details of her life in New York. Certainly, as I watched Jack Stout amble down Main Street that morning, I had no expectation that the information he'd bring back to Port Alma would be of any great importance. Nor did I want it to have any such gravity. It was only the surface of Dora's life I sought to probe, not the black depths I later found.

And yet, in some way, perhaps I should have sensed that

the ground was already trembling beneath my brother's feet, should have seen at least that much in the look on my father's face as he and I sat in his front parlor three days later, playing our weekly game of chess.

'I spoke to William yesterday,' he told me, reaching for a pawn, then drawing back, taking a bishop instead. 'He just came by for a chat, but the subject turned somewhat serious.' My father was in his late seventies, and in old age, liked to think of himself as deeply sagacious, the sort of man a son would go to for advice, though he clearly understood that for any real guidance, Billy would certainly turn to his mother.

'So, what'd Billy have to say?' I asked idly, more intent upon plotting my strategy, hoping for checkmate within five moves.

He sat back, twined his fingers together. 'He was asking about children.'

'What was he saying about children?'

'Just general things,' my father answered. 'Having them. Raising them.' He placed his hands firmly on the armrests, a pose he associated, I think, with statues of great men. 'He seemed extremely intense, Cal.'

I continued to study the board. 'Billy's always intense, Dad.'

'But what's got him suddenly thinking about children?'

'True love,' I answered with a cynical smile.

'That never did run smooth,' my father said.

I expected him to add some grave remark, assume the worldly tone he often took with me, convinced of how alike we were, he and I, how different from Billy and my mother, we the truly knowing ones, steeped in life's unflattering realities, they forever pursuing golden shards from the Holy Grail. But instead, he remained silent for a moment, then told a story I'd never heard before.

'It certainly didn't run smooth for your mother and me,' he began. He shook his head at the difficult life they'd lived together. 'Not even during the courtship.'

'That's supposed to be the best time, isn't it?' I asked, though with little actual interest, my attention on the board, where I had a knight in peril.

'Supposed to be,' my father replied. 'I guess it is for most couples.'

I reached for my queen. 'But not for you?'

'No, not for me. Your mother never made it easy.' He smiled softly. 'But she was such a jewel, Cal. No one else like her. No one in the world. I didn't want to let her go. But what could I do? From the way she acted, I couldn't see that she gave a damn whether I came or went. So I finally told her that I couldn't go on with her the way it was. I said, "Mary, I guess it has to come to an end with us."'

I lowered the queen to the board.

'I used practically those very words,' my father went on. 'While we were walking along Fox Creek, not that far from where she went to live. I said, "Mary, it's time for us to part."'

'What'd she say?'

'Nothing,' my father answered. 'She just looked at me. Like I was a mannequin in a store. Finally, we walked over to my buggy and I drove her home. Neither one of us said anything all the way. When I pulled up to her house, I didn't even walk her to the door. I just said, "Well, good-bye, Mary." And she said, "Good-bye, Walter," and got out of the buggy. She said it almost cheerily. Like I was a cousin, or just someone who'd dropped by and taken her for a buggy ride. She walked straight to her house. Didn't so much as glance back at me.'

A terrible emptiness had swept over him after that, my father told me, a misery like none he'd ever known. 'You've never felt it, Cal,' he said assuredly, equally convinced that I never would, certain that not even the sharpest arrow could pierce me as deeply as it had once unexpectedly pierced him. 'Mary was everything. And she was gone.'

Or so he'd thought. Until he came home from the *Sentinel* one afternoon, still heartsick, to find a note slipped beneath his door, folded into a white envelope that bore no name, no address.

'I thought it was one of those anonymous tips I got about once a year,' my father told me. 'Usually somebody informing on a local politician or shopkeeper.'

But it had been from her.

Four lines.

> *Before your love be all rescinded,*
> *Or strikes the hour when we part,*
> *Can you not break me till I'm mended?*
> *Crack the will of my unwilling heart?*

'There's nothing like loneliness, Cal,' my father said, 'to bring you to your knees.'

I knew then what he'd been getting at all along. 'Do you think Billy's that lonely, Dad?'

'Not anymore.' His eyes fell toward the queen I'd placed so perilously near his last remaining knight. 'Not anymore,' he repeated softly. 'Who is she, Cal?'

*

I told him her name and the few things I knew about her, but left out the fact that only a couple of days earlier I'd sent Jack Stout on a mission to find out more about Dora March. Even so, my father appeared quite satisfied by what he'd learned from me. He seemed eager to meet Dora, perhaps even half convinced that my mother had been right all along, that for such a one as Billy, there could be but one true love.

The next day I thought only infrequently of either my brother or Dora. There was plenty of work to do, sorting through the cases Hap had assigned me, deciding what prosecutions should be brought, how they might best be conducted.

Night was closing in by the time I pushed aside my paperwork and left for home. Hap had long since departed, but others were afoot on the streets of Port Alma, mostly closing up their shops, heading home.

A sea fog had moved in an hour or so before, and the moon was little more than a smudged light behind a bank of clouds. The metal sign at Madison's General Store creaked in the breeze that swept in from the bay, and far away, a dog briefly sounded a lonely, hollow wail, then fell silent. Beyond that, nothing save the crunch of my boots on the hard-packed snow.

I headed past the grocery and the hotel, nodding to the neighbors I glimpsed through their lighted windows, then moved on along the edge of the town's small park, its wooden benches piled with snow. Through the haze, I could scarcely see the old wharves that rose on the other side of the park. Only the great revolving light at the top of MacAndrews Island made any dent in the fog, its white beam circling in from the sea, flashing briefly on the great gray stones of the jetty, finally running along the slender cement lip of the seawall.

That was when I saw her, a woman standing at the far edge of the park, poised at the verge of the wall. She was facing the ocean, and in my brief glimpse of her before the light swept on again, she seemed to be waiting for something or someone to reach out from its vast depths.

I stopped and waited as the light made its slow circle. When it returned, I saw her once again. Then darkness swallowed her as the light moved on. I waited, watched, but when the light made its third circle, crawling along the seawall, she was gone. The place where she'd stood was empty, the park and the jetty both deserted, with nothing moving anywhere, nor any sound, save for the distant surge of the sea.

I started homeward again, tugging my collar up against the rising wind. I'd made it nearly to my car when I saw the woman emerge briskly from the shrouded alleyway that led from Main Street to the wharves. She swung swiftly to the right, like a creature on the run. She didn't see me, and in the fog I'm not sure I would ever have guessed who she was. For she seemed very nearly carved out of that same roiling density, her long coat blending with it perfectly, so that nothing impeded my sense of her having been formed out of the smoky cloud that surrounded her, save for the flicking tongue of my brother's dark red scarf.

Chapter Ten

The telephone rang just as I stepped into my office the next morning.

It was Billy.

'There's something you need to know,' he said.

I was quite certain that this 'something' I needed to know had to do with Dora March. But I was wrong.

'It's about Carl Hendricks,' my brother told me. 'Did you know he was married before?'

I tugged off my overcoat and slung it over the nearest chair. 'That's not a crime, is it?'

'He had another daughter too. She was killed. It happened around twenty years ago. She fell off the seawall right here in town.'

An image from the night before flashed through my mind, Dora, in the dense fog, poised at the edge of the seawall, facing the impenetrable water that swept out toward MacAndrews Island.

'I'd like to talk to you about this, Cal,' Billy said. 'Are you free?'

I could hear the urgency in his voice. 'Yeah, all right. Just give me a few minutes to get settled in.'

The clock had not yet struck nine when Billy arrived. He was carrying the battered leather briefcase my father had given him the day he'd turned the management of the paper over to him. Once he'd taken his seat in front of my desk, he opened it and took out a crumbly, yellowed copy of the *Sentinel*.

'Hendricks was only twenty-seven years old when it happened,' he said as he slid the paper over to me. 'The child was three.'

While he waited, I read the article. It was clear that the *Sentinel* had given the incident quite prominent coverage at the time. My father had selected a bold typeface for the headline. From all appearances, he'd also done a workmanlike job of running down the details of the story. I learned that Hendricks's first wife had died of tuberculosis in Royston Hospital in December 1917. According to the article, Hendricks had then moved to Port Alma, where he'd lived on Pine Road with his younger sister. On the day in question, March 4, 1917, Hendricks had come into town for supplies. He'd planned to go directly to Madison's, he'd later told authorities, but the child, whose name was Sophie, had gotten 'cranky,' and so he'd taken her along the wharf, then back to one of the benches that faced the seawall and the bay. Once there, he'd put her down and let her crawl about. At that point, a stranger had come up to ask directions. They'd talked briefly, then the stranger had departed. It was only then that Hendricks had noticed his little girl was missing.

'I talked to Dad last night,' Billy said when I looked up from the paper. 'He remembered quite a lot. He said that Hendricks continued to live with his sister after his daughter died. In the very same house that burned down.'

'What happened to the sister?'

'As far as Dad could remember, she moved out west somewhere. After that, no one knows. She just disappeared.'

'Into the mist,' I said, long used to the disappearance of such witnesses, how they vanished into the ether, taking all hope of truth and justice with them. I handed the paper back to my brother. 'What are you getting at?' I asked a little impatiently, thinking of the casework piled on my desk.

'Well, as it turns out, Hendricks's second wife – Molly's mother – died about three months ago.'

'So Carl's not a lucky guy. So what?'

'It was three months from the time of his first wife's death until his first daughter was killed.'

The nature of Billy's suspicions, how dark and terrible they were, suddenly became clear, but I still felt no need to entertain them myself.

'Killed? You mean murdered? Is that what you're getting at?' I laughed. 'Does the word "coincidence" mean anything to you?'

Billy stood his ground. 'Do you want to hear more, or not?'

'Go ahead,' I said without enthusiasm.

'I checked the weather on the day the little girl disappeared. It was clear but very windy, so the ocean was probably whipping up quite a bit. In any case, there wouldn't have been many people out near the water.'

'Except for that stranger.'

'Who was never found.'

That didn't surprise me. 'Did anybody actually see Hendricks near the wall?'

'No.'

'And no one saw the kid either?'

'No one saw anything.'

'Well, there must have been some sort of official investigation.'

'Not much of one,' Billy replied. 'I found the police report. Carl Hendricks was the only witness. The police took him at his word.'

'Which leaves you where?'

'Wondering about that little girl.'

'I gather you don't accept Hendricks's account of what happened to her?'

'I have reason to doubt it.'

I was beginning to get exasperated. 'Other than coincidence, exactly what reason do you have?'

'Sophie Hendricks had withered legs,' my brother said. He waited for me to speak, then added, 'The lip on the seawall is twenty-eight inches high. She couldn't have climbed it.'

'And you're telling me that nobody raised that point when the child died?'

'Hendricks had just moved to Port Alma a few weeks before. It was winter. Sophie had probably never been seen by any local people. Except all bundled up. If that's true, then no one would have noticed her legs until spring.'

'I'm presuming the body was swept out to sea?'

'Never recovered. Yes.'

'Then, how did you find out about the little girl's legs being withered?'

He seemed almost reluctant to tell me. 'Dora,' he said finally. 'Dora found a picture. At the house. Among all that rubble.'

He reached inside his briefcase again. This time he came out with a photograph. It was badly scorched, but the central image was clear, a small child with curly hair, propped up in a chair, clothed only in a white diaper, perfect from the waist up but with legs disproportionately small and undeveloped, the feet curled. Dangling at the end of Sophie Hendricks's tiny legs, they looked like small, rounded flippers.

'Her name is on the back,' Billy said.

I turned the picture over, read what was written there: *Sophie, 2 years, 3 months*, then set it on my desk. 'So, your idea is that Hendricks threw his daughter into the ocean?'

'I don't know, Cal. I don't think anyone will ever know. But I'm worried about the other daughter. The one he has with him now. Molly.'

'There's no evidence that Carl's ever hurt his daughter,' I said firmly. 'And certainly none that he tried to burn her alive in that fire.'

For a moment there was silence, then Billy said, 'The blanket. The one he said he used to beat back the fire. It wasn't singed or scorched. It didn't even smell of smoke.'

In my mind I saw Dora standing in the snow, the charred remains of Carl Hendricks's house before her, the blanket a soggy mass at her feet.

'Look, Billy, I'm not going to say that Hendricks couldn't have thrown his first kid into the sea. Losing his wife, left with a crippled child. Maybe he snapped. It could happen. And I'm not going to say that he didn't try to burn up the second one. But there's absolutely no evidence of either crime. Nothing to hang a charge on. Not even arson. Much less murder, in the case of the first child. Or attempted murder, in the second.'

'You don't have to charge him, Cal.'

'What do you want me to do, then?'

'Protect Molly.'

'For Christ's sake, how?'

'You could go out there. Talk to Hendricks. He's living in that little shed behind the house. Just by dropping by, you'd let him know that you were keeping an eye on him. That would give us time to find out more.'

'Us?'

'Dora and me,' my brother said without hesitation. 'It was Dora who first had doubts.'

I suspected that those doubts had been based on nothing more than the look she'd glimpsed in Molly Hendricks's light blue eyes. 'You know, Billy, it's not really my job to be poking into Carl Hendricks's affairs without any proof at all that he's actually done anything wrong.'

'But it would be worth it if we were right,' Billy shot back. 'It wouldn't even be out of your way, Cal. It's Saturday. Hendricks's place is right on your way.'

'On my way?'

'Well, you'll be going to Royston tonight, won't you?'

'Yeah, I'm going to Royston.'

'So why not just drop by Hendricks's place? You know, on your way to Royston.'

I could find no reason not to. And I knew that Billy wouldn't leave until I'd agreed to do what he asked. 'Okay,' I said.

Billy left immediately, and for the rest of the afternoon I worked to set my office in order before the weekend. There'd been more to do than I'd expected, however, so that it was well past seven before I finally managed to get away.

I drove down the deserted main street of Port Alma, then along the road I took to Royston each Saturday evening, a flask of whiskey in my jacket pocket and the vague image of a woman in my mind. On the way, I crossed the rickety wooden bridge that stretched over Fox Creek, then swept by the Hooverville that lay beyond it. I could feel the urgency building in me, desire like a whip at my back. I was eager to get to Royston. But I'd told my brother that I'd drop in on Hendricks, and so I did.

In the darkness I could make out only that no light burned in the small shed in which Hendricks and his daughter had taken up residence. I saw no sign of Hendricks, no sign of Molly, and so I quickly pulled back onto Pine Road and headed once again toward Royston and the woman who waited for me there.

She lived with four other women in a house where the smell of the sea wafted through the carefully swept hallways and tidy, surprisingly well-appointed bedrooms. The surrounding area was a worn and wholly disreputable part of town, moon-swept but otherwise unlighted, a labyrinth of narrow lanes and alleyways, patrolled by skinny dogs and scruffy cats. At night I could hear the laughter at the seaman's bar next door, along with the inevitable fistfights that poured out onto the old brick streets. Beyond the windows a steady stream of trawlers swept across a swath of black water, their decks heaped with mounds of gray netting.

Maggie Flynn met me at the door. She was now the sole proprietor of the establishment her mother had maintained for nearly fifty years. Edna Flynn had been driven from Ireland by the Great Hunger. She'd come to Canada on a coffin ship, Edna said, then drifted south, where she'd finally found work as a charwoman at a rooming house in Royston. Slowly, by small, nearly imperceptible steps, the rooming house had turned bawdy. Edna had never formally lent herself to that particular task, as she often said, but on occasion she would 'take a fancy' to some young sailor, and together they'd drift upstairs to one of the bedrooms that ran down a long gaslit corridor. In the morning, a few coins inevitably lay neatly beneath the lantern on the bureau. Since Edna was by no means dull, she'd early realized that this added up to prostitution, and yet, even after she'd become the sole proprietor, incontestably a madam, she'd never allowed anyone, neither her customers nor any of her 'girls,' to use that term in connection with what took place in the upper rooms of her house on Blyden Street.

Her daughter Maggie had no such reservation, however. Once her mother was dead and buried, all pretense that the men who tramped up the wooden stairs came for 'social' purposes went out the window with as little ceremony as a tub of fish heads. Still, Maggie seemed to prefer the 'regulars' to the transient seamen who came but for a night and were never seen again. The regulars, mostly older men from neighboring towns, often married, with businesses and professions of their own, these were the 'heart and soul' of her operation, Maggie said, and I always believed that she'd chosen that phrase purposefully, because it conveyed the high regard for permanence and stability that creatures like ourselves, impermanent, unstable, doomed by time to disappear, yearn for without surcease.

She was wearing a bright dress of royal blue that evening, a dress I'd never seen. The rest was familiar, however, a rawboned woman whose hair would have been gray but for a dye of strawberry blond, and whose breasts would have dropped quite noticeably had they not been laced up in an old-fashioned corset. But for all that, Maggie had a curiously quiet, almost contemplative manner, not at all that of the rowdy, loudmouthed saloon matrons portrayed in western movies.

Ten years had passed since the first time I'd turned up at Maggie's door, and hardly a week had since gone by without my returning to her house on Blyden Street. I was a regular now.

'Hello, Cal,' Maggie said as I took off my hat.

'Good evening, Miss Maggie.'

She led me inside. 'Welcome home,' she said.

I took my usual seat in the parlor, poured a whiskey and lit a cigar, then waited, quite contentedly, for a woman to descend the stairs, cross the room, and with all the innocence of a blushing virgin, take my hand.

She came down a few minutes later, then led me back up the stairs. Halfway down the corridor to her room, we passed the bathroom, its door casually open. Mr Castleman, dressed in black wool pants and a white undershirt, stood before a mirror, straightening himself up after his latest activities. A pair of suspenders dangled to his knees as he combed the few remaining strands of his hair. He glanced at me as I strolled by, nodded courteously, and continued grooming himself.

Farther down the corridor, I saw Polly Jenks alone in her room, slowly fastening her garters. She smiled thinly as I passed, then plucked two bills from the bureau.

Once in our customary room, I stretched out on the old fourposter and glanced about the room my customary lady had prepared as I preferred it – no candles, no flowers, no photographs on the Victrola.

'Polly's leaving,' she said matter-of-factly.

'Oh, yeah? Where's she going?'

'Back home. Iowa. Says she's getting too old for it.'

'Well, she's been at it a long time. She's probably pretty tired.'

She gave me a quick, suggestive smile, then lied through her teeth. 'I'll never get tired of you.'

She stepped behind a translucent screen and began to undress, folding each garment carefully as she removed it, then laying it over the top of the screen. Once naked, she put on the bright red silk robe she'd bought in Portland. She'd had it only a couple of years, but it was tattered at the sleeve, worn at the lapel. I'd never learned whether she wore it because she thought men liked it, or because she liked it herself, fancied it gave her a touch of class.

She'd taken her hair down, and it fell in a dark brown wave over her shoulders. She shook it playfully, like a girl, though the lines around her eyes, the slight sag beneath her chin, put the lie to any pretense that we could steal a single second from the clock. She had a plump, well-rounded body, the sort that, depending upon the position, either rode heavily upon you or provided an ample cushion for your weight. I guessed her age at around forty-five, though I'd guessed almost the same nearly ten years earlier, when I'd first showed up at Maggie Flynn's. In truth, I no longer cared how old she was, or that her body had lost its tone, or that her breath had grown more labored during sex, a line of sweat forming on her brow and along her upper lip. I had reached that whoremaster's plateau where nothing was felt but what lay between my legs, all other flesh but a sea of flesh, soft and serviceable, but hardly different from my hand.

'So, what's new in Port Alma?' she asked as she curled onto the edge of the bed and began to untie my shoes.

I mentioned the only thing that came to mind. 'We had a fire.'

'My goodness,' she said, feigning shock. 'I bet the whole town came to see it.' She set my right shoe under the end of the bed, then started untying the left one.

I plucked the cigar from my lips and pressed its still faintly glowing tip into the little glass ashtray on the table beside the bed. 'My brother thinks it was arson. That a man was trying to kill his little girl.'

Her fingers stopped for an instant, then started again. 'Let's not talk about that,' she said. She drew off the second shoe, placed it beside the other, then crawled up the bed and pressed herself down upon my chest, her mouth poised just over mine. 'It must be really interesting though, your job.'

'Not really. And the pay's lousy.'

She smiled and tossed her hair. 'Well, you manage to have enough for me.'

'Barely.'

She kissed me once, then remembered and pulled back. 'Oh, sorry. I forgot.'

'It's all right.'

'I usually remember that you don't—'

'It's all right,' I assured her.

She lifted herself up and let the robe fall open, now working to get back into the rhythm of our sessions. 'So, what's my name tonight?' she asked.

It was a routine we'd acted out for years. I'd pick a name for her, usually from ancient drama or mythology, tell her the story behind it. 'Antigone,' I said.

'That's a pretty name,' she said. 'What's her story?'

Billy's face swam into my mind, more innocent than his years, still battling lost causes, still believing he would win them. I felt all my tenderness sweep out to him, embrace him and wish him well, and I knew that no feeling would ever touch me more deeply than this, a true and decent hope that it would all come to him in the end, every wild hope and foolish dream. 'Antigone loved her brother,' I said. 'He was all she ever knew of love.'

Chapter Eleven

I left Blyden Street at the usual time, offering my usual good-bye, 'See you next week,' as I stepped out the door.

Once away, I got in my car and headed in the general direction of town. The road was unpaved and pitted, as though the city fathers had decided to make it as difficult as possible for men like me to escape the bars and whorehouses in which they'd spent the night.

It was a Sunday morning. The canneries were silent, nothing moving but the gulls and the sea. Farther along, the shanties and rusty warehouses of the waterfront gave way to the homes of the dock and cannery workers, small, wood-framed, with cramped, snow-covered yards hemmed in by unpainted picket fences.

Once downtown, I pulled up to Carpenter's Café, took the booth in the front window, ordered the special of eggs, bacon, toast, coffee. The waitress was in her forties, with brown hair pulled back and wound into a bun. Her upper arm jiggled as she scribbled the order upon the pad.

'Anything else?' she asked.

'No.'

The local paper lay folded on the table. I opened it, scanned a story about FDR's latest scheme to save the nation, another about a boat that had run aground on the beaches to the north, then folded the paper again.

By that time breakfast had arrived. I ate it listening to the first church bells summon the faithful to morning Mass. I could feel a cloud settling over me, and to escape it, I quickly drained the last of the coffee and returned to the street. But rather than get in my car and go directly back to Port Alma, I decided to take a walk.

I didn't know where I was going. Nor did I care. I simply headed up the hill, into a neighborhood of homes that had clearly seen better days. Even from a distance I could see paint peeling from their wooden clapboards, roof edges curled backward, strips of caulking that drooped from beneath rotting windowsills.

At the top of the hill, I turned back to observe the view. Below, the town spread out in a tangle of streets, a crescent bay beyond it, ragged lines of sea foam tumbling over the wintry beach.

I was still staring at the town and the bay when I heard the slap of a screen door. I turned and saw a woman stroll out onto a wooden porch. I recognized her right away. It was Rachel Bass, Hap's widowed cousin. She stood on the same porch she'd occupied in his photograph, the rusty tin thermometer still nailed in place beside her shoulder.

She was wearing a dark green dress that fell almost to her ankles, but otherwise she looked much as she had in the picture Hap had given me and that now rested somewhere in the clutter of papers in my desk drawer. She remained quite still for a moment, the broom in her right hand, then began to sweep the porch.

The screen door slapped again a few seconds later, and a small girl darted out of the house. The child scrambled down the stairs, leaped onto a rusty tricycle, and began careening about on a sidewalk that had only recently been cleared of snow.

She played alone for a while; then, as if something had silently called to her, she turned and bounded back up the stairs, rushing past her mother and into the house.

For a time I waited, expecting the child to return. When she didn't, I strolled over to where Rachel Bass continued to sweep.

'Good morning,' I said.

She looked toward me, lifting her arm to shield her eyes from the sun.

'I'm Cal Chase,' I added. 'I work for your cousin. In Port Alma.'

She came closer and lowered her arm, so that I could see that her eyes were dark blue. 'You work for Hap?'

'Yes,' I replied. With nowhere else to go, I added, 'He showed me a picture of you.'

She smiled. 'I guess Hap's out beating the bushes for me.'

'I recognized you as I came up the road,' I told her.

'You're walking?'

'My car's down the hill.'

'So, what did Hap tell you?'

'I know that you lost your husband. That you have a daughter.'

She pointed toward the house. 'I rent rooms. That's how I make a go of it.'

'You once taught school, Hap said.'

She nodded. 'Years back.' She leaned on the broom and continued to study me. 'What are you doing in Royston?'

I had no choice but to lie. 'I decided to take a drive. You know, get out of Port Alma.'

'Looking for adventure.'

'I guess.'

A silence fell between us, one we both tried to breach at the same instant.

'Look . . .'

'Well, I . . .'

We laughed.

'You go ahead,' Rachel said, smiling.

'Well, when I saw you, I remembered your picture. Just thought I'd say hello. I'll tell Hap we ran into each other.'

She smiled quietly. 'You do that,' she said.

I shrugged. 'That's all, I guess.'

She knew I was leaving, perhaps had swung by only to take a look, window-shop, nothing more, and that somehow, according to my own secret scale of things, she had failed to measure up. Even so, she took it in her stride.

'Well, I'm glad to have met you,' she said. She offered her hand. 'Good-bye, Mr Chase.'

I pumped her hand, then released it, turned and headed back down the hill to my car. I knew she was watching me, perhaps even hoping that I might swing around, stroll up to her again, boldly invite her to dinner or a dance. In earlier years I might have done just that, followed the normal route of courtship, marriage, parenthood. But by then I felt sure that I'd walked the rogue's path far too long ever to abandon it, that the call of romance was one I would never hear, nor, if I heard it, be foolish enough to heed. That world was for Billy, strewn with roses and punctuated with breathy, melodramatic sighs. I could imagine my mother looking on approvingly as he sank deeper and deeper into the trough of such romance, offering me only a sidelong glance, a whispered judgment: *Stay with your whores, Cal. You lack the heart for more.*

Snow fell thickly as I left Royston. It continued to fall for the next hour, growing more dense as I neared Port Alma.

It was as I approached Pine Road that I thought once again of Molly Hendricks, saw her in my mind as she'd last appeared to me, a small figure crouched and freezing as she trailed behind her father, leaving tiny footprints in the snow.

As I came to a halt in Hendricks's driveway, the snow suddenly stopped and a burst of sunlight swept down upon the blackened heap that had once been the house. Beyond the rubble, the shed stood, all its somber details brilliantly visible in a dazzling light, its weathered roof, the rusty tools nailed to its clapboard sides, two tiny windows, each covered with what appeared to be thick woolen blankets.

I'd gotten halfway to it when I noticed that there were no tracks in the snow around it. Clearly, neither Hendricks nor Molly had been outside for a time. They might be huddled in the shed, of course, but no smoke came from the black pipe that pierced its roof, and in the cold, it seemed unlikely they would have remained inside without a fire.

I tapped lightly at the door. When no one answered, I stepped over to one of the windows. The blanket appeared to have been put up hastily, leaving an uneven space of nearly two inches above the sill. I peered inside.

In the shadows I could see Molly Hendricks lying faceup on a sagging cot. Her eyes were closed, her face colorless save for the slender line of blood that ran from the left corner of her mouth, then gathered in a frozen pool near her head.

Inside, I found them both, Molly with a single bullet hole at the back of her head, her father sitting upright in a wooden chair no more than five feet away, a smear of dried blood caked around his mouth and spreading in a black stain across the front of his shirt. The bullet had gone through the roof of his mouth, exited at the rear of his skull. His eyes were wide open, so that he looked shocked, perhaps horrified, either by the force of the explosion or by his first glimpse of the world that awaited him, no less cruel and inadequate, on the other side.

Billy was waiting on the curb, stamping his feet in the deepening snow when I pulled up at the *Sentinel*. He was not alone. Dora stood beside him. Puffs of condensed air burst from her lips, and even after my brother had ushered her into the backseat of my car, she looked deathly cold.

We said nothing as we headed toward Pine Road, nothing as I guided the car into Carl Hendricks's drive. In that silence, Dora seemed truly distant and inscrutable, like a statue that draws light into it rather than giving it off, darkens whatever space it occupies.

After discovering the two bodies, I'd gone directly to my office, of course, called Hap, told him what I'd found in the shed, then phoned the *Sentinel* and given Billy the same details. 'I'm going back out there,' I told him. 'You want to come?'

'Yes, of course,' he'd replied.

'I covered Molly's face,' I told Billy as we got out of the car. 'I left everything else the same.'

Dora had gotten out along with us, and was now standing beside the car, her arms gathered protectively at her chest, flakes of snow gathering on her shoulders and clinging to her hair. 'You want to see this?' I asked her.

'No, I don't,' she answered firmly, sinking her hands into the pockets of her thin coat. 'I'll stay here.'

Billy and I walked past the remains of the gutted house, then to the shed. 'I hope you're ready for this,' I warned him as I opened the door.

For a time he gazed at Molly Hendricks. Then he turned to Carl, flinching suddenly. 'Good God,' he whispered.

'Isn't very pretty, is it?' I asked.

His eyes returned to Molly. 'She's just a child. You always wonder how someone could hurt a child.' He looked at me. 'But then, most people can't. I guess that's what we cling to.'

That was true enough, although I knew that I'd long ago accepted such lethal mayhem as the inescapable result of our disordered nature, and which no scheme for improvement, no matter how trivial or vast, would ever change one whit or in any way undo.

Billy bent forward, touched a curl of Molly's hair.

Watching him from the door, I sensed the tenderness he extended toward everything, an almost primordial sympathy, something taken with us out of paradise.

He straightened, moved to the stove and touched it. 'It's been cold for a long time,' he said softly.

'My guess is, they were already in here when I came by Saturday evening. Already dead, I mean.'

'Probably,' Billy said. He looked at Molly again. 'Poor thing' was all he said.

A moment later, we walked out into the swirling snow.

'I guess Carl just couldn't figure any way out,' my brother said.

'Then he should have thought a little harder.'

'People get trapped in things, Cal.' He glanced toward the car, Dora standing beside it. 'She was terrified that this was going to happen.'

I ducked my head against the cold, thought of old Ed Dillard, now this. A thought passed through my mind: *Death follows her.*

Hap pulled into the drive just as Billy and I reached my car.

'T. R.'s on his way,' he told me. He looked at Billy. 'Well, I guess you were right. There *was* something wrong here.' He glanced toward Dora, his gaze lingering on her briefly, so that he appeared to recognize her distantly, like a photograph he'd once seen in a book. Then he stepped away, moving purposefully toward the shed. Halfway to it, he snapped a branch from a bare sapling. He slapped it softly against his leg as he walked the rest of the way, scattering a burst of snow.

I gave the little shed a final glance, then looked over to where Dora and my brother stood together. Billy was talking quietly, no doubt describing what he'd seen inside it. Even served cold, it would be a disturbing vision, and I expected Dora to do the usual womanly thing upon receiving it, either collapse in my brother's arms or bury her weeping face into his broad shoulder.

She did no such thing, however, only nodded from time to time, as if in response to quite ordinary news. It wasn't until after Billy had stepped away that I saw her body tighten suddenly, grow taut, rigid, as if to squeeze back into its cage whatever raged inside her.

Chapter Twelve

A few days of unseasonably warm weather thawed the ground enough to bury Molly Hendricks six days later. Hap thought someone from the office should make an appearance at the funeral, and since my brother had to some extent been involved in what Hap called 'the Hendricks matter,' he gave the job to me.

The ceremony, such as it was, was almost over by the time I got there. Standing at a distance, I could see Billy and Dora gathered with a few of Hendricks's neighbors from Pine Road.

Reverend Cates conducted the funeral with his usual solemnity. The course of every life, he said, followed a strange and unknowable direction. We might work to probe the mystery, but it would always elude us. For we were lost, like sheep in a deep valley, wandering in the darkness, without guidance or direction, driven here and there by mere circumstance, undone by pure chance. The darkness was impenetrable, and so we groped and stumbled, fell into traps and snares. We had been brought here to suffer, he told the small gathering, to be broken into submission, wounded again and again, so that we might find within those wounds the force and grace of love.

When it was over, Reverend Cates grabbed a handful of snow-encrusted earth and tossed it onto the plain wooden coffin the citizens of Port Alma had managed to buy for their murdered daughter. After that, we headed in ragged lines down the hill to the main road. Only Billy lingered at the grave, no doubt gathering thoughts for the column he'd write later that day, leaving Dora to make her way down alone.

'Well, you were right, Dora,' I said as I came up behind her. 'About Molly, I mean. That her father intended to kill her. My brother told me that you sensed things.'

I'd meant it as a kind of praise, a recognition of her intuitive powers, but I could see she had little use for compliments. Still, I did not relent.

'What did you sense in Molly Hendricks?' I asked, my tone suddenly insistent. 'That she was going to be hurt?'

'That she'd already been hurt.'

'And that looked like . . . what?'

'Helplessness. Like someone was holding her down.'

'Why didn't I see it?'

She didn't answer, but I saw the answer in her eyes: *Because it's never happened to you.*

'I saw you, you know,' I told her. 'At the seawall that night. In the fog.'

Dora held her attention on the black, wrought iron gate at the bottom of the hill. 'You walk at night,' she said. It was not a question.

'Sometimes.'

She appeared to take my answer as confirmation of my solitary habits, the improvizations I had built to hold my life together. I sensed that she'd built a similar structure, erected walls and fences to keep in what she needed, keep out what she could not endure.

'I prefer the night,' I said.

'Why?'

The question seemed innocent enough, and yet I felt that I was suddenly under interrogation, like a suspect in a detective novel, squirming in his chair, the naked bulb shining cruelly overhead. 'I've never really thought about it,' I answered. 'I suppose I like the solitude.'

'Do you draw at night?'

'Draw?'

'Billy says you draw.'

I laughed. 'I haven't drawn anything in years. He means when I was a kid.'

'Did you keep them?'

'Yes, I did. I hung them in my study.'

'I'd like to see them sometime.'

'I wouldn't bother. They're not any good. I'm not the artist type. And even if I were, I'm not—'

'Not what?'

To my surprise, the answer pained me. 'Gifted at anything.'

She smiled quietly. 'Neither am I,' she said.

We walked on down the hill in silence, said good-bye at the bottom of it. I headed for my car while Dora remained in place, standing by the old iron gate, waiting for my brother to join her there. It was perhaps the last time I felt that she was no more than she seemed to be, of few words, with an edginess that was clearly more intense than most, but still well within the range of other women I'd known, no less likely to get over whatever it was Billy felt so certain had happened to her.

I gave her no further thought as I drove back into town. Once there, I went directly to my office, hoping to catch up on my work.

But when I arrived, I found Jack Stout coming down the corridor that led to my office. He'd just delivered Charlie Younger to Sheriff Pritchart.

''Afternoon, Mr Chase.'

I could tell by the congratulatory sparkle in Jack's eyes that he'd brought news from New York.

'I had some luck on that job you gave me. About that woman. Dora March.' He said her name with a curious emphasis.

I ushered him into my office, offered him a cigar, which he took but didn't smoke, slipping it into his shirt pocket instead.

'What did you find out?'

'Well, she lived at that residence hall, all right,' Jack said. 'Tremont Residence Hall for Women, it's called.' He took a scrap of paper from his pocket, soiled, sticky. 'An old woman runs the place. 'Bout sixty, I'd say. Name of Mrs Posy Cameron.' He looked up from the paper. 'That's who I talked to.'

'Did she remember Dora?'

'Well, sort of.'

'Sort of?'

'Remembered that she'd lived there.' He glanced at the note again. 'But not much about her.'

I remained silent, waiting. I knew there was more.

'She gave me something though,' Jack said. 'Something the woman left in her room. Mrs Cameron kept it in storage, thinking Miss March might send a forwarding address. But she never did.' Again he reached into the pocket of his jacket, drew out a magazine, rolled up and held curled by a rubber band. 'So she gave it to me,' he said as he handed it across the desk. 'Told me to give it to Miss March, but I figured I'd give it to you first.'

I stripped off the rubber band and let the magazine unroll in my hand. It was called *Astonishing True Stories*, and seemed to be a religious publication of sorts, with lead lines that suggested tales of miraculous cures, unexpected rescues, answered prayers, the reappearance of the dead.

'I was flipping through it on the way home, and I found a story you might be interested in.' Jack's tone darkened somewhat, as if it were not a magazine at all but some creature he'd stumbled upon in the deep wood, neither snake nor scorpion, but small and deadly anyway, something he'd never seen before. 'Page thirty-one.'

I began leafing through the pages, strange pictures flashing here and there, a boy with three arms, a dog riding a goat, a boa coiled around a dugout canoe.

'The story's about a little girl,' Jack said. 'Left out in the open.'

I found the story and began to read it, following the first sightings, a little girl running naked in the wilderness, her skin brown and leathery, the soles of her feet thick as shoe soles, but graced, as the magazine's only color illustration made clear, with a wild mane of long, blond hair.

'It's the second page that has the punch,' Jack said.

I turned the page, found what he meant. 'Dora March,' I said.

Jack grinned. 'That's what they named her. Them doctors.'

I nodded, then read on, followed the story as far as the magazine presented it, the fact that it was English doctors who'd finally claimed her, brought her to London from the Spanish Pyrenees, where she'd first been sighted, named her Dora, from *d'oro*, Spanish for 'of gold,' meaning the color of her hair, and Marzo, also Spanish, for the month she'd first been sighted, and which the English had later Anglicized to 'March.' In a final rendering, 'Dora March' squatted naked in the corner of a bare room, scrubbed clean, her legs drawn up against her chest, her waist-length hair gleaming in the hard white light.

'Looks like her, don't it?' Jack asked.

'Looks like who?'

'That woman at the *Sentinel*. You think it could be her, Mr Chase?'

'You didn't get to the end of the article, did you, Jack?'

'No, sir.'

'This little girl was found in Europe. In 1889.'

Jack peered at me wonderingly.

'She died twenty years ago.'

Jack grinned. 'Well, couldn't be Dora, then,' he reasoned.

'No, it couldn't,' I replied.

'Just a coincidence, you think? Them having the same name?'

I took a five-dollar bill from my wallet and gave it to him. 'If you don't mind, I'd like to keep this whole thing between us.'

He plucked the cigar from his shirt pocket, wrapped the bill snugly around it, and returned both to his pocket. 'Sure, Mr Chase,' he said with a wink. 'Stuff like this, I'm a regular fence post.'

For the rest of the afternoon I considered how I should tell my brother what I'd learned about Dora. It was not as strange a tale as Jack Stout had imagined, but it was curious nonetheless. There was certainly reason to believe that she'd plucked her name out of a magazine. There had to be a reason for her doing such a thing, it seemed to me, a true identity that she had reason to conceal. Until Billy knew that reason, he could not know her.

I was still pondering exactly how I was going to break all this to him when I pulled up in front of his house later that evening. Night had fallen, and from the street I could look directly into the lighted dining room, see him moving about, putting a cluster of flowers on the table. Two candles flickered in a crystal candelabrum, the very one my mother had given him years before, insisting that it should be used only for 'romantic occasions.' Because of that, I had no doubt as to what was going on. My brother was preparing to receive Dora, making everything just right.

I got out of my car and started up the little cement walkway that led to his door, *Astonishing True Stories* rolled up in my coat pocket. I was utterly intent on revealing, for whatever it might be worth, exactly what Jack Stout had found. Then, out of the darkness, I heard my father's voice as clearly as if he were standing beside me, repeating the words he'd said in his parlor a few days before: *There's nothing like loneliness to bring you to your knees.*

At that instant, it struck me that Billy had finally reached the point in his life when he wanted nothing more than to put an end to his romantic longing, place his heart on the red nine, and spin the wheel.

Who was I to stop him?

And so I went back to my car, pulled myself behind the wheel, then glanced toward my brother's house a final time, fully expecting to see him still busy with his preparations. He was in the dining room just as before. But he was no longer alone. Dora stood beside him, helping him set his table, chatting quietly with him until he suddenly turned and left the room, leaving her to stand alone, holding an empty goblet, a slender figure in a plain white dress. In such a pose, she seemed little more than a wisp of breath, not at all robust, and wholly inadequate to Maine. In this harsh land, lashed by wind and sea, I felt certain she would wither.

But she bloomed.

PART THREE

Chapter Thirteen

It began with the smallest bud, Dora's flowering, then opened steadily after that, so that by spring of '36, I could hardly imagine that she'd ever seemed in the least insubstantial to me, someone to be dismissed without consequence, a woman who might come and go, leave no lasting mark behind.

During the preceding winter, I'd seen her only rarely, usually in company with my brother. I knew that she continued to work at the *Sentinel*, always at the copy desk, a very able grammarian according to Billy, but with no interest in actually composing stories. From time to time I'd glimpsed her within the throng of locals who shopped in Madison's on the weekend, but had always stepped away quickly, feeling no need to address her. Once Billy had suggested that we all 'go out' together. Rather than refuse, I'd reminded him that I would surely be the third wheel in any such gathering, since I had no woman to 'go out' with in the sense he meant.

And so it was not until early April that I found myself alone with her for the first time since we'd strolled down the hill from Molly Hendricks's frozen grave. She'd rented a small cottage at the edge of town by then. I'd gone there as a favor to Billy, who'd asked me to pick her up that evening. Earlier that day, he'd gone to the state capital to cover some new plan for social improvement that FDR's followers in the legislature had devised. Typical of my brother, he'd gotten swept up in the debate, no doubt offering his own wild scheme, left later than he'd expected, then broken down on the way home, his old Ford barely lurching into a service station before it expired altogether. He'd called to tell me that he'd be arriving late for our customary Wednesday night dinner with our father.

'We'll just wait for you,' I told him. 'Dad certainly won't mind lingering over a second drink before supper.' I laughed. 'I doubt even a third would cause him much alarm.'

'Yes, I know,' Billy said. 'But I'd planned to bring Dora.'

By then I knew that Billy had already brought Dora around to visit with The Great Example. My mother had received her with great warmth, he said, given every indication that she found Dora as remarkable as Billy himself did. She had even advised him to be bold in his pursuit of her. In my mind, I could see her doing exactly that, urging Billy forward in a wild, romantic quest, certain that he could maneuver whatever tangled road lay ahead.

I was less certain as to what my father might think of Dora. Over the last few years he'd taken to 'wintering' in Virginia during February and March. He had only recently returned to Port Alma, and so had not yet been introduced to Dora. Once that meeting had taken place, I suspected that my father's opinion of her, as well as his advice to Billy, would be considerably more guarded than my mother's. He would temper enthusiasm with warning, point out that life was a long road filled with pits and snares, love a thing that had to flex and bend in order to negotiate it. I could hear his voice rise sagely in the parlor: *Reason is still our only guide, Billy, regardless of what your mother contends.*

'Dora will be at her house,' Billy told me. 'Would you mind driving her to Dad's?'

I had no desire to do it, of course. During the long snow-bound months following Jack Stout's return from New York, I'd purposely kept away from Dora. I could not imagine that a light would not soon go on in my brother's head, reveal at least one or two of what I suspected must be scores of both small and large deceptions. A confrontation would ensue, then a vastly overdue parting of the ways.

But spring had now arrived and nothing of the kind had happened. Dora's spell was still upon Billy.

I arrived at her house at just after six o'clock that evening. It was on a narrow lane on the outskirts of town, distant and somewhat secluded, bordered by woods all around, with only a few equally isolated cottages along the same untended road, most of them scattered along a rocky inlet so inhospitable it could scarcely be called a beach at all.

I'd never taken any note of Dora's cottage, but when I arrived to pick her up, I was struck by how small it was, little more than a converted shed.

At my knock, the door opened slightly and a pair of green eyes peered through the slit.

'Cal,' she said, the door opening more fully now.

'Billy's been delayed,' I told her. 'He sent me to pick you up.'

'Come in,' she said.

For various reasons, I'd been in the houses of the

richest people in and around Port Alma, its few doctors, lawyers, and owners of banks, fishing fleets, and canneries. For equally various, usually profoundly different reasons, I'd also seen the life of our state's eternal poor, the wilderness hovels that crouched on rocky hillsides, homes that looked oddly pilfered, made of tin and discarded wood scavenged from nearby sawmills and boatyards. They were little more than huts, hardly distinguishable from the stacks of firewood piled beside them. But for all the poverty I'd seen, I'd never been in a dwelling place as unadorned as Dora's. Even the poorest of the poor did something to relieve their bleakness, hung a family photograph on the wall or placed a colored bottle in the window to catch the light. But Dora had done nothing of this sort. There were no pictures or paintings on her walls or mantel. Not so much as a vase to hold a sprig of winter holly. For furniture, she had only two plain ladder-back chairs and a wooden table. It was a place so devoid of even the simplest comforts, I felt a grim awe that any life could will such bleakness upon itself.

Dora, however, appeared entirely indifferent to her surroundings. In fact, she seemed well accommodated to them, so that I got the impression she'd lived in such bareness before, like the wild child whose name she'd taken, accustomed to a life ruthlessly reduced to fundamentals.

'Would you like some tea, Cal? There's some left.'

'All right,' I said.

She moved to the kitchen at the rear of the house, leaving me alone in the front room. From where I stood, I could see that the kitchen held a black cast-iron stove, a small sink, and a hand pump. A few utensils lay in a neat row on a white towel beside the pump, one of them the long knife my brother would later draw from his wounded chest.

'Sugar?' Dora called from the kitchen.

'No.'

The bedroom door was slightly open, and inside it, I saw a bed but no mattress, only a frame and bare wooden slats. A large chair rested beside it, spread with pillows and draped with a blanket.

I was still peering into the bedroom when Dora returned, two teacups in her hands. She noticed me staring into the room, no doubt realized how bizarre it appeared, grim as a dungeon, the sort of place people were taken to have confessions beaten out of them.

'I sleep in the chair,' she said. She handed me the tea, then walked to the bedroom door and closed it. 'I have trouble lying down.'

'How long have you had this trouble?'

'Since I was a little girl,' she answered.

She added nothing else, but I immediately imagined a terrible injury, the 'thing that had happened to her,' about which Billy had speculated so darkly, and that he seemed to consider part of her romantic allure.

'Was this in New York City?' I asked.

She looked at me as if I'd breached a wall she'd not expected to be so vulnerable.

'Billy once mentioned that you lived in New York,' I explained.

'Not when I was a child. Only recently.'

'I lived in New York too. While I was in law school.' Cautiously, I probed the darkness. 'Where did you grow up?'

'California.'

'I've never been there.'

She sipped her tea. 'I haven't met your father.'

It was a clear attempt to change the subject. I knew I'd gotten as far as I could, that the door into her past, like the one to her bedroom, was now firmly shut.

'Well, since my mother left him he's taken on a few aristocratic pretensions,' I told her. 'You've visited my mother a few times, I understand. With Billy, I mean.'

'Yes.'

'He goes almost every day now,' I said.

'You don't?'

'No,' I said. 'I'd visit her more often, but I'm not sure I'm always a welcome sight.'

'What gives you that idea?'

I smiled, trying to make light of it. 'Well, sometimes, when I come into her room, she looks like a cold blast hit her. Dad's the one who's always happy to see me. He reads a lot, and we talk about what he's been reading. He was more or less my tutor when I was a boy. My mother tutored Billy.' I felt a sudden, curious ache that my family had been divided so starkly, like a body flayed open, the wound unhealed. Again I retreated to a less disturbing subject. 'So tell me, are you glad you came to Port Alma?'

'I like it here. It's remote.'

'Do you plan to stay?'

'No,' she said resolutely. 'I'm only passing through.'

Only passing through.

Something in the certainty of her tone told me that this was true, that for reasons I would probably never know, Dora was one of life's pariahs. I felt something stir in me, something small, a tiny tremor of feeling for all who were like Dora, inexplicably driven from place to place, rootless, solitary, invisible whips forever at their backs.

'I'm sorry to hear it,' I said. 'That you're just passing through.'

Our eyes locked briefly, then she glanced toward the window. 'A fog is coming in,' she murmured.

'Yes, it is,' I said. I took a final sip from the cup and set it down. 'We'd better go while we can still see the road.'

We drove back through the town, then out along the coastal road, a wall of evergreen rising on one side, the sea crashing on the other. The road turned inland less than a mile beyond town, wound through a series of rocky hills, and ended in my father's driveway.

He was already standing at the door as we came up the steps, dressed to the nines in a dark suit and bow tie, a sure sign of how special he considered the evening to be.

'Ah, you must be Dora,' he said brightly. 'Come in. Come in.'

She stepped into the foyer, her attention lighting briefly on a portrait of one of my forebears, his severe likeness trapped in a heavy wooden frame, a man with silver hair and stern features, utterly proper in his black coat and starched white collar.

'Obadiah Grier,' my father told her, pleased by her interest. 'William's grandfather. Looks like he's just condemned a witch, doesn't he?' He laughed. 'Actually, he was quite a nice old man. Used to bounce William on his knee. Cal too.' He placed his hand on my shoulder. 'Of course, Cal never enjoyed that sort of thing, did you, Cal?'

He waited for me to respond, engage him in our usual

badinage. When I didn't, he turned to Dora. 'May I take your coat, Miss March?'

She gave it to him, but he only passed it over to me. 'Hang it in the front closet, Cal,' he said as he escorted Dora into the sitting room.

Cradled in my hands, Dora's coat felt even lighter than it appeared, designed for a climate where the seasons changed far less radically than in the north. A label had been crudely stenciled inside the coat: *Lobo City Thrift*.

Lobo, I thought, recalling the origins of her hand-picked name. Spanish for wolf.

My brother arrived an hour later, plunging hurriedly through the front door, gay and energetic as ever. He walked directly to the fire and warmed his hands, greeting each of us in turn before his eyes settled fondly on Dora. 'I see Cal got you here safely.'

'Yes,' Dora said with a smile that rose with an unexpected brightness from the dark net of her face.

Billy's eyes swept over to me, and I could feel the great affection he had for me. I knew it was the love of the righteous for the prodigal, but I also knew that at that moment his greatest wish was that I someday find what he now seemed unshakably certain he had found.

But there was no mention of such things that evening. Instead, we chatted about his day, the legislative debate currently raging, what might ultimately come of it. For a while we even discussed the weather, how soon summer would be upon us, how quickly it would pass.

As the clock chimed eight, we took our seats at the long cherry wood dining table my father had set with a pretentious formality, everything in its proper place, little silver salad forks and Bordeaux glasses for the wine.

My father took his customary place at the head of the table, the chair at the other end of it left vacant, as if in reverence for my mother. Billy and Dora were placed side by side, Dora directly across from me, my brother facing the empty chair to my left, the one that would have been taken by my wife or lover.

Dora sat erect, her hands in her lap, like a child at table in a boarding school. I felt her eyes drift toward me, then slip away.

'Well, has my father given you the family history yet?' Billy asked her, smiling happily.

She shook her head.

'Well, the Griers are a lively group,' he said.

'But the Chases are a criminal clan,' I added.

Dora glanced toward me. 'Crime interests you?'

'Not really, no,' I said.

'A certain kind of crime would,' Billy said.

'Really, and what kind of crime would that be?' I asked him.

'One that was philosophical in some way. Abstract.'

I shook my head. 'I don't think so.'

'What kind of case would interest you, then, Cal?' my father asked.

Before I could reply, my brother offered an answer of his own. 'A murder case. Some horrible murder case.'

'No, not a murder case,' I told them. 'Most murder cases are quite ordinary. The motivations are usually predictable. Love or money, for the most part.' I shrugged. 'Nothing that would make for a great case.'

'So what would make a case great?' Billy asked. 'For you, I mean.'

'I've never really thought about it. But I suppose it would have to involve something important, some idea or—' I stopped, unable to put my finger on it. 'Some principle that would make me—' Again I stopped, still searching for the right answer.

Then, out of nowhere, Dora found it.

'Sacrifice something,' she said.

I had never thought of it that way, never sensed, other than inchoately, that I wished to be called to any greater purpose than the lowly office I maintained. And yet it was true. She had seen it, the fact that for all my professional dispassion, I longed for something fierce and noble, something for which I would put everything at risk.

'You're right,' I said to her.

Billy gazed at me, amazed. 'Really? I never knew you felt that way.' He turned to Dora. 'I think you know Cal better than I do.'

Dora's eyes remained on mine. 'Yes, I think I do,' she said.

She added nothing else, and the conversation quickly moved on to other things. And yet, for the rest of the evening, I felt curiously vulnerable and exposed, like a small animal snatched from the undergrowth, the predator's black talons already sinking in.

After dinner, we gathered around the fire. Dora and Billy sat together on the brocade sofa my father had bought some years before. It had a mahogany frame and was covered in a wine-red velvet, a taste for the luxurious he felt entirely free to indulge, buying silver and crystal, expensive furniture and a large Oriental carpet, all of it designed to give him a sense that he was, at last, the lord of a great estate. For Dora's sake, he commented expansively upon almost every article in the room, from the tinkling chandelier to the old grandfather clock that ticked loudly in the corner.

I could hardly imagine a more boring recitation, but through it all, Dora showed a peculiarly intense interest in even the most banal aspects of my father's conversation, how things were made, for example, where they came from. Even his travels, limited as they were, engaged her, his recent sojourn in Virginia as wondrous as one of Sinbad's voyages.

As for Dora herself, she spoke almost exclusively about books, presenting fictional characters, even the most minor ones, as if they were real, the shopkeepers and seamstresses in Balzac, the milling throng in Dickens. But of the caravan of actual individuals anyone of her age should have encountered in real life by then, she had almost nothing to say.

The evening came to a close at just before eleven. At the door my father took Dora's hand. 'It was a pleasure, my dear,' he said as he kissed it ceremoniously. 'I hope you come again.'

'Thank you,' she said, smiling up at him. 'So do I.'

With that she turned and headed down the walkway, Billy at her side. I saw him take her arm as they neared the stairs at the end of it.

'Charming girl,' my father murmured as we stood together and watched them go, two figures moving through the dense fog to where my brother's car rested like a pile of rusty scrap at the bottom of the stairs. 'Quite charming, don't you think? And lovely.'

I tossed what remained of my cigar into the yard. 'Charming and lovely, yes.'

'Billy's quite taken with her.'

'By all indications.'

My father smiled. 'His mother must be pleased. She's always expected such a woman to turn up.'

I shrugged. 'And now, at last, she has.'

'It's an illusion, of course,' my father said. 'But there's a sweetness to it.' A curious wistfulness settled over him. 'And who knows, Cal. Maybe Dora is the woman who was born to love Billy all his days.'

A different possibility flashed into my mind like the glint of a knife. 'Or born to break his heart,' I said.

Chapter Fourteen

For the next few weeks, I watched Dora from a distance. Each time I visited the *Sentinel*, I found her working at her desk. She never greeted me with more than a quick nod. On other occasions, when I ran into her in a local store, she would say only 'Hello, Cal' and go on with her shopping. Sometimes, I noticed her striding alone by the seawall, her eyes on the bay, MacAndrews Island, the charred remains of the Phelps mansion that lay atop it, its blackened chimneys rising like gun barrels against the overarching sky. Plotting her next move, I thought.

As for Billy, he now lived in the full radiance of romantic anticipation. So much so that one warm Saturday afternoon in early May, as we played a game of croquet on my front lawn, he even ventured the hope that I might find such happiness too.

'Happiness,' I said. I gave one of the wooden balls a hollow bang. 'So you're happy now?'

'Yes, I am,' Billy said.

'You're happy with Dora?'

'I'm happy *because* of Dora.'

'And you've learned a lot about her, I suppose?'

Billy paced from one ball to another, then knelt down, eyeing the angle of his shot. 'Enough.'

'Enough for what?' I asked absently.

Billy got to his feet, slapping bits of grass from his

trousers. Instead of answering me, he said, 'I was thinking of dropping by Mother's cottage later this afternoon. Take a walk along Fox Creek. Would you like to come along? With Dora and me, I mean.'

A warning sounded suddenly at this suggestion, like the snapping of a twig behind me in the dark, but I said nothing.

Billy made a grand swing. The ball shot forward, swept beneath a metal goal. He crowed with pleasure. 'I want Dora to see the cottage. Get some sense of what Mother was like before the stroke. How vibrant she was.'

'Well, for God's sake, don't tell her what happened.'

'What do you mean?'

'The way she was when I found her.'

'Why not?'

'Because she was so . . . she looked so . . .'

'She looked human, Cal.' He saw that all talk of the horrible condition in which I'd found our mother still disturbed me, and shrugged. 'Anyway, Dora and I plan to go out to the cottage later this afternoon. I thought you might want to join us. We wouldn't stay for very long. I know you need to . . . I mean, it being Saturday, I know you have things to do in Royston.'

He meant that I could linger on Fox Creek for only a little while before heading for my weekly rendezvous with my whore.

'I really would like you to come along, Cal,' he added emphatically. 'We don't get together as often as we used to. And besides, I'd like you to get to know Dora better. Come on, Cal, join us.'

There was no way to refuse the brightness of his smile, the innocence of his offer. For a moment, he was a young boy again, urging me to help him take his homemade raft to Fox Creek. And so I agreed.

I got to Fox Creek a few minutes before the appointed time. The little house in which my mother had chosen to spend her final years stood nestled in a grove of evergreen. I could imagine her sitting on its small porch, humming a scrap of Mozart, a book of poetry in her lap. The Great Example in the fullness of her solitude. I thought of how often I'd worked to please her, to shine somehow in her eyes, perhaps prove that what I lacked in passion I made up for in reason, that she and Billy could survive and flourish only in a world that men like my father and me, cool-headed and realistic, had made safe for dreamers. And yet, for all my effort, I knew that I'd never gained any portion of the sweet regard she'd so generously heaped upon my brother, never felt in me the deep delight she took in him.

Some aspect of this dark truth was probably in my face when Billy and Dora arrived, though my brother was too much in love by then to allow anything to dampen his own exultant mood. I could see it in the lightness of his stride as he came toward me. In finding Dora, Billy seemed to believe that he'd grasped something amazing, that rare form of love that flowers ever more beautifully as beauty fades, endures every shock and sorrow, the green vine of his romance already aging toward a ruby richness, his love, at last, like wine.

'Wonderful day, isn't it, Cal?' He was dressed in linen trousers and an open-collared white shirt, his head topped with a rumpled felt hat, a figure truly splendid, very nearly radiant.

'Yes, it is,' I said, my eyes moving reflexively to Dora. She stood beside him in a long-sleeved dress with slightly puffed shoulders. Like all her attire, it seemed selected for the maximum of coverage.

'Hello, Cal.' She glanced about, taking the general lay of the area, her eyes following a line of purple crocuses that had just sprouted along the edge of the creek. 'What a lovely place.'

Billy pointed toward the cottage. 'We've kept it as a memorial to our mother,' he said to Dora. 'All her things are still there.'

'Most of them,' I said, referring to the fact that Billy was continually taking some little token from it, a napkin or a bud vase. 'I guess you know by now that my brother calls her The Great Example.'

'Which she is,' Billy said quite seriously.

With that, he led us across the lawn, mounted the wooden stairs, and opened the door of the house in which I'd found my mother in her helpless sprawl. It was a vision that met me at the threshold, so that I suddenly recoiled and stepped back onto the porch, leaving my brother and Dora to explore the cottage.

From my place just outside the door, I watched as the two of them drifted slowly about the cottage, Billy occasionally lifting some curio my mother had accumulated. I noticed Dora move her finger along the side of the little desk by the window. She seemed to be gathering something from it, my mother's thoughts and memories, as if such things lay like a film of dust upon the objects we left behind.

As the minutes passed, Billy grew increasingly expansive, spinning tales of The Great Example, utterly unmindful that I remained outside, still shaken by the memory of my mother's lying faceup, those yellow stains, the smell, the filth, the horrible indignity of it all.

He walked into another room, leaving Dora behind just long enough for her to glance in my direction, glimpse the seething in my eyes. In a single fluid movement, seamless as a breeze, she swept over to me, touched my arm, then whispered, 'What's the matter, Cal?'

'The way she looked when I found her,' I said. 'Why can't I get it out of my head?'

'Because you love her.'

'So does Billy, but—' I stopped, still unable to speak the truth.

Dora waited.

And it came.

'But she loves him back,' I said. 'Sometimes I think she even taught him how to love. You know, with all his heart.'

'What does she teach you?'

I smiled thinly. 'The opposite lesson, I suppose.'

'Which was?'

'How to live without it.'

I expected Dora to offer some small commiseration, perhaps a counterargument of some kind. But instead of a well-intentioned, banal aside, the words dropped from her mouth like shards of ice. 'There are worse lessons than living without love.'

'Do you think so?'

She started to answer, but at that moment Billy sailed onto the porch and grabbed her hand. 'Let's walk over to the bridge,' he urged.

It was only a short walk to the bridge, my mother's cottage still clearly visible behind us. Some of the bulbs my mother had planted here and there were beginning to inch their way into the spring air, scattering sparks of red and gold across our path.

'This is where my father proposed to my mother,' Billy told Dora as he led her to the center of the bridge, a rickety, unstable old thing that shook slightly as they walked onto it. When they reached the center, he let go of Dora's hand, leaned over the wooden rail, stared into the rapid water below. 'I made a raft once. Tried to sail all the way across.' He looked up and grinned at me. 'Remember, Cal?'

'I remember that you saved a little girl's life instead,' I said, recalling the gleam and glory of his dive. 'Have you told Dora about that?'

'No,' Dora said. 'He hasn't.'

Billy smiled. 'We did it together,' he told her. 'Cal and I.'

'You're the one who plunged in after her,' I reminded him.

He gazed at me affectionately. 'But you're the one who plunged in after *me*.'

With that, he seized Dora's hand again, tugging her off the bridge and along the water's edge.

'I still sometimes wonder what Mother thought about,' Billy said once we'd reached the spot where she had spent long hours, reading silently on a small red blanket.

'The past,' I said.

He looked at me quizzically. 'Why not the future?'

'She didn't have a future by then.'

'Of course she did,' Billy replied. 'She'd left Dad. She'd chosen to live her own life. Her future was completely open.'

'No future is ever open,' I said bleakly.

Billy shook his head and laughed. 'You are a dark force, Cal. You are truly a dark force. Isn't he, Dora?'

She kept her eyes on the water. 'Yes.'

We sat down beside the water, Billy and Dora close together, I apart, my back pressed against a tree.

Seeing them so close, my brother's arm at Dora's waist, filled me with a strange unease, a restlessness that finally drove me away from them, where I stood alone, smoking idly, now eager to be on my way to Royston, the sweet oblivion of a brothel bed.

'I want to get something from the cottage,' Billy said suddenly. He hastily got to his feet. 'I'll meet you two at the car.'

With that he bounded off toward the cottage, leaving Dora and me beside the water. I scooped up a small stone and plopped it into the creek. When I glanced back toward the cottage, Billy was coming out of it, carrying a small blue vase.

'He keeps taking things from the house,' I said. 'Pieces of her.'

Dora looked at me pointedly. 'Be careful, Cal,' she said.

'Of what?'

'Of needing love too much.'

I laughed. 'I think it's my brother who has that problem.'

Her eyes were very still. 'No,' she said. 'It's you.'

No one had ever spoken to me with such disturbing intimacy, and all during the drive to Royston that evening, I replayed the moment, the stillness in Dora's eyes, the way she'd said 'It's you' with such certainty that it was me, rather than my brother, who was perilously in need of love.

I was still brooding on what she'd said when I arrived

on Blyden Street at just after six. Night had fallen, the lights of the town shimmering on the water. I could hear the piano in the bar next door, the steady hum of the crowd inside.

Maggie Flynn sat on the porch as I came up the steps, fanning herself languidly in the warm night air. She'd pulled her dress up, and her large round knees shone like pale orbs as she drifted back and forth in the old wooden swing.

'I'd just about given up on you, Cal,' she said.

Normally I would have gone directly upstairs, but an inexpressible heaviness pressed me down upon the step. I took off my hat, fanned my face, then lit a cheroot. 'I'll go in shortly.'

'Want a drink?' Maggie asked.

'Not yet.'

I blew a column of smoke into the night air.

Maggie eyed me closely. 'How long you been coming here, Cal?'

I took another draw on my cigar. 'Twelve, thirteen years, I guess.'

'Long time. You still single?'

'Yeah.'

She smiled and nodded. 'You were just a kid when you first showed up.'

'I was twenty-one.'

She laughed. 'A kid to me.' The laughter trailed off. 'You look a little out of sorts tonight.'

'Just tired.'

'Maybe you're getting tired of us.'

'Why do you say that?'

'It happens,' she said with a shrug. 'A man starts needling more.'

'I don't need more.'

Maggie's gaze was piercing. 'Don't be so sure. It hits you like a hammer.'

I felt a strange alarm, rose quickly, tossed my cigar into the street, and went inside. My regular met me in the front parlor, poured me a drink, then escorted me up the stairs. Down the corridor we passed Polly Jenks's room, empty now.

'Polly finally quit,' she said. 'Left on Wednesday.'

'So who does Mr Castleman see now?'

'Me,' she answered airily.

In her room, I took my usual position, lying on my back in the bed while she undressed behind the screen.

'Do you want another drink?' she asked when she emerged.

'No.'

'You got here late,' she murmured as she curled on the bed and began to untie my shoes.

'I had more work than usual.'

'Something big?'

'Not really.'

'So, there's nothing new in Port Alma?'

The answer sprang from my mouth before I could stop it. 'My brother's in love,' I said.

'That's nice,' she said cheerfully. She drew off the second shoe, placed it beside the other, then crawled up the bed and sat down beside me. 'You like the woman, the one your brother's in love with?'

'She's interesting.'

She leaned forward, her lips poised at mine, but careful not to kiss me. Her breath smelled faintly of meringue.

'Well, that's enough about *her*,' she said. She got to

her feet, let the robe fall open, then took it off entirely and sat naked upon me. 'You're here to be with me.' She unbuckled my belt, gently tugged it from my trousers, and twined it sensually through her stubby fingers. 'To have a good time.' She took my hands and cupped her breasts with them. Sitting astride me, peering down, she was utterly confident of her skills, an Eve who'd learned the lessons of the ancient garden, taken charge of the serpent, knew just how it would answer her command. She raked her nails languidly over my chest, pretending to find me desirable. Then she bent forward and whispered in my ear. 'Who am I?'

My mind had already begun to wander. 'What?'

'My name. Who do you want to be with tonight?'

It never left my lips, but the way it flashed into my mind, so swiftly and spontaneously, should have rung like a fire bell in the night.

Dora.

Chapter Fifteen

We think of our destruction as something that falls upon us abruptly, in a sudden rush of wind and fire. But I've come to believe that our fall slinks through the undergrowth instead, creeps from one place to the next around the little shelter we've built until, at last, it finds the single rotted board we neglected to replace, the crevice we left unsealed, that place in the dark it can nudge through, and slither in.

And yet, for all that, I could have avoided it. From the moment I'd stepped into Dora's cottage that rain-swept afternoon, whispered her name, then glimpsed my brother in the shadows at the other side of the room, I'd recognized the one thing I could have done to prevent the catastrophe that had instantly overwhelmed me. I could have stayed away from Dora. I could have controlled my own steadily building impulse and determined never to be alone with her. I might even have taken a passionless pride in such self-control.

At first, I tried to do exactly that. I dove into the petty cases Hap tossed onto my desk as if they had the gravest importance. I stopped walking by the *Sentinel*. Had I seen her coming toward me, I would have crossed to the other side of the street. At home, safely alone, I sank into my books, and occasionally the bottle.

But as the days passed, Dora intruded upon me. While

hunched over some document in my office, I'd lift my eyes, certain she was in the room, and be disappointed – even angry – when she wasn't.

And so, one warm June evening, as I sat on my front porch, finishing off a second brandy, I called to her as she walked past the house, no doubt on the way home from the *Sentinel*. It was the first time in a month that her name had passed my lips.

'Dora.'

She stiffened, as if a hand had gripped her shoulder from behind.

'It's Cal,' I said, rising from my chair, waving my glass slightly. 'Here. On the porch. I didn't mean to startle you. I just happened to see you passing by.' An idea came out of the blue, kicked up, as it has since seemed to me, by a cloven foot. 'I thought you might want to see my drawings. The ones Billy told you about.'

She hesitated for an instant, perhaps to gauge my intent. Then she nodded and came up the stairs.

'I was on my way home,' she said when she joined me.

'I thought so,' I said. 'Is Billy still at the office?'

'No, he's gone to Royston. To buy paper.'

A salty night breeze toyed with a strand of her hair. I grew bold enough to return it to its place. 'So, you're alone for the evening.'

'Yes.'

I smiled. 'You once asked me if I liked solitude. Do you?'

She peered at me distantly. 'I'm used to it.'

'You must have lived alone for quite some time, then.'

'Long enough not to be afraid of it.'

'Years, I suppose.'

'Yes, years,' she answered, as if challenging me to ask her more.

Instead, I retreated back to an earlier subject. 'Well, let me show you those drawings.'

We walked inside the house, down the corridor, and into my study. It was the room in which I spent most of my time, and which, over the years, I'd turned into a kind of inner sanctum. Thick curtains were drawn over the windows, and an Oriental carpet covered the wide pine floors. The room had been decorated according to my taste, which tended toward heavy furniture and somber colors. Billy had always found the room uncomfortable, teasing that it reminded him of a funeral parlor.

'What a quiet place,' Dora said as she entered it.

'Billy calls it my tomb.'

She looked at me. 'More like a burrow, I think.'

'Well, I'm the only one who burrows here, that's for sure.'

The drawings hung in various places on the walls, some well lighted, some in shadow. There were a few still lifes, but most were of stone walls and wooden fences, rigid pastorals that portrayed the security of limits.

As I watched, Dora walked from one drawing to the next, always taking time to stop, gaze, ponder. She seemed remarkably at peace as she moved about the room, as if she inevitably felt safer and less exposed in worlds created by others, particularly imagined ones, where nothing real could intrude upon her, seize her unawares.

'Not very exciting stuff, I know,' I said when she'd looked at the final picture, a stone wall that ran through an otherwise open field.

She smiled, then made a second sweep of the room, this time eyeing the books rather than the drawings.

'I like the way you look at books, Dora,' I said as I came up behind her.

'They gave me a place to go.' She drew a single volume from the shelf, opened it. 'I remember this.'

I looked at the title. Pascal's *Pensées*.

'He says that people are unhappy because they prefer the hunt to the capture,' Dora said.

'And you think he's right?'

'Not for everyone.'

'How about you?'

'Not for me at all,' she answered bluntly.

'Then you must find Billy very refreshing.'

'Why do you say that?'

'Because all he's ever wanted to find and capture was his one true love.'

She lowered her eyes to the book. 'William is noble' was all she said.

My brother's character suddenly struck me as a vaguely charged subject. I decided to leave it. 'I know your secret now.'

Her eyes darted toward me.

'You're a Catholic,' I said with a smile. 'Only Catholics read Pascal. My mother, before she left the Church. And a few odd ducks like me.'

She closed the book and returned it to the shelf. 'Thank you for inviting me in, Cal.'

'If you saw anything you'd like to read . . .'

'No.'

I smiled. 'And, of course, the drawings are for sale.'

She laughed. 'Even that one?' She pointed to a small, rather crude drawing of a young girl with long, dark hair, dressed in white, her figure ghostly, vaporous, almost translucent, something the slightest breeze would have torn apart. 'It's different from your other drawings.'

'It should be,' I said. 'I didn't draw it.'

'Who did?'

'Billy.'

'Who is she?' Dora asked.

'She's no one,' I said. 'She's imagined.'

Dora glanced at me quizzically.

'Billy thought of her as his . . . how shall I put it? His damsel in distress, I suppose.'

She laughed again, a quick, self-conscious laugh, which, for all its slender brevity, seemed to lift her like a wind. 'You don't like it, do you?'

'No. I hang it only because Billy gave it to me.'

'Why don't you like it, Cal?'

'Because the woman is unreal. An illusion.'

Dora smiled quietly. 'Pascal would understand.'

'Yes, he would.'

She said nothing else, but only stepped away and headed for the door.

'Would you like a drink?' I asked quickly. 'Tea. Coffee.' I lifted my half-empty glass. 'Something stronger?'

'No. I'd better be getting home.'

'Well, good night, then,' I said when we were on the porch again.

'Good night.'

I stood and watched as she headed back down the walkway to the street. She seemed curiously self-possessed as she moved through the darkness, and I recalled how, only a few short months before, I'd stood outside my brother's house, pronounced her far too frail for Maine. Now she seemed carved of native stone. So much so that I could not imagine how my brother might ever penetrate, much less win her.

And yet, even at that moment, he'd already hatched a plan.

I learned about it two weeks later as Henry Mason, Billy's employee at the *Sentinel*, and I sat in Ollie's Barber Shop. It was late in the afternoon, only an hour before closing, a blue evening shade already falling beyond the twirling barber pole.

'I guess you heard about the new arrangement,' Henry said, his breathing somewhat labored, as it always was, his voice coming through a shaky wheeze.

'What arrangement?'

'At the paper.'

Henry was in his late sixties, a frail, sickly man, surrounded by a consumptive air, so that he seemed forever on the brink of physical collapse. His wife had left him years before, and since then he'd been the sole support and caretaker of a retarded daughter, Lois, who, now in her forties, often wandered from her home, sending Henry in all directions looking for her. 'What will she do when I'm gone?' I'd often heard him ask my brother plaintively. 'Who'll take care of Lois then?'

'The arrangement with Dora March,' Henry said, then coughed into his fist.

'What about her?'

'Well, you know how William is.'

'What do you mean, Henry?'

'The way he's never taken much interest in running

the paper.' He cleared his throat, shifting in the chair, his bony fingers gripped to its padded armrest. 'I mean, the day-to-day affairs.'

'What does that have to do with Dora?' I asked just as Lloyd Drummond, Ollie's second-string barber, began applying a thick white lather to my face.

'She can write checks now,' Henry replied. 'Write checks from the company book. William never let anyone do that before.'

Ollie stepped over, snapped a wide white cloth, then draped it over Henry's chest and lap.

'He says he wants to bring her more into the business,' Henry said anxiously. 'I think he wants to show her how much he trusts her.'

'Trusts her,' I repeated, almost to myself.

Lloyd flipped open the straight razor. Its long, flat blade winked in the light.

'She always worked the copy desk before,' Henry added. 'But now—' He stopped suddenly. 'Well, William can do whatever he wants at the paper.'

'Yes, he can.'

Ollie took a pair of clippers and a comb from the shelf below the mirror, eased Henry's head forward, and began to clip at the nape of his neck.

'I mean, if he wants to turn things over to a stranger, then, well . . .'

'She's not exactly a stranger, Henry.'

'No,' Henry said quietly, averting his eyes somewhat. 'Not exactly.'

'What's bothering you?' I asked. 'About this new arrangement.'

The question released a dam in him. 'I can't help it, Cal. You know how I feel about William. He's like a son to me almost. But he's the type of person that someone has to look out for. *You* know that.'

He waited for some type of confirmation. When I offered none, he continued. 'Anyway. We all do the best we can. All of us at the paper. We keep an eye on him. For his own good. Then . . . all of a sudden . . . this woman . . .' He heaved a weary sigh. 'But it's none of my business what he does. What he lets Dora do, I mean. But you know the way she is, Cal. It worries me. Him giving her access, you know, to the money.'

'What do you mean, the way she is?'

He turned my question over in his mind. 'The way she reacts to things. It's strange. Unstable.'

'What are you getting at, Henry?' I felt my patience slipping.

Henry glanced about. 'Take the other day. We were cleaning out the back issues. Taking them downstairs.'

Ollie passed between us. After he'd stepped away, Henry said, 'So we were talking about some of the old papers. The old stories. Wally and me. What was the biggest story the paper ever covered. That sort of thing. And the Phelps mansion came up.'

'You mean, what happened there.'

'That's right.' Henry nodded, wheezing slightly. 'Twenty years ago. The murders.'

The murders.

I'd heard of them all my life, how Simon Phelps and his wife had been slaughtered, their daughter Abigail taken into the groundskeeper's shed, butchered there, then the great house set afire. I could even recall the name of the man who'd done it. It was a name whispered as a warning to the children of Port Alma for over twenty years, finally turned into a scary little rhyme:

> *Be good or he'll get you.*
> *Cut your throat, do you in.*
> *Then vanish in the shadows*
> *Evildoer. Auckland Finn.*

'Wally really went into the details,' Henry went on. 'Especially about little Abigail. What was done to her. The way Finn had taken her out to the shed, held her down, cut her up.' His features tensed. 'That's when we noticed Dora. She'd been sitting there all along. At her desk, like always. None of us had noticed her . . . She was pale as a sheet, Cal. Pale as a sheet. We just looked at each other, Wally and me. We didn't know what to do. It was strange, the way she looked. So . . . unstable. She looked like she couldn't move, like she was being held down. Living through it herself. Like she wasn't even in the same room with the rest of us. But in that shed, you know.' His eyes were fixed in grim amazement. 'With Abigail.'

'Did my brother see this?'

'No. He was in his office.'

'Did Dora say anything?'

'No,' Henry answered. 'She just came back to herself after a little while. Then she got up, walked away. Got about as far as she could get from anybody else.' He offered a pointed gaze. 'But you could see the terror was still in her.'

All that evening, I tried to get the vision out of my mind, Dora in the grip of terror. I recalled the conversation we'd had as we'd walked down the hill from Molly Hendricks's grave.

What did you sense in Molly Hendricks? That she was going to be hurt?

That she'd already been hurt.

And that looked like . . . what?

Helplessness. Like someone was holding her down.

Why didn't I see it?

In my mind, I repeated the answer that had flashed into her eyes: *Because it's never happened to you.*

By midnight, I could no longer stop myself. I closed the book I'd been trying unsuccessfully to read for the last four hours and made the short walk from my house to the paper's offices.

Felix Miller was just finishing up his nightly cleaning duties when I arrived.

'It's past midnight, Mr Chase,' Felix protested as he opened the door.

'I know. But I need to look up something, Felix. In the back issues. For a case I'm working on.'

'They moved them back issues down the basement.' Felix eased backward, tugging the door along with him. 'I'll show you where they are.'

He led me to the basement stairs, unlocked the door, and turned on the light.

'You don't have to hang around after your work's done,' I assured him as I headed down the stairs. 'I can let myself out.'

It didn't take long for me to find the issues I wanted, begin to review the same grim story of a family's slaughter. It had happened on November 12, 1915, and the *Sentinel*'s front-page coverage had begun the following day, my father having selected a special typeface, not only bold and black, but cut in a style similar to that seen on old tombstones in the town cemetery: *Phelps Mansion Scene of Fire and Carnage.*

He'd made other embellishments as well. A large photograph of the Phelps mansion, stark, massive, poised grandly atop MacAndrews Island. Photographs of the individual victims were positioned around it, rather like a wreath, the faces staring out from oval frames, like cameos, and hung with a not very artful rendering of black crepe. Beneath the photographs, my father had composed a single grim line: *Three Dead in Brutal Slayings.*

The photograph of Simon Marcus Phelps, thirty-five, showed a thin, nearly skeletal man, the bony structure of his skull so prominent, his face seemed draped over it like a cloth. His dark hair was slicked down and parted severely in the middle. The eyes behind his wire-rimmed glasses were so small and round, they gave him a fragile and unhealthy look.

Dressed in her finery, with large bright eyes, Madeline Inez Phelps seemed as robust as her husband appeared sickly. She held her head erect, the chin slightly lifted, in the style of English matrons posed in the reading rooms of their country houses, but the corners of her mouth tilted upward in a youthful, perhaps slightly coquettish smile. Her hair was done up in a typically Edwardian mass of carefully arranged dips and swirls, but even so, Madeline Phelps appeared extraordinarily vibrant, filled with the life she was about to lose.

But it was the picture of Abigail Dorothy Phelps that most captured my attention. She was eight years old, dressed formally in a white blouse, her throat encircled by a delicate swirl of lace, her hair so light that even in the black and white photograph it seemed to shimmer. She wasn't smiling, and so looked somewhat severe, a pose the children of the wealthy were often taught to assume in those days. And yet, despite the formal attire and mirthless face, Abigail Phelps gave off a sense of that innocent mischief for which she was, according to my father's accompanying article, *'well known and much treasured by the residents of MacAndrews Island, as well as the loving parents who were also murdered.'*

The savagery of the murders had been awesome, and although I'd known of the deaths from the time I was a boy, I'd never actually looked into the details of what had happened on MacAndrews Island on November 12, 1915.

On that day Simon Phelps returned to Port Alma after a week-long business trip to New York City. He'd taken the overnight train back to Portland. Witnesses had placed him in the smoking car with several other men until almost midnight, when he'd finally retired to his Pullman car. He'd arrived in Portland at just after six A.M., then driven south through a steadily building rain and nearly gale-force winds, so that it was already midafternoon when he finally reached Port Alma. Two witnesses saw him get out of the car and fight his way to the town pier, wind and rain tearing at his coat and hair. At the pier, he found his boat, the *Little Abigail*, empty, then strode to the battened-down office of the harbormaster, Samuel Clark, and inquired into the whereabouts of the young groundskeeper he'd recently employed. Phelps's exact words were quoted in my father's article: *'Have you seen a young man at my boat? He has long, red hair. His name is Auckland Finn.'*

Auckland Finn, as it turned out, had spent most of the afternoon waiting at the Seaman's Tavern. He'd sat in a back corner, witnesses said, downing one dark ale after another while the storm mounted and raged outside. By all accounts, Finn had been quite drunk by the time Simon Phelps pushed through the tavern door in search of him. According to several witnesses, Phelps fiercely berated Finn for his drunkenness. Finn responded no less sharply, though with considerably more profanity, an exchange my father described simply as '*having words.*' The altercation lasted for no more than a few minutes, after which Simon Phelps slammed back to his boat. Ignoring the harbormaster's warning, he'd sallied forth into the storm, leaving Finn alone and fuming in the Seaman's Tavern.

Nearly an hour later, Simon Phelps had arrived at his great house on MacAndrews Island. He'd looked '*quite angry and upset*' according to Louise Payne, the family cook, and the only servant left in the house, the others having been sent home to their families because of the approaching storm.

At dinner that evening, Simon Phelps spoke of his business trip, and of the torturous journey from Portland to Port Alma, according to Louise. Then, rather suddenly, he turned to his wife and said, '*By the way, we'll be looking for another groundskeeper. I fired Auckland this afternoon.*'

Louise left the mansion at approximately eight o'clock that evening. By then the storm was raging even more violently than before, rattling windows and banging doors, the wind so loud and howling, it sounded like '*a bunch of squealing pigs.*'

And she said more. My father quoted her at length:

After dinner, Mrs Phelps asked me if I wanted to stay there at the house. But I said no, I had a family of my own waiting for me at home. And so I wrapped myself up good and proper and headed toward the road. It was about eight. Dark as midnight already, that's for sure.

Dark, to be sure, but not dark enough to have kept Louise from seeing a figure stagger up the very steps that led from the beach to the crest of the island.

It was Finn. Our groundskeeper. He came stumbling up them stairs and saw me at the gate. For a second, he just stared me cold in the eye, bold as brass. Then he grumbled something and pushed by me. I smelled liquor on his breath.

At that point Louise had turned her own steps toward home. She'd never see Auckland Finn again.

The exact time of the killings had never been determined, only that they had taken place at some point between eight in the evening, when Louise Payne met Auckland Finn at the cliffside gate, and just after five the following morning, when a local fisherman spotted the mansion in flames.

Later that same afternoon, the charred remains of Simon and Madeline Phelps were pulled from the smoldering ruin. Abigail, however, remained missing. Speculation arose that Finn had abducted the child and taken her with him. That ended when, just before nightfall, her body was found in the groundskeeper's shed. She'd been strapped, facedown, on a workbench, her blouse pulled up to her shoulders, her back flayed open.

At that point, the only remaining mystery was the whereabouts of Auckland Finn. Part of that mystery had been solved the morning following the blaze. A twenty-five-foot schooner, the *Laura Booth*, had been stolen from the marina. Four witnesses had seen its dark blue sails fluttering in the dawn air as it slipped away from MacAndrews Island, the flames of the Phelps mansion already visible at the crest of the island. One witness had seen a man at the foremast. He had red hair, and was later identified as Auckland Finn.

For the next three months, authorities along the entire East Coast searched for the *Laura Booth*, everyplace from the rocky inlets of Maine to the lush tropical maze of the Florida Keys. My father dutifully reported dozens of 'suspected' sightings during that time, one in Cape Cod Bay, another in the Chesapeake, still others in the tidal estuaries of the James River. The schooner was seen as far out as Bermuda and as far inland as Cape Fear, a ghost boat forever drifting in and out of tidal fogs and swamp mists, the *Laura Booth* with its blue sails, piloted by a figure whose red hair now hung to his shoulders.

By the following year, the *Laura Booth* had become a vessel of dark renown, routinely added to any list of macabre sea tales, from coffin ships to the fate of the *Flying Dutchman*. It might have passed entirely into legend had it not been found on August 17, 1918, drifting aimless in San Francisco Bay.

By then she hardly looked herself at all. The blue sails were gone, replaced by nondescript ones of white. The boat had been repainted, its name changed to the utterly ordinary one of *Wanderer*.

But where was Auckland Finn?

No one knew, my father diligently informed his readers, although everyone suspected that Finn had climbed into the small four-person lifeboat that had once been lashed to the *Laura Booth*, and rowed himself to shore somewhere along the rocky coast of northern California.

It was very late when I returned the old *Sentinel* editions to their wooden cabinet. I'd read everything available about the Phelps murders, and yet I still had no idea why Dora had reacted so violently to our local tale of murder and escape. Nor did there seem any way for me ever to know.

And so, when I left the *Sentinel* a few minutes later, I intended to go directly home. Then, quite unexpectedly, a powerful urge overtook me, a need, strange as it seemed, to be near Dora, feel her presence physically, as if, in some demented way, I wanted to assure myself that she was real. And so I turned, almost without willing it, like a figure on a music box, and headed toward her cottage.

When I reached it, I could see a yellow light burning in Dora's bedroom window. I saw nothing else until she suddenly glided past the window, her body draped in a dark red robe. From my place among the trees, I saw her bend forward to blow out the candle on the table beside her chair. At that instant, the robe slipped from her shoulders, and I glimpsed her back, the deep scars that gouged it. In the silence, I heard her voice, *Because it's never happened to you*. Words that should have come to me in warning, but formed a siren song instead.

Chapter Sixteen

A song that was still echoing in my mind six months later when I pulled up to my father's house, the old man a spectral figure now, lost in grief and intoxication.

He sat in the parlor, the same closed room where we'd placed my brother's coffin, the smell of funeral flowers still faintly in the air, along with the scent of my father's whiskey. The drapes had been drawn since Billy's death. It seemed to me that the shadows in which he sat hour after hour had by then come to possess my father, that he'd chosen to be entombed within them, as dead as his murdered son.

'Any luck, Cal?' he asked wearily.

'Not much.'

'Who'd you talk to?'

I gave him the names of the people I'd spoken with since beginning my search for Dora.

'Preston Forbes?' my father asked. 'He wouldn't be any help.'

'No one was.'

He took a sip of whiskey. 'The gods use us for their sport, Cal.'

He seemed to fear that any less mythical speculation might overwhelm him, compel him toward some desolate land where even the classical and biblical references that had anchored him for so long would prove no more than windblown straw.

And so he preferred to focus on the small details of Billy's death, revisiting them continually.

'There must have been a lot of blood,' he said.

'Yes.'

'Stabbed in the heart. That would explain so much blood.'

Billy had actually been stabbed in the chest, the blade passing smoothly between two ribs, then into the soft tissue of his left lung. He'd pulled the knife out himself, then tossed it across the petal-strewn floor.

'Terrible,' my father muttered.

I saw my brother on his back, eyes open, glaring, a hand lifting toward me, his blood gathered beneath him, so that he seemed to float on a thick red stream.

'Terrible,' my father repeated. He tightened his fingers around the glass. 'His eyes were open,' he said as he brought the glass to his lips.

'Yes, they were.'

He lowered his head briefly, then lifted it. 'William was high-strung.'

At Billy's funeral he'd stood stoically in his black suit, his eyes fixed on the granite tombstone as if it were the accuracy of the dates carved upon it that really mattered, the cold precision with which they recorded the all-too-brief circuit of my brother's life.

'Like his mother.' He pondered this, then added, 'Emotional. Dora brought his emotions to a head. He was so taken with her.'

'He didn't know her.'

His eyes cut toward me, struck by the firmness of my last remark. 'Did you know her, Cal?'

In an instant, she was before me, staring at me blazingly, as she had on that last night, *I can't, Cal. I can't.*

'No one knew her, Dad.'

He studied me briefly, his eyes very still. Then he said, 'T. R. came by.'

'I thought he might.'

'He said he'd had a word with you this afternoon. He had some questions for you, he said. He didn't like the answers you gave him.'

'They'll have to do.'

My father leaned forward unsteadily. 'He's worried about you, Cal. About what you're doing. Tracking her down. I'm worried too. The way you look. I don't want to lose another son.'

'I'm going after her,' I said.

'How can you do that, Cal?' He didn't seem surprised, only doubtful of my success. 'You have nothing to go on. No way to find her.'

'I'll go to New York first,' I told him. 'To where she lived before she came here.'

'And do what?'

'Find something maybe. A direction.'

'What if you don't find one?'

'Then I'll head west.'

'West,' my father repeated softly. 'Because of that book you found.'

'It's the only lead I have.'

To my relief, my father asked nothing more about my plans. Instead, it was a favor he wanted.

'If you find her, Cal, don't hurt her. William wouldn't have wanted you to hurt her.' He took another sip from the tumbler, letting the whiskey's warmth draw him toward oblivion. 'He loved her. Remember that. He loved her with all his heart. He'd expect you to do the right thing.'

In my mind, I saw my brother as he'd faced me at the final moment, heard his one-word question: *Cal?*

My father lowered his head, his mind churning briefly before it threw up a reference. 'She was like Mephistopheles,' he said when he looked up again. 'Not always in Hell, but always of it. A born deceiver. A thief. A liar.' His eyes bore into me. 'You could smell brimstone in her hair.'

And in mine, I thought.

'Seduced him,' my father muttered bitterly. 'Made him fall in love with her. Then stole from him. Stabbed him in the heart.' Something in his mind sparked through the approaching stupor. 'T. R. thinks she didn't do it by herself.'

'He told you that?'

'Thinks she had an accomplice.'

I shifted restlessly, eager now to be on my way.

'He thinks there was another man in Dora's life,' my father persisted. 'Besides William.'

'There was only one man in Dora's life,' I told him.

'T. R. thinks William might have gotten wind of it. This other man.'

My brother's question taunted me: *Is it you?*

My father nodded blearily, giving up on the idea that it would ever be solved, that he would ever know the source of his son's death, the dark collusion from which it had sprung. 'When are you leaving?' he asked.

'Tomorrow morning.'

He made no objection to my going. 'I'll miss you, Cal' was all he said.

*

It was only a short drive to my mother's house, the farewell I owed her before my departure.

Emma was surprised when she saw me at the door.

'Is Mother sleeping?' I asked.

Emma waved me inside. 'She don't sleep like she used to. Maybe you can ease her.'

The only one who could ease her, I thought, is dead.

She lay on her back, dressed in a white nightgown, her hair a silver curtain in the lamplight. Her blue eyes fell upon me as I came into her room.

I took her hand. 'I'll be away for a little while,' I told her.

She gazed at me without expression.

'Not too long, I hope,' I added.

She remained entirely motionless, grief like a weight slowly crushing her to death.

'She's 'bout stopped talking,' Emma told me. 'Mostly just stares out the window. Looking for something.'

Her dead son, I thought. The full substance of her hope and joy.

'Where you headed, Mr Chase?' Emma asked.

'I'm not sure,' I said.

My mother's eyes flared. 'Cal?'

I leaned toward her. 'I'll be back soon,' I promised. She struggled to lean forward, ran out of strength, and drifted back. Her lips moved but no sound came. After a time, she closed her eyes. Seconds later they fluttered open again. 'William,' she whispered, her eyes fixed upon me. 'William loved you, Cal.'

I saw my brother's eyes as he'd gazed at me in the final moments. 'I know,' I said.

'Loved you . . . Cal,' my mother repeated.

I took her hand.

'And you loved him,' my mother added.

I felt something squeeze together deep inside me, like fingers around the handle of a knife.

'You would have saved him if you could,' my mother said. 'But I . . .' She lurched forward, eyes glistening. 'I . . .'

'Try to sleep,' I told her softly.

She drew in a labored breath, offered no resistance as I pressed her back into her pillow.

I left her, locked in silence, a few minutes later, went directly home and packed a valise, intent upon leaving Port Alma as quickly as I could. But I found I couldn't leave without making one more visit. And so, for a little while, I walked through the bare rooms of Dora's house, careful not to glance at the stain that swept out from the place where my brother's body had lain. In the bedroom the chair still remained by the window, the pillow propped up against its wooden back, the imprint of her body still pressed into it, a ghostly form that gave no sign of where she'd fled.

When I'd had enough, I walked to my car and drove to my house. For a few minutes, I paced about my study, sometimes halting to peer at one of my drawings, follow a sketched wall across a frozen field. Then I poured myself a final drink, knocked it back pleasurelessly. I could feel nothing but the tumult of the past few weeks, could conceive of nothing beyond them but my search for Dora. For a moment, I felt myself shrink to a tiny, aching center of anger and regret. I saw my brother's body, splattered with blood. And Dora, pale and unsmiling, her eyes upon me as fiercely as they'd been at our last meeting, her words no less virulent: *We can't do this.*

At first light, I strode to my car and tossed my valise into the seat behind me. As I pulled away from my house, it seemed fitting that I was traveling light, stripped of everything but a few clothes and some money, the book Dora had left behind, along with the only purpose left to me now, an order endlessly repeated in my mind: *Find her.*

The snow had stopped and a clear blue sky hung above me as I drove out of Port Alma, noting the seawall where Billy and I had spent so many hours, the stone jetty we'd run along as boys, he forever in the lead, always happiest, it seemed to me now, at its very edge. I saw him in his final moments, sprawled across the wooden floor, his eyes growing dim as they stared wonderingly into mine, his question carried on a faint breath: *Cal?*

My answer had sounded only in my mind.

Because there's something you don't know.

PART FOUR

Chapter Seventeen

In New York, I found a hotel just off Broadway. It was small and intimate, its lobby adorned with plaster statues of Greek figures and lit by a modest chandelier. It was the sort of place where assignations no doubt took place, and there might have been a time when I could have imagined Dora and me meeting here, deciding what to do, how to do it, finding a way that did not end in murder.

'Sir?'

I looked up, realized that I'd drifted once more into a grim meditation. 'What?' I answered.

The man behind the desk eyed me suspiciously, as if I were the one in flight, leaving bloody tracks across the pale blue carpet.

'Our dining room is to the right,' he said. 'Will you be dining with us this evening?'

I was tired and hungry, but the lash struck again: *Find her.*

'No, I won't,' I replied, took the key from his hand, and went directly to my room.

The room was spare, with nothing but a bed and small bureau, a worn carpet on the floor. I locked the door behind me, then walked to the window and looked down at the street. A dirty snow lined the gutter, blackened by soot and car exhaust, people slogging through it, clutching bags, packages, the collars of their coats, the wind forever howling at their backs. In every face I searched for Dora's.

The Tremont Residence Hall for Women was only a block away. It was an ugly brick building, five stories high, with a spacious vestibule finished with two sofas and a few tables and chairs. Potted plants stood here and there, along with reading lamps at almost every chair. It looked like the student lounges I remembered from my college days.

The man who approached me was short and stocky, with the cauliflower ears of an ex-prizefighter and a body that rolled toward me heavily, like a cannon ball. He introduced himself as Ralph Waters, and although he offered a friendly smile, his gaze remained steely, full of silent warning. Here was the guardian of women against the dark obsession of disordered men.

'Is there something I can do for you?'

I told him my name, where I'd come from, and that I wanted to see the woman who ran Tremont Hall.

'I believe her name is Cameron,' I added.

'Mrs Posy Cameron,' Waters said respectfully, as if her married status were a royal title. 'She'll want to know what this is about.'

'Tell her it's about a young woman who once lived here.'

One eyebrow arched. 'And that would be?'

'Dora March.'

The name registered in his eyes, but Waters said nothing of what it had sparked in his mind. Instead, he pointed to a wooden bench nearby. 'Have a seat,' he said, almost as a policeman would address a felon, my appearance perhaps so changed since my brother's death and Dora's flight that I now gave off a criminal air.

At the bench, I watched as Waters headed toward the back of the building. He knocked at a closed door, then stepped inside.

While I waited, the residents of Tremont House came and went. Most of them were in their twenties. They glanced at me furtively as they passed, somewhat fearfully, so that I felt like a wolf among them, grim and predatory, a creature they should, at all cost, avoid.

Posy Cameron appeared a few minutes later. She was in her sixties, I supposed, a small but imposing woman, who dressed with a clear eye to modesty. Even from a distance, she gave off a no-nonsense authority, which, along with the look of command she offered the young women who greeted her as she made her way across the room, reminded me of Maggie Flynn, the sort of woman for whom young women felt, in equal measure, a daughter's trust and fear.

I rose as she came up to me.

'Mr Chase?' she asked.

'Yes.'

She seemed to glimpse the grave task I'd set myself.

'Perhaps we should speak privately,' she said, then led me into a small, uncluttered office, its walls lined with neatly arranged shelves and cabinets. There was nothing on her desk but a note-pad, a telephone, and a few pencils, all carefully lined up along one side. A photograph of President Roosevelt hung in a large wooden frame on the wall behind her, his jaunty grin determinedly at odds with the gloomy state of things.

'Please, sit down,' Mrs Cameron said. She lowered

herself into the plain wooden chair behind her desk. 'This is about Dora March, I understand?'

'Yes, it is.'

'You're not the first person who's made inquiries about Miss Dora March,' Mrs Cameron told me. 'Another man came by some months ago. He was also from Maine, as I recall. He said he worked for the district attorney.'

'So do I,' I told her, the lie tripping from my mouth as easily as the truth.

'Doing what?'

'Looking for Dora March.'

'Has something happened to Dora?'

'Not just to Dora.'

'Well, the other man only asked questions about Dora,' Mrs Cameron said. 'He didn't mention anyone else. Any other problem. I take it the information I gave him was not enough.'

'At the time, it was.'

'But now you need more?'

I saw my brother stumble backward, his eyes wide, unbelieving, no doubt astonished, in his last instant, that his love could end this way.

'Since then there's been a murder,' I said.

'A murder?' Mrs Cameron asked unbelievingly. 'And you think Dora had something to do with it?'

'She was the last person to see the victim alive.' I kept my voice steady, gave no hint of what the words themselves summoned up in me.

'A man was killed,' I said. He returned to me in all his splendor, first as a boy rolling in the grass, then a young man singing duets with our mother, and finally as I'd seen him in his last hours, emboldened by romantic certainty, a man of diamond purity, a heart swelled with romance. 'He loved her,' I added softly.

'Loved Dora?' Mrs Cameron asked.

I saw them together on the old wooden bridge that spanned Fox Creek. 'Yes,' I said.

Mrs Cameron nodded. 'I see.' She studied me like one waiting for the pool to clear, catch a view of its dark bottom. 'What makes you think Dora had something to do with this man's death?'

'She fled the scene,' I answered in what was left of my official voice. 'That's why I'm looking for her.'

Mrs Cameron continued to watch me warily, perhaps suspecting the very motive I labored to conceal. I took out a notepad, hoping it would give me a purely dispassionate appearance, suggest that I was just a man doing his job, with only the faintest connection to the one he sought.

'You told Mr Stout, the other man, that Dora March stayed here only around a month,' I said.

'Yes.'

'Do you know where she came from?'

'No.'

'Did she make any friends in the residence?'

'Not that I know of. She kept very much to herself.'

'You never saw her with anyone?'

'No,' Mrs Cameron said. 'She always seemed rather distant, Mr Chase. I had the feeling that she really didn't want to have any sort of relationship. That she preferred being alone.'

I saw Dora rise from the moist ground, brush the sand from her dress, then stretch her hand toward me.

'I don't think she wanted to be alone,' I said before I could stop myself.

Mrs Cameron looked as if I'd suddenly confirmed a faint suspicion. 'So you knew Dora?'

My own voice sounded in my mind: *Don't go, Dora. Not yet. Please.*

'Yes, I knew her.'

Mrs Cameron's eyes were two small, probing lights.

'A little,' I added, then glanced down at my notebook, away from Posy Cameron's penetrating gaze. 'Do you know why she left New York so suddenly?'

'No,' Mrs Cameron answered. 'She didn't say a thing to me about it. But I had the impression that the city disturbed her. The crowds. The noise.'

My question: *What do you want, Dora?*

'I felt that she might have come from a very different sort of place,' Mrs Cameron continued. 'With more space. That she wanted . . .'

Her answer: *Peace.*

'A more tranquil setting,' Mrs Cameron said. 'In any event, that New York wasn't the place for her.'

'Did she ever mention her family?'

'No.'

'Do you know if she ever got a job of any kind?'

Mrs Cameron shook her head. 'She paid the rent on time, that's all I know.'

'You have no idea where that money came from?'

'No.'

'And after she left, you never heard from her again?'

'Not a word.'

I had only one other place to go. 'She left a book behind. I think she must have had it for a long time. There was a label inside. It said that the book came from the library of a man named Lorenzo Clay. Did you ever hear her mention that name?'

'No.'

'Carmel, California, did she ever mention living there?'

Mrs Cameron shook her head. 'What was the book?'

'Just a book of poetry,' I answered.

Mrs Cameron looked surprised. 'Poetry. I wouldn't have expected Dora to care much for poetry.' She saw something in my eyes, something deeper even than the weariness and grief, perhaps some glimmer of the passion I had known. I could see that she was bringing it together in her mind, connecting the flying strands of my own story, thought she now knew why I was tracking Dora March. 'Of course, you no doubt knew her much better than I did.'

I felt Dora's lips on mine, pressed hard, then drawing away swiftly, like someone alarmed by her own deep need.

'Dora is a suspect, I take it?' Mrs Cameron asked.

'She's the only suspect.'

'Because she "fled the scene," as you put it?'

I saw her rushing through the rain, the brown suitcase hanging heavily from her hand, her coat flying as she raced through the wood, then out onto the road, toward the white pillar that marked the Portland bus stop.

'Yes,' I replied.

'But are you sure she was really fleeing? Maybe she was—'

'Someone saw her.'

Henry Mason's sedan drew up beside her, the door opened. I heard Henry's wheezy voice: *Where are you going, Dora?* For a moment, I felt myself poised behind the wheel of Henry's car, my question quite different from the one he'd asked: *What are you running from, Dora?*

'Of course, a woman can run away from many things,' Mrs Cameron said. 'The women here at Tremont House are often running away from something. Poverty. Bad families.' She looked at me pointedly. 'Even love.'

Even love, I thought, then felt Dora pull herself out of my embrace, stride toward the door, open it, and step out into the darkness. Where would a woman go, I wondered, if she were fleeing that?

Chapter Eighteen

It was a long drive to California, plagued by fierce weather and badly tended roads, a tale of breakdowns and delays, my car rattling ever more loudly with each passing mile, its once-bright sheen finally buried under layers of dust and grime.

As the days wore on, I began to break the monotony by picking up hitchhikers along the way. They were ragged and bereft, carrying scarcely little more than the stories of themselves, chronicles of loss and dispossession, the love or hatred they had left behind. They spoke of fires, floods, drought, of closed factories and confiscated farms. Wives and children appeared briefly in their stories, then fell away in rancor, betrayal, early death. While they talked, they slapped dust from their hats, scraped mud from their shoes, cleaned their nails with pocketknives. They carried matches to light their fires, tin skillets to heat their suppers, and ice picks to fight off men yet more desperate than themselves. They never asked for money, or for pity, or to spin their tales for longer than I cared to listen. When the ride was over, they got out of the car, nodded, wished me luck. 'Hope I didn't bore you,' they would often say.

They never did. For each had, in his way, told a different story. And yet, in time a single theme emerged, that people were equally undone by things both great and small, from our grandest passions to our most petty needs, events as vast as war and as small as a misplaced note. In my own version, as I came to realize, the great thing was Dora in her dark allure, the small one nothing more than a tiny broken gear.

At first no one noticed. There was a slight smudge on the 'n' and 'm' as the paper ran off the press. A small gear had cracked in the mechanism that turns the inking cylinder, thus slowing its turn just enough to smear the ink sufficiently for the human eye to catch it. After looking over the damage, Billy decided that the old press was falling apart in various ways, and should simply be retired. But Henry Mason informed him that there wasn't enough money to buy a new press, that replacing the broken gear was my brother's only option.

Billy left for Portland on the morning of August 3, spent most of the day tracking down exactly the right gear. He'd finally found it late in the afternoon, then headed back toward Port Alma. About halfway home, caught in a driving rain, the car had begun to skid, then spin, turning in full, slicing circles until it had finally careened into a ditch half filled with muddy water.

Billy was found slumped over the wheel, bleeding and unconscious, and taken to the nearest hospital.

I answered the phone at just after nine that evening.

'Calvin Chase?'

'Yes.'

'This is Dr Goodwin. I'm calling from Portland General Hospital. You're William Chase's brother, is that right?'

'What's happened?'

'Your brother was in a car accident,' Dr Goodwin told me. 'He's—'

'Dead?' I blurted out.

'No,' Dr Goodwin said. 'But he's hurt quite badly.'

'Is he conscious?'

'Yes, but he's sleeping now.'

'When he wakes up, tell him I'm on my way.'

'One thing,' Dr Goodwin said quickly. 'He repeated a name several times. Perhaps his wife?'

'My brother isn't married.'

'Dora,' Dr Goodwin said. 'That was the name.'

'Tell him I'll bring Dora with me.'

I arrived at her house ten minutes later, knocked at the door, then heard the creak of the wooden floor as she moved toward it. The door opened, and she stood before me, her hair free and falling to her shoulders, her body hidden beneath a long white sleeping gown. 'Cal,' she said.

'I'm sorry to disturb you, but—'

'What's wrong?'

'Billy's been in an accident,' I told her. 'It's pretty serious, the doctor said.'

'Where is he?'

'In Portland. At the hospital there. He asked for you.'

'Come in. I'll get dressed.'

She headed for the bedroom, opened the door, and stepped inside. In that brief instant, I saw a single candle burning on the narrow table opposite the bed. A small porcelain figure rested just to the right of the candle, a little girl, naked on a gray stone, her legs drawn up to her chest, her back obscured by a curtain of long, blond hair.

Seconds later, Dora emerged, now in her dark green dress. 'I'm ready,' she said.

I stepped to the door and opened it.

'Is your father coming?' she asked as she went through it.

'No, I haven't told him yet,' I said.

She looked up at me quizzically.

'I want to see how Billy is doing first,' I explained.

I can no longer say whether that was actually true, or whether, deep within the darkened chamber a different thought held sway, that I merely wanted to be alone with Dora in the night, feel that nothing stood between us but the electric air.

We drove through Port Alma, then up the coastal road, a night-bound sea at our right. Against that utter blackness, Dora's face was pale and still, an ivory cameo. I tried not to look at her, tried to suppress the tumult that rose in me each time she came into view. I even worked to maintain my silence, since each time I heard her voice, I felt myself fall deeper into the pit. I had never known anything like this before, and I didn't like it in the least. I wanted only to regain my footing once again, leave all thought of Dora March behind, return to my books and my brandy and my whore, let my brother win her if he could, then smile happily as I tossed the rice on their wedding day.

And yet, when I spoke, I felt a sinister purpose in what I said.

'I warned him about that old wreck. Especially about the brakes. But he just wouldn't listen.' My eyes slid over to Dora. 'You know how he is? Like a little boy.'

Although my words had been aimed at my brother's carelessness, the way he'd endangered himself simply by letting things go, I recognized that I'd shot them like arrows meant to unhorse a rival knight, send him sprawling into the mud before his lady's eyes.

When Dora said nothing, I struck again.

'He's careless. He's always thought of himself as invulnerable. But he was always getting hurt when he was a boy. Mother was forever bandaging a finger or putting his arm in a sling. I think he sort of liked that, being mothered.'

Dora's silent gaze remained fixed on the road ahead, so I retreated into another pose, that of the kind and faithful brother. 'But he always pulled through,' I added. 'And he'll pull through this time too.'

'Yes, he will,' she said determinedly, as if by will alone she could make it so.

An hour later Dr Goodwin escorted us into Billy's room.

He lay in a narrow metal bed, his head swathed in bandages, blood soaking through the gauze, his eyes black and swollen, a body suddenly small, frail, broken, utterly *physical* in the sense of being composed exclusively of flesh, capable of being scraped, torn, battered. I saw his soul as well, like his body, no less naked and exposed, doomed to a thousand shocks and terrors. And yet, for all that, I didn't rush over to him, take his hand, let him know that I was at his side.

It was Dora who did all that.

'William,' she said softly, then swept over to his bed and clasped his hand.

He stirred slightly, and I could see a subtle movement beneath his closed lids, as if he were searching for her, like a child in a darkened room.

'It's Dora,' she said quietly, not as a call for him to awaken, but only to let him know that she was there.

His fingers curled around Dora's fingers. She leaned forward and kissed him on the forehead.

We stayed for hours in his room, left it only when Dr Goodwin returned, two nurses just behind him. 'I need to do an examination,' the doctor told us. 'There's a waiting room down the hall.'

It was a plain area with wooden chairs and a checkered floor. Ashtrays here and there. A single large window faced the hospital's asphalt parking lot, the black tar slicked with rain.

'He can stay with me when he leaves the hospital,' I said. 'In the room upstairs.'

'He's lucky to have you, Cal.'

I shook my head. 'No. He's lucky to have *you*.'

I instantly realized that inadvertently I'd revealed a glimpse of my true feelings for her, touched her, almost physically.

She seemed to feel a dark heat rising from me. 'I'll do what I can for him,' was all she said.

'I'm sure you will,' I said, then detailed how much I, too, was willing to sacrifice for my brother, all of it geared to demonstrate the depth of my devotion to him.

'Over the years, I've gotten used to taking care of Billy,' I said, then echoed one of my father's biblical references, 'I am my brother's keeper.'

It was a role I'd played so long, and cherished so devotedly, a sentiment I'd expressed with such convincing sincerity that even months later, as the lights of Carmel, California, glittered distantly in the dark hills, I could still almost believe that it had been true.

Lorenzo Clay was not hard to find, since, as it turned out, he was one of the richest men in Carmel. He lived in a large house on a rocky beach, its grounds bordered by a high white wall topped with red slate and protected by a towering wrought iron gate.

The entrance door opened and a swarthy man in a dark, carefully tailored suit walked to the gate. 'Yes?'

'My name is Calvin Chase,' I said. 'I'm here to see Lorenzo Clay.'

'Is Mr Clay expecting you?' He spoke with a slight accent.

'No.'

'Well, then, I'm afraid that you'll have to—'

'I'm investigating a murder.'

The man's face tensed. 'A murder?'

'In Maine, two months ago.'

'What would that have to do with Mr Clay?'

I handed him the book. 'The person who last saw the victim alive had this book. As you can see, it once belonged to Mr Clay.'

He looked at the book, even flipping through the pages while he considered what he should do. Finally, he glanced up and said, 'Just a moment.'

He went back into the house, carefully closing the door behind him. While I waited, I gazed out over the wide grounds of Lorenzo Clay's estate, heard Dora's voice repeating once again the thing she'd claimed most to need: *Peace*. I saw my hand take hers, draw her to her feet, our eyes, in that instant, fixed in a terrible collusion, all hope of future peace cast to the wind.

The door opened and the man returned to the gate. 'Mr Clay would be happy to see you,' he informed me.

He unlocked the gate with a large brass key and led me down the walkway, up a short flight of stairs and into the house. It had a spacious foyer, a marble floor partially covered by a wide Oriental carpet. If Dora had actually lived here, I could not imagine the adjustment she had made, the route that had taken her from such wealth and luxury to her spartan cottage in the wood.

'Mr Clay is in his study,' the man told me as we swung left and headed down a long corridor. At the end of it, he opened a door, stepped to the right, and gestured me inside.

'Mr Calvin Chase,' he said formally, then backed away, leaving me alone with Lorenzo Clay.

He sat behind a massive oak desk strewn with books and papers, the brocade back of his chair rising several inches above the top of his head. I couldn't tell how tall he was, only that he was quite obese, with a thick neck and arms. He was completely bald, and had practically no eyebrows, so that he looked as if he'd been dipped in acid, all his features melted into a doughy mass. His eyes were hazel and perfectly round, small coins pressed into the dough.

'I hope you'll excuse the disorder. I wasn't expecting any visitors today.' He nodded toward a chair. 'Please, have a seat.'

I did as he asked, glancing about the room as I lowered myself into one of the two chairs that faced Clay's desk. There were no cases filled with curios, no sculpture. Only a few small oil paintings hung on the walls, all other space taken up by towering bookshelves. For a moment, I imagined Dora drawing books from their shelves, touching them in the way she'd touched mine, as if they were small and alive, tiny, purring things.

'Would you like something to drink?' Clay asked.

'No. Thank you.'

He held the book I'd brought from Maine in his hands. 'You're correct in what you told Frederick,' he said. 'This book certainly once belonged to me. You've come a long way to return it.'

'That's not why I came.'

He seemed to hear the stark tone in my voice, dead and without inflection.

'So I was told,' he said quietly. He placed the volume on his desk, then slid it toward me. 'Frederick mentioned that it has something to do with a murder.'

'Yes.'

'When did this murder take place?'

'Last November. The twenty-seventh to be exact.'

'And you've come all the way from Maine?'

I nodded, caught my own profile reflected in the window glass to my left, a gaunt figure, gnawed to the bone.

'That's a very long way,' Clay said. 'The victim must have been someone quite important.'

'The victim was my brother.'

For the first time, Clay's tiny round eyes appeared capable of something other than suspicion. 'I'm sorry,' he said. He lifted the book. 'And this book is connected in some way to your brother's murder?'

'The woman who owned it, she was—' I stopped, saw her in my mind, the two of us alone in her small, bare house, her eyes aglow in the firelight. 'My brother was in love with her.' I felt my hands cup her face, draw it toward mine, so close that as I spoke, my breath had moved her hair: *I won't let anything stop me.*

'She went by the name of Dora March.' I recalled her tiny signature in the ledger books, proof positive both of her larceny and of how little it had mattered to me, how easily I'd dismissed it, love, more than anything, a process of erasure. A terrible heaviness fell upon me, the awesome weight of what I'd done.

'It was all a lie,' I said.

'A lie?'

'Her name. Everything.'

'How do you know?'

'She had a magazine.' The garish pages fluttered in my mind, a wild child huddled in a corner, her thin brown legs drawn up to her chest, blond hair falling to the floor. 'It had an article in it. About a young girl. The girl's name was Dora March.'

'She took her name from a magazine article?' Clay asked, clearly intrigued.

'Yes, she did.'

'Do you have a picture of this woman?'

'No.'

'What did she look like?'

'She was in her late twenties, I think,' I said. 'It was hard to tell exactly how old she was.'

'Why?'

I saw her face me mutely, sound my black depths, realize in a fearful instant how far I'd go to have her.

'She seemed older than she looked,' I told Lorenzo Clay. 'More experienced.'

'In what?'

The word came from me before I could stop it. 'Pain.'

Once again Clay's eyes softened. 'I see.'

I could feel myself fading, turning into dust, and so I acted quickly to reconstitute myself, draw life back in again, as if on a gasp of breath.

'When she first came to Port Alma, she had short hair,' I said. 'It's longer now. Blond.' The sheer paucity of what I actually knew of Dora nearly overwhelmed me, but I went on. 'She had green eyes. And she wore reading glasses.'

'It's really not a lot to go on, is it, Mr Chase?'

'No,' I admitted. 'But it's all I have.'

'Is she a suspect in this murder?'

A series of images slashed through my mind, a woman running through the rain, a car drawing up beside her, a question she could not answer: *Where are you going, Dora?*

'She ran away,' I said. 'That's all I know.'

Clay glanced down at the book. 'I suppose you thought I might be connected to this woman.' He seemed amused by such a notion. 'Well, that would certainly have been a new experience for me. I might actually have enjoyed it. Being thought of as a criminal.'

'Most people don't enjoy it,' I said dryly.

All humor drained from his heavy face. 'No, I suppose not.'

I lifted the book, held it in the air between us. 'Do you have any idea how Dora March could have gotten this?'

'Well, I often give books away,' Clay said. 'Usually to hospitals, asylums, prisons. In the case of that particular book, I can only tell you that it didn't come from my library here in Carmel.'

'It says Carmel.'

'Yes, it does,' Clay said. 'But if you look at the label closely, you'll notice a small D in the left-hand corner.'

I looked at the place he indicated.

'The D means that it came from the old Dayton ranch,' Clay said. 'I sold that ranch several years ago. At that time, I got rid of the contents of the house. In all likelihood, the books were donated to whatever private or public institution my staff could find in the general area of the ranch.'

'And where is that?'

'Out in the desert,' Clay said.

Dora's lips whispered in my ear, *Sometimes, when the wind blows over it, the desert sounds like the sea.*

'Where in the desert?' I asked.

'Near a little town called Twelve Palms. It's about a hundred miles east of Los Angeles. Do you know that area of California?'

'No.'

'It's very beautiful in its own way,' Clay said. 'I enjoyed having a place out there. But my wife never felt comfortable at the ranch. She simply couldn't get it out of her mind. What happened there, I mean.' He leaned back slightly. 'A whole family was killed. By this drifter and his girlfriend. Then they tried to burn the house down.' He smiled. 'They'd have gotten away with it. But they made one very big mistake. They left a living witness. A little girl.' The air around him seemed to darken suddenly. 'My wife insisted she kept seeing the child at the top of the stairs. Because that's where they left her. To die, I mean. All cut up.'

'Cut up?'

'Her back. All cut up.'

It flooded over me like a wave, a surmise as wild as any my brother had ever had. I saw Dora standing in the darkness, the lights of Carl Hendricks's shabby, burning home shining in her eyes, then later, as the red robe had dropped from her shoulders, revealing a field of scars.

'How old was the little girl?' I asked.

'Eight, perhaps.'

'Do you remember her name?'

'Shay, I believe. Catherine Shay.'

'Do you know where she is now?'

'No,' Clay answered. 'She could be anywhere. It's been twenty years, Mr Chase. Why are you interested in Catherine Shay?'

I held myself in check, said only, 'The woman I'm looking for, her back was badly scarred.'

Clay nodded thoughtfully. 'And since she seems to have come from somewhere near the Dayton ranch, you think this woman might be Catherine?'

'Not very likely, I know, but . . .'

'But it's all you have left to go on?'

'Yes.'

'Well, if you think there's a chance of it, you should talk to Sheriff Vernon over at Twelve Palms,' Clay said. 'He could give you more details. He might even know where Catherine is. You can mention that you spoke to me. Vernon will do what he can.'

I rose to leave. 'Thank you, Mr Clay.'

Clay walked me to the door, offered his hand.

'I hope you find the woman you're looking for, whoever she is,' Clay said. 'I admire the lengths you've gone to to track her down, traveling such a distance and so forth.' His final words cut through me like a blade. 'You must have loved your brother very much.'

Chapter Nineteen

You must have loved your brother very much.

We'd brought him home from the hospital three weeks after the accident. By then he'd regained some of his strength but still needed a great deal of assistance. He'd broken both legs, and although he could hobble about on crutches, his sense of balance had been impaired by the crash, so that he was nonetheless quite unsteady on his feet.

Still, he had remained adamant about returning to his own home rather than moving in with me or our father. Both of us had been more than willing to take him in. At first, we'd even insisted that he live with one of us, but at each insistence, Billy had grown more adamant in his refusal.

By then we'd all noticed how much he'd changed. It had been evident almost from the moment he'd regained consciousness, and it had become more so during the weeks that followed. He was less able to read and concentrate, and he seemed far more troubled, as if some dark music were forever playing in his brain.

But even worse was the air of suspicion that seemed continually to surround him, blotting out the peace he'd once known, the delight he'd been able to take in small things, and finally that sense of trust he'd extended so generously in the past. It was as if all of that had been flung out of him as the car spun round and round, leaving him still whirling in its aftermath.

And so it didn't surprise me one evening only a few days before he was set to return to Port Alma that he suddenly decided he wanted to leave the hospital immediately. 'I want to go home, Cal,' he insisted. 'I don't like being kept here.'

'I don't think that's a very good idea,' I told him. 'I mean, you can barely get out of bed, much less . . .'

'Someone will help me.'

'I'll help you, but I think—'

'No,' he said sharply, a tone he'd come to use increasingly during his time in the hospital. 'I want to go home.'

'All right,' I said. 'You can stay with me until you—'

'Stay with you, why?'

'So I can—'

'Keep an eye on me? Why is that important to you, Cal?'

'Keeping an eye on you is not important to me at all. I'm just trying to think of what would be best.'

'Best for me?'

'Of course.'

'I want to go home. That's what would be best for me. My own house. Not a strange place.'

'My place would hardly be strange.'

He shook his head with exaggerated force. 'No.'

For an instant, he looked like our mother, no less determined to take his own course, live where he pleased, as he pleased, no less confident that he knew his own mind, could chart his own course. I knew I would be no more successful in persuading him than I had ever been in persuading her.

'All right,' I told him. 'If that's what you want.'

And so, a week later, my father and I bundled him up, took him out into a light rain, and drove him back to his house in Port Alma. On the way, he stared vacantly at the road, save for the curve where he'd lost control of his car almost a month before. 'Right there,' he said as we went around it. 'Right there's where it happened.'

There was no sign of where he'd gone off the side of the road, the rain having long ago washed away the tracks of his skid, but in his mind, Billy seemed to see the accident play out again. His whole body grew rigid as we approached the curve.

'It broke, you know,' he said once we'd rounded it.

'What broke?' I asked.

'The part that guides the car.'

'The steering cable?'

'That's right.'

'How do you know that?'

'The policeman told me. The one who came to the accident.' He looked at me intently. 'He said it was strange. The way it broke. For no reason.'

My father and I exchanged glances.

'Sometimes things just happen, Billy,' I said.

My father leaned forward. 'William, you need to relax,' he said, patting him gently on the shoulder. 'Just relax and let your mind settle down.'

Billy's face remained troubled, but he said no more about the accident. Instead he asked, 'Why didn't Dora come with you?'

'She's getting the house ready,' my father told him.

'Why? Did something happen to the house?'

I glanced into the rearview mirror, saw the worried

213

look on my father's face. 'No,' I told Billy, 'it's just that you've been away for so long.'

'It got dusty,' my father said. 'It needed to be cleaned.'

Billy fixed his eyes on the road, his features drawn, concentrated, as if he were deciding on some grave issue. 'Is Mother all right?'

'She's fine.'

'I'll need to visit her.'

'Of course,' I said. 'As soon as you get settled in.'

Dora was standing on the porch when we arrived, one hand clutching the other, like a woman in waiting. She seemed at home in the role, as if she had been long schooled in service. Billy waved to her, but I saw no pleasure in his eyes.

'Steady now,' I said as I tucked the crutches beneath his arms.

He took hold of the hand grips, his eyes fixed upon Dora as she made her way toward us, her blond hair falling to her shoulders, a vision that struck me so powerfully at that moment that I briefly lost control.

'She's beautiful,' I said.

Billy's eyes shot over to me, a simmering alertness in his mind, so that I felt like a shadow beyond the fire line, another creature stalking his terrain.

'You're a lucky man,' I added quickly, offering a broad smile. 'A very lucky man.'

Billy turned his gaze toward Dora, his expression now curiously altered.

It was a change Dora perceived instantly. She slowed, giving my brother time to adjust to her approach, clearly sensing what he most needed to regain was trust.

'Hello, William,' she said when she reached him.

He nodded, his eyes upon her with a fierce intensity,

like someone trying to penetrate the nature of her disguise, where the real face ended, the illusion began.

'Your room is ready,' she added. Then, very softly, 'Welcome home.'

She stayed with Billy for the next few hours, while my father and I remained downstairs, where we briefly busied ourselves with various chores, then retired to the small front room.

'Well, it's good to have him home,' my father said as he lowered himself into the old wooden rocker my brother had retrieved from our mother's cottage on Fox Creek.

I leaned forward, lit the fire. 'I talked to Dr Goodwin before we left.' The kindling began to crackle and burn, filling the room with a vaguely orange light. I watched it a moment, then turned my back to the flames. 'He doesn't know what to expect. From Billy, I mean.'

'So he could stay this way?'

'Yes. Or he could get better overnight. There's no way to tell.'

My father rubbed his eyes softly. 'Of all people,' he said. 'Of all people, William.'

'He could recover quite soon,' I added, now trying to put the best light on what Dr Goodwin had told me. 'I mean, there's no real impairment. Of his intelligence.'

'It's not his intelligence I'm worried about,' my father said.

'No.' I took the metal poker from its stand and needlessly churned the fire. 'We'll just have to see what happens.' I returned the poker to its stand, then took a seat. 'He wants to go back to work as soon as possible.'

'As soon as possible? What does that mean?'

'I really don't know. I suppose that's up to Billy to decide.'

My father looked at me solemnly. 'He shouldn't rush things, Cal,' he said. 'The people at the *Sentinel*, they'll be expecting the William they remember, the one who was so . . . He's not ready. We both know that.'

'But what can we do about it?'

My father considered the question, then, without offering an answer, pulled himself to his feet. 'I'll sleep on it, Cal,' he said. 'I'm tired now.'

I walked him to the door, followed him out onto the small wooden porch. The rain had stopped, the clouds parted, a brilliant moon glistened on the leaves.

'He'll get better, Dad,' I said. 'He'll be all right, believe me.'

He shook his head. 'Why is it always the ones who love life, Cal? Your mother. Now William. Why is it always the ones who love life that are taken? The ones who want so much from it, give so much to it?'

'They aren't taken any more than others. Dad. It just seems that way.'

He nodded slowly. 'Seems that way, yes. Because they're the ones we miss.'

I sat down beside Billy's fire, and let my eyes roam about. Despite my long familiarity with the general physical disarray in which my brother lived, I was still amazed by the sheer density of the clutter, the way he'd turned a spacious room into a cramped one by stacking books and papers all about. He'd given strict orders that nothing be moved in his absence, and the hard edge of his tone as he'd said it had been the first sign that something had been dislodged from his character, the gentleness that had always seemed so inseparably a part of him. We had all obeyed him, of course, tidied up as much as we could without actually altering the chaos in any measurable degree.

It was a disorder that had often annoyed me in the past but which now I looked back on with an unmistakable longing. For it seemed part of a brother who was now disturbingly altered, and whose future I could no longer predict.

After a time, I picked up a book and began to read, though an hour later, when I heard Dora padding down the stairs, I could not have told anyone a single detail of what I'd actually read.

She stopped at the entrance to the room, the dying firelight reflected in the lenses of her glasses.

'William wants me to stay a little longer,' she told me. 'He wants me to read to him.'

I gestured at the engulfing clutter, stacks of books and magazines, piles of newspapers. 'Well, you've got plenty to choose from.'

'He mentioned one book in particular,' Dora said.

'Does he have a clue where in all this mess it might be?' I asked, surprised by the edginess in my tone.

'It's at my house,' Dora said. 'He brought it over the day before the accident.' She turned to leave. 'I'll be back in a few minutes.'

'Let me get it for you,' I said quickly. 'It'll make me feel useful. Besides, I need a walk.'

'All right,' Dora said. 'It's on the mantel.'

It was the first week of September, a fall chill already in the air, and I found myself dreading the approach of winter, a dread I'd never experienced before. In the past,

I'd always looked forward to its raw cold, the way it drove everyone else inside, left the snowbound streets to me. But as I made my way toward Dora's house that night, I found that I no longer welcomed the coming freeze. I'd even begun to see it as something I'd favored because of the isolation it had forced upon me, a wall of winter added to my other walls.

Dora's house was completely dark save for the one lantern she'd left burning in the front room. The door was unlocked, as almost all doors remained in those days, and I could see the book my brother had asked for in the place she'd indicated, lying on the mantel. I picked it up, saw that it was one of his boyhood favorites, *Two Years Before the Mast*, the sort of youthful, romantic adventure tale he'd all his life preferred. It was a brand-new edition, and from the cracking sound of the spine as I opened it, I knew that Dora had yet to begin it.

Her own book lay on the chair beside the fireplace, an anthology of poetry she'd opened to Matthew Arnold. There, underscored in black ink, were Arnold's most famous lines, the bleakest, as they had always seemed to me, in all the history of verse, a final, terrible admission made on the shores of Dover Beach, that in all the wide, wide world, there was neither faith, nor hope, nor certitude, nor any end to pain, and against whose black tide was set only the pledge of two people to be true to one another.

Suddenly, like a blow, I felt the whole structure of my long resistance to Dora collapse. It was the single most searing emotion I had ever felt, so powerful and shuddering that I knew it had come from the deepest, most needful and explosive part of me, a place that Dora

March had entered and in which she would forever dwell. And I thought, *This is what it is, then. This is what it is to be in love.*

It was still raging through me when I returned to Billy's house, a storm twisting through my mind, leaving all behind it in fearful disarray.

I could hear him talking quietly as I made my way up the stairs. He fell silent when I entered his room, his gaze leveled upon me oddly, as if he suspected that I'd lurked outside his door for some time, been secretly listening as he talked with Dora.

'I brought the book you wanted,' I told him.

'Book? What book?'

I laid it on the foot of his bed. '*Two Years Before the Mast.*'

He nodded but said nothing, so that I reflexively glanced toward Dora.

She sat beside his bed, her hair a wave of gold, her eyes soft but oddly penetrating behind the lenses of her glasses. For a moment, I could not draw my gaze away. When I did, I saw that Billy was watching me closely, squinting slightly, like someone struggling to bring a vaguely troubling image into focus.

I forced a light tone into my voice. 'You went absolutely crazy when you read that book the first time,' I reminded him.

He continued to peer at me quizzically.

'You wanted to go to sea that very day,' I teased. 'You must have been what? Ten?'

His eyes remained very still. I felt pinned down by their dark concentration, a small, wriggling thing.

'Well, I'll leave you to your reading,' I said to him.

Then I looked at Dora, felt my earlier tumult surge again, pressed it down, said only, 'Good night, Dora.'

She nodded. 'Good night, Cal.'

Billy had begun to talk again by the time I reached the bottom of the stairs, and for the next hour, as I sat in his study surrounded by his belongings. I heard his voice above me, speaking softly to her. The very intimacy of it worked like a steadily building charge in my blood.

It was nearly midnight when she came down the stairs again. I heard her footsteps, and darted quickly into the hallway.

She was standing at the front door, about to open it.

'You have a way with him,' I said.

'He is very vulnerable right now.'

'I know. I sometimes think that if he were to stumble, he'd break into a thousand pieces.'

She drew her coat from the peg by the door. 'He's trying to put things together again. Sort things out.'

'Things like me.'

I was very near her now, could smell her hair, her skin, all but feel her breath on my face.

'I know it must be hard for you,' she said. 'The way William is.'

'You're very good with him, Dora. I hope he knows how lucky he is.'

She seemed to catch the fire in my eyes, decided to ignore it. 'He wants to visit his mother,' she told me as she reached for her scarf.

'I don't suppose he wants me to come along.'

I felt her gaze as softly as if it were her hand upon my face. 'He'll come back to you, Cal.'

I shook my head. 'It'll never be the same, Dora.'

She drew the scarf around her throat. 'Yes, it will. He

has to find a way back into his life. Everyone does. After a tragedy.' She turned toward the door, started to open it but stopped when I spoke.

'He once told me that something tragic happened to you.'

She faced me. 'Something tragic?'

'That you'd suffered some terrible . . .'

'Why would he think that?'

'Maybe he just wanted to,' I answered. 'Suffering lends an air of mystery, you know.'

She looked at me uncomprehendingly. 'What could be less mysterious than suffering, Cal?'

It was the saddest question I had ever heard. For once in my life, I had no ready answer.

'I guess it's finding happiness that's the real mystery,' I said. 'Finding love.'

She opened the door and stepped out onto the porch.

I followed behind her until she reached the stairs. 'I hope you find it, Dora,' I told her. 'Love.'

Her face was masked in darkness, impossible to read, leaving the meaning of her final words in terrible uncertainty.

I have.

Chapter Twenty

Twelve Palms was a small, sweltering town, little more than a single street, surrounded by a limitless expanse of cactus and tumbleweed. A range of mountains loomed in the distance, dark and jagged, suspended in rippling waves of heat.

There was a general store and a small hotel, both wood-framed, a barbershop with a rusted metal sign, and at the very end of the town, a tumbledown corral attached to an abandoned barn. Old cars, limned in a fine white dust, were scattered about the main street, toys in a sandbox town.

Near the end of the street, a one-story adobe building stood on a lot that would have been entirely bare were it not for a few sprigs of parched grass and a dusty palm. A storm fence glimmered in the hard sunlight, erected no doubt because the building contained, according to the weathered sign that swung languidly from two rusty lengths of chain, both the sheriff's office and the local jail.

The sheriff was slumped in a metal chair at the front of the building. He was a short, stocky man, with slick black hair, thinning at the top, and skin so brown and leathery, it looked as if he'd been hung out in the sun.

'I'm Calvin Chase,' I said.

He took off his hat, hung it over one knee. 'Charlie

Vernon.' His eyes flicked over my scarecrow frame and hollow eyes. 'If you're looking for work, I don't have any. Nobody does around here.'

'I have work,' I replied.

'Not one of them Okies, then?'

'I'm from Maine.'

'Maine? I guess you've got a good reason to come so far.'

'Yes, I do.'

He returned the large, western-style hat to his head, then pushed it backward with a single finger. 'So, Mr Chase, what can I do for you?'

'I'm looking for a woman.'

Vernon grinned. 'Ain't we all.'

'I think she might know something about my brother's death.'

The grin vanished. 'How'd your brother die?'

'He was murdered.'

Vernon's face remained expressionless. 'Back in Maine?'

I nodded.

'And you think this woman might be out this way?'

'I don't know where she is. But I think she might have come from this area.'

'Why's that?'

'She had a book that came from around here. The Dayton ranch.'

His eyes narrowed. 'Fred Dayton's ranch?'

'When Lorenzo Clay owned it.'

'You know Lorenzo Clay?'

'I spoke to him. He said you might be able to help me.'

Vernon suddenly appeared more accommodating,

though only slightly, not a man who would grovel before wealth and power, only one smart enough to know who had it and who didn't.

'What was this woman's name?'

'I don't know. The one she used came from a magazine.'

'With no name, I don't see how I can be of much help.'

'What can you tell me about Catherine Shay?'

A light flickered in Vernon's eyes. 'What's Catherine Shay got to do with anything?'

'The woman I'm looking for said she was from California,' I told him. 'And she had scars on her back.'

Vernon's eyes widened. 'Are you telling me you think this woman might actually *be* Catherine Shay?'

'I'd like to make sure she isn't.'

'Well, I can tell you this, Mr Chase. If this woman is Catherine Shay, you got no hope of finding her.'

'Why not?'

'Because Catherine has spent her life making sure no one knows where she is.'

I saw Dora as she so often appeared, moving quickly through the darkness, perpetually in flight. 'Why?'

'Because of Adrian Cash,' Vernon answered. 'The man who cut her. She's spent her life hiding from him. So even if I knew where Catherine was, I wouldn't tell you.' He worked to regain his earlier, more languid manner, his voice now as slow and steady as the swing of an old saloon door. 'What do you actually know about Catherine anyway?'

'Only what Clay told me.'

'Which was?'

'That she was at the Dayton ranch the night the family was killed. And that she was assaulted.'

'Assaulted doesn't begin to describe what happened to Catherine Shay,' the sheriff said. 'That's why she's been on the run for twenty years. That's why she's changed her name a dozen times, roamed from coast to coast.'

I waited, said nothing, confident he would go on.

'Catherine heard everything, you see. She was in the house the whole time the others were being killed. Hiding in a little room down the hall from the kitchen. She was already on her way back to the kitchen when it started.'

I saw a little girl step into an unlighted corridor, then stop, shrink back.

'She heard this girl say, "I'm hungry, do you have some food?" That was Irene Dement. The girl Cash had been living with. After that, all hell broke loose. People being tied up. People being murdered. Catherine heard all of that.'

Then abruptly it had stopped, the last moans fading away.

'Once everybody was dead, Cash and Irene started robbing the place. They went through closets, drawers, that sort of thing. Picked up the stuff they got caught with a month later. Myra's pearl earrings. Fred's leather gloves. Catherine heard all that commotion too, of course.'

I felt that I was with her now, in that dark room, a little boy myself, huddled in the same inescapable blackness, locked in the same mute terror.

'They stuffed what they could in a couple of feed sacks, then they left. Catherine didn't see them go. But she heard the screen door bang shut, heard them talking as they headed away from the house. Cash was cussing Irene, telling her what a dumb bitch she was, stuff like that. Then, nothing.'

A little girl's voice whispered in the silence, *They're gone*.

'She waited a little while, then she came out of the room,' Vernon said.

I saw her rise, walk to the door, open it softly, peer into the dark corridor.

My voice was a boy's, *Don't go*.

She looked at me, her green eyes curiously assured, *They're gone*.

I was at the door now, watching her move slowly down the corridor, toward a single square of light that came from the distant kitchen. In a frantic whisper, I said, *Come back. Please, come back.* She turned to me, her long, blond hair shining in the light, *I can't*.

She walked straight to that kitchen,' Vernon said. 'Saw what had been done to them.'

Fred Dayton, gagged, tied to a chair, head pulled back, mouth agape, eyes open, throat cut. Myra Dayton, gagged, hands behind her back, tied to the door, body slumped forward at the waist, her long, dark hair dangling toward the floor, a pool of blood soaking her feet. Sally Dayton, gagged, tied facedown across the kitchen table, throat cut, back slashed.

'It scared the daylights out of her, of course, and so, instead of going out the kitchen door, which was right in front of her, Catherine turned and ran toward the front door, fast as she could.'

I saw her streak past, a little girl in full flight, her

blond hair flying wildly behind her. My own boyish warning sounded softly in the dark, *Hide!*

'She made it to the front door,' Vernon said. 'Even got it partway open. That's when she saw them coming back.'

I saw them too. Adrian Cash striding toward the house, Irene Dement trotting, doglike, at his side.

'Catherine didn't know why they were coming back to the house until they got close enough for her to make out what Cash was saying:

> *Four plates on the table*
> *Somebody else is in that house.*
> *Somebody else.*
> *Alive.*

'She knew they were coming back for her,' Vernon said. 'The fourth plate, you might say.'

And so she ran, first back to the bathroom, then to the study, finally back through the living room, now racing frantically through the darkness, bumping into chairs and tables until she reached the stairs, dashed up them, and curled into a desperate ball, her eyes searching the darkness around her until the front door opened and she saw a yellow shaft of light sweep the downstairs rooms.

'They found her at the top of the stairs,' Vernon said. 'That's where it happened to her. When it was over, they left her for dead. Set the house on fire. Somehow, Catherine came to. She managed to get out, crawl all the way out into the desert. She stayed there, watching neighbors fight the fire until Tom Shay came roaring up. Then we heard this little cry and there she was, standing about a hundred yards away, naked from the waist up, covered with blood. She said, "Papa." That was all.'

Later, however, she had said considerably more.

'Catherine was a real bright little girl,' Vernon went on. 'Smart as a whip. Sort of artistic in a way, liked to draw. She gave a description of Cash and Irene that had every detail you could think of.' A triumphant smile broke over his face. 'That's how the border patrol caught them. Because Catherine had given such good descriptions.'

The trial had begun in less than a month, and ended in less than a week.

'Catherine showed the jury exactly what they did to her,' Vernon said.

I saw her rise, turn her back to the jury, saw her blouse drop from her shoulders.

'You should have seen Cash when she did that,' Vernon said. 'He leaped up and pointed his finger. Yelled, "You're mine" to her. "You're mine."' He drew an exhausted breath. 'Far as I know, she's still hiding from him.' He was staring at me thoughtfully, as if trying to determine if he should tell me more. 'Catherine never got over it. That's what I'm trying to tell you. She's had a rough life. You know, wandering from place to place. Always afraid.' The last revelation seemed most to pain him. 'She's had a few run-ins with the law. Stole some money here and there.'

I saw Dora's name in the ledger books of the *Sentinel*, the paltry sums she'd stolen.

Vernon shrugged. 'Each time, Tom tracked her down and brought her back. But she always left. Couldn't get Cash out of her mind. Always running from him.'

'Why?' I asked. 'Cash was caught, wasn't he?'

'Yeah, he was caught,' Vernon said. 'But he wasn't killed. Got life in prison. That's what drove Catherine crazy. That he was alive, and that he'd yelled at her that way. She was just a little girl, remember.' His mouth twisted into an angry sneer. 'I blame Hedda Locke for that.' He saw that the name meant nothing to me. 'Cash's lawyer. That woman charmed the jury right out of their seats. Told them what a terrible life poor Adrian had had.' His anger flashed, a leaping fury. 'Got the trial transferred over to Lobo City. Even tried to make herself look older so the jury wouldn't think she was just a kid, fresh out of law school. Wore long dark dresses. That sort of thing. Even a pair of gold-rimmed glasses.'

Chapter Twenty-one

She took off her glasses as she came into the room. 'William's getting better,' she said.

Nearly a month had passed since we'd brought him home, and all that time I'd worked to remind myself again and again that the feeling I had for Dora could never be revealed, nor acted upon, that I had no choice but keep my yearning to myself.

'He's getting stronger, yes,' I said.

She took a chair near mine. 'He thinks he can go back to work in a week or so.'

'Perhaps,' I said with little emphasis, working to conceal the tumult her mere presence called up in me, the way everything about her, her eyes, her voice, lit their own separate fires.

I remained silent for a time, then said, 'But what if he can't? What if he can't ever go back to work? What if this suspiciousness never goes away?'

I related an incident of the day before, how my brother had suddenly heard our father moving about downstairs and had immediately demanded that I go down, check what he was doing.

'He seemed to think that Dad was going through his things for some reason,' I told her. 'That he was looking for something. But Dad was only clearing a few things away here in the study.'

'Did you tell William that?'

'Yes.'

'Did he believe you?'

'I don't know if he did or not. That's why, as far as his going back to work, how can he do that? How can he ever do that if he can't trust his own father? Not to mention me.'

'He mistrusts himself, Cal,' Dora said.

'Maybe so, but the fact is, he can't go back to the *Sentinel* until he gets better.' I tapped the side of my head. 'Up here.'

'That will come,' Dora said confidently.

'What if it doesn't? What would you do?'

She looked at me quizzically.

'I mean, do you think you could take over the paper?'

Her answer was crisp and sure. 'No.'

'Why not?' I offered a faint smile. 'I mean, let's face it, Billy was never much of a manager. I'm sure you'd be a far better one.' I waved my hand over the chaos of the room he insisted that we leave untouched. 'I rest my case.' I looked at her pointedly. 'The fact is, Billy's still a little boy when it comes to keeping things in order. The *Sentinel* included.'

Dora said nothing, but merely rose and began to gather up her things. 'I'll be back tomorrow morning.'

I couldn't bear to see her go, had come to dread every moment she was not in view. 'Would you mind if I walked you home?' I asked.

She didn't seem alarmed by the prospect, nor to have the slightest inkling of my feelings for her, how feverish they had become by then, a boiling tide inside me.

'All right,' was all she said.

We made our way down the walkway, she close at my side, our bodies almost touching.

'By the way, did you ever get a new coat?' I asked.

She shook her head.

'You'll need one with winter coming on.'

'The one I have will do.'

'Perhaps I could get you one,' I said tentatively. 'You've been so good to Billy. I'd like to . . .'

She smiled. 'That's very nice of you, Cal, but I won't need a coat.'

We continued on, past Port Alma's main street, its few small lights flickering distantly behind us, then turned on to the narrow road that led to Dora's house. The moon was full and bright, enough to light our way.

As we walked, I began to feel and hear every sight and sound to a strangely heightened degree, all my senses suddenly on point, the night wind more delicate, the whispery movement of our bodies more tender, the whole world immeasurably soft and frail, as if caught in a hushed suspension, awaiting my next move.

I felt my hand reach for Dora's, then hesitate and draw back. It was a kind of fear I had never known before, and it seemed both anguished and infinitely thrilling.

As we neared her house, I could hear the sea churning softly in the distance.

'It's a beautiful sound,' I said. 'The sea. Especially at night.'

'Yes, it is.'

'Does it help you sleep?'

She shook her head. 'No.'

I inched toward the forbidden. 'What would?'

'The desert,' she replied. 'Sometimes, when the wind

blows over it, the desert sounds like the sea. Very peaceful.'

'You've lived in the desert?'

'When I was a little girl.'

She glanced up at me. Her hair glimmered in the moonlight. It was all I could do not to touch it.

'You must have been a beautiful little girl, Dora.'

Something tensed in her eyes, but she said nothing. Instead, she tilted her head toward the stars.

I knew that the passage of the years would surely modify the pain I felt when I was with her, smooth its sharp edges, and yet, at that moment, as I stood beside her in the darkness, saying nothing of what I actually felt, I could not imagine that this ache would ever end, that there would ever be a time when I no longer felt it.

All of that surged within me, but once again I managed to contain it, give no hint of the rising water I was drowning in.

'Well, good night, then,' I said.

She didn't turn, didn't go. Instead, she held her place, still looking up at the night sky. And I thought, *She doesn't want to go in. She wants to be with me. Here. In this darkness.*

'I had a telescope when I was a boy,' I told her. 'I learned all the constellations. But I've forgotten most of them since then. Except for Diana.'

She laughed, a soft, tripping laughter that seemed to lift her toward some world she'd only glimpsed before.

'What's so funny?'

'I thought she might be the one you remembered.'

'Why is that?'

'Because she's the huntress,' Dora said. 'She would appeal to you.'

'Why would a huntress appeal to me, particularly?'

'You'd like the hint of danger.'

'Not at all. I like everything safe.'

She cocked her head almost playfully, a gesture I'd never seen before. 'I don't believe that,' she said.

'I can prove it.'

'Go ahead, then,' she said in mock challenge.

I released truth like an arrow aimed at her heart. 'I go to whores.'

A darkness gathered in her face.

'It's the only kind of "romantic" relation I've ever had,' I added. 'And what could be safer than that? No risk. No risk at all. Of anything.'

She smiled very delicately, and to my surprise took my arm and urged me forward, toward the house, leaves tumbling before us in small, frantic circles.

'I'll always remember you, Cal,' she said.

There was an unmistakable finality in her voice, so I realized absolutely that she was going, that she had always known she would be going, perhaps even known the date of her leaving on the day that she arrived in Port Alma. That was why she'd have no need for a new coat. Because by winter, she would be gone. It was also the reason she'd so emphatically refused even to discuss taking over the *Sentinel*. She was going. She was leaving me behind like something whirling in her white wake. And there was nothing I could do about it.

And so, at her door I said only, 'Well, I've brought you safely home.'

'Good night, Cal,' she said, then disappeared into the house.

I walked to the edge of the yard, stopped, and turned. I saw her step to the window, draw the curtains together. Then, one by one, the lights went out inside. And yet, I didn't leave. Instead I remained in place, watched the darkened windows, imagined her beyond them, sinking down upon her pillows, lying sleepless in the darkness, perhaps thinking of that very desert she'd mentioned minutes before, the one place where she'd found peace, and to which, I knew now, she would soon be returning.

And so, when Hedda Locke turned toward me, her face framed by the desert landscape that swept out beyond her window, I imagined that it might be Dora, the same green eyes upon me as they had been that night, a pair of gold-rimmed glasses held delicately in her hand.

But it was an entirely different woman who faced me, older, and clearly quite ill.

I took off my hat as I stepped into the room. 'My name is Calvin Chase,' I said.

She leaned forward, squinted. 'You can go, Maria,' she said to the small, plump woman who'd escorted me into the dusty room where she lay. Despite the suffocating heat, she was wrapped in an Indian blanket, her fingers curled around a steaming cup of coffee.

'Sheriff Vernon told me where to find you,' I said when Maria had left us.

'He must have been surprised that I came back.' Hedda fingered her blanket. 'Everybody was. The return of the prodigal daughter.'

Her hair was jet black but streaked with iron, her eyes sunken, two rheumy, dark pools. She started to speak, stopped abruptly, and coughed into a dark red handkerchief. Once the spasm had passed, she brushed her mouth roughly, then lowered her hand into her lap.

'Sorry,' she said almost bitterly. 'I've not been well.' She glanced out the window, into the blinding sunlight beyond it, a white-hot sweep of desert sand. 'I didn't want to come back here, but I owned this little house. Free and clear.' She shifted slightly and a pair of small brown feet peeped from the blanket. 'They said it would help me. Coming back here. The climate. The dryness.' She fanned herself with an open hand. 'A good place to die.'

I saw something of the thwarted life she'd lived, felt the death that would soon bring it to an end. 'I'm sorry,' I told her.

She looked at me intently, like someone studying a map. 'Maria said you came all the way from Maine.'

'Yes.'

'What are you looking for, Mr Chase?'

'Catherine Shay.'

The oldest of her wounds opened before my eyes.

'So this is really about Adrian Cash,' she said. 'What I did to Catherine by saving his life. You'd have thought him being locked up would have been enough to ease her mind.' She fell silent for a moment, then said, 'Tell me, do the people in Twelve Palms still believe I fell in love with Adrian?'

'I don't know.'

'Well, suppose I did. You can't help who you fall in love with, can you?'

I heard my own fated pronouncement: *I love you, Dora.*

'No,' I said. 'You can't.'

'Well, just for the record, I fell in love with my duty, not Adrian Cash,' Hedda said. 'My duty as a lawyer. And they never forgave me for it.' She wiped a line of sweat from her upper lip with her hand. 'End of story.'

'It's not the end of Catherine's. She's still running from him.'

She squinted slightly. 'You look like a priest, Mr Chase. One of those worldly priests.' She sucked in a raspy breath. A hot breeze rustled the blanket at her feet, sent tremors through her hair. 'You know the type. A fallen, fallen man.'

I saw Dora's house swing into view, blurry through the sheeting rain, my brother's car in the muddy driveway, felt my feet press down upon the sodden earth, my body move forward through silver wires of rain.

'The type who can't forgive himself,' Hedda said.

The stairs creaked as I went up them, a chorus of tiny, aching cries.

'Something eating at him. Something he did.'

The door was partly ajar. I stopped, a moment, nothing more, then pressed my hand against it, called her name, *Dora*.

'Something . . .'

Then stepped inside, searching for her in the dim light, finding someone else instead.

'. . . terrible.'

William.

Hedda's eyes now bore into mine so fiercely that for an instant I believed she'd seen the images in my mind. 'Well, I'm like that too,' she said. 'Fallen. Because of what I did. Saving Adrian Cash from the hangman. What that did to Catherine.'

The only words I could muster were 'Help me find her.'

'You shouldn't have much trouble doing that,' Hedda said bluntly. 'She's not hiding anymore.'

'Why not?'

'Because Adrian Cash is dead. Died three months ago in the state prison.' She turned toward the small table that stood beside the couch.' He willed me his entire estate.' She pulled open a drawer, reached inside, and drew out a battered silver ring. 'This is it,' she said as she handed it to me. 'All he had left.'

I turned the ring over in my fingers.

'I don't know where Catherine Shay is, Mr Chase,' Hedda said. She plucked the ring from my fingers, her eyes still on me intently. 'But I'm sure her father knows that Adrian is dead. That Catherine is safe now. And so, like I said, she doesn't have to run anymore, hide anymore. My guess is, her father's probably already gotten in touch with her, told her to come home.'

I suddenly felt Dora so near to me that I could all but feel her breath in my hair. 'Home?' I asked.

Hedda nodded toward the window. 'Not far from here.' She pointed toward a line of dark, ragged cliffs that rose in the distance. 'She's out there somewhere. With her father. In the mountains.'

At that moment, as I've since calculated, she was sitting on a granite stone, her legs drawn up beneath her, peering into an icy mountain stream.

Chapter Twenty-two

Billy was at the window when I came into the study.

'How are you doing?' I asked.

'Fine,' he answered softly. He continued to stare out into the yard. He was fully dressed, sitting in an upright chair, both hands on the handle of his cane, massaging it rhythmically.

'You're low on firewood,' I told him. 'I'll get some from the basement.'

He continued to stare out the window.

'It won't take long,' I assured him. 'I'll try not to disturb you.'

He said nothing until I turned to leave. Then he said, 'That woman, the one you visit in Royston. Do you ever feel anything for her, Cal?'

'No.'

'Nothing at all?'

'Nothing.'

'You don't confide in her?'

'No, I don't.'

'Do you want to?'

'She's a whore, Billy. I don't pay her to listen to my troubles. Besides, I don't go there anymore.'

'You don't? Why not?'

'I guess I've . . . well . . . I don't know why.'

He looked at me with genuine puzzlement, then said, 'Cal, who do you talk to?'

'I talk to you.'

'No, you don't. Not really. Not anymore.' His gaze became oddly tender. 'At least not about yourself.'

'Then nobody,' I told him. 'If not you, then nobody.'

He glanced about, suddenly agitated, like someone trapped in his own mind, scrambling to leap free of the web it had become, gray and knotted, a tangle he could not escape. Then something shot into his brain, so that he abruptly focused his attention upon me again.

'Do you talk to Dora?'

'No.'

'Does she talk to you?'

I shook my head.

Again he lapsed into silence. I waited, not wanting to draw him out on so disturbing a subject.

'Dora doesn't talk to me either,' he said finally.

I faked a laugh. 'What do you want her to tell you? Some deep, dark secret? Maybe she doesn't have one.'

'I think she does.' Again his mind seemed to flutter about. 'Do you remember what Mother used to say, that everyone wants at least one thing in life that doesn't change?'

I remembered it very well. She had said it during our last visit before her stroke. 'And that we want that thing to be love,' I said.

'Yes, love,' Billy said thoughtfully. He paused, then added, 'Dora doesn't confide in me, Cal. If you love someone, you confide in them, don't you?' He didn't wait for an answer. 'She's hiding something, Cal. Something she's afraid for me to know. But there's nothing that would change the way I feel about her. Nothing at all.' He looked at me imploringly. 'I love her, Cal.'

If I'd ever doubted the depth of my brother's love for Dora, any such doubt would have ended at that moment. His pain now came from the possibility that the one he'd finally found to love might not love him back.

'I know you do,' I said softly.

He seemed to glimpse the world we'd once shared, the love and trust we'd once known. 'You'd help me if you could,' he said with his old confidence that I was still the brother he remembered, the one who'd dove into the water so many years before, who'd always swum out to save him.

'Of course, I would,' I told him in a voice that no doubt sounded brotherly to my brother, sweet, devoted, having nothing but his best interests at heart, as Iago's voice must have sounded to Othello.

I spent the next hour doing a few final chores, bringing firewood up from the basement, coal for the old iron stove he'd never removed from his study. By then Billy had gone upstairs, so that as I worked, I could hear the soft tap of his cane as he paced back and forth within his room, brooding, as seemed obvious, about Dora.

Once I'd finished the work, I shouted a quick 'Good night,' listened for his reply, then, when none came, headed out the door. I'd just reached the stairs when I saw Henry Mason pull up to the curb.

'I think Billy's sleeping, Henry,' I said as I came up to him.

'Sleeping? He just called me.'

'Called you?'

Henry's pale face seemed even more ghostly in the dark air. 'He says he's coming back to work.'

'When?'

'Soon, I guess. He wants to see the books.'

'The books? He doesn't know anything about the books.'

'I know,' Henry said. 'But he wants to see them.'

I glanced into the backseat of Henry's car, saw the ledgers stacked in a single cardboard box, a weight far too heavy for a man as frail as Henry Mason to bear up the stairs.

'I'll take them to him,' I said.

Henry did not resist the offer. 'Whatever you say, Cal.' He opened the car door, then stepped aside while I lifted the box to my shoulder.

'Sorry for the trouble, Henry.'

Henry looked at me worriedly. 'Is William . . . is he . . . all right?'

'He's fine,' I assured him, then turned and headed up the stairs.

Billy was sitting in bed when I came into the room.

'Henry brought these,' I told him. 'Where do you want them?'

'Just put them on the bed.'

I placed the heavy box at the foot of the bed. 'Well, good night again,' I said.

'Good night, Cal,' my brother said, then, just as I turned away, he grinned his old grin, the one I'd seen so often in his youth, the one he'd never failed to give me when I shared a piece of candy or offered him a turn at some game I was playing with my older friends, a grin I'd not seen since his accident, and which seemed, in every way, to summon back a bright and innocent world, the brotherhood we'd once known, and which in my wild innocence I had thought would last forever.

I went directly home, made dinner, then went to my study and tried to read. But as the hours passed, the room's solitary atmosphere began to oppress me. I heard my father's words again, *There's nothing like loneliness to bring you to your knees,* and wondered if I had reached that point where solitude itself became an accusation.

By eight the sound of my own breath had driven me from the house, sent me pacing aimlessly, with no particular destination in mind, so that it seemed almost providential when I suddenly noticed Dora coming toward me, her long black skirt flowing like a dark wave over the walkway.

'I was on my way to William,' she said when she stopped before me.

'I saw him earlier this evening,' I told her.

'How was he?'

'Fine. At the moment he's going over the books.'

'What books?'

'The accounting books. For the *Sentinel*. He asked Henry to bring them over.'

'Why did he want to see the books?'

'He's preparing to go back to work, I suppose.'

I expected her to nod briskly, continue on her way. But she remained in place just long enough for me to recall my last meeting with my brother, the things he'd said about Dora.

'Dora? Do you think we could have a talk?' I asked.

Before she could refuse, I added, 'Billy's quite focused on the *Sentinel*'s financial records at the moment. It's probably better to leave him alone until he gets tired of them.'

I touched her arm, moved her down the walkway, heading now in the opposite direction from my brother's house.

'Billy and I had a talk this afternoon,' I began.

She didn't look at me, but I sensed a subtle tension come over her.

'About his feelings for you,' I added quietly, laying little emphasis, letting my words fall upon Dora like flakes of snow, with no indication of the dark suspension in which I hung.

We walked on a little way, then I stopped and faced her. 'You know what those feelings are, don't you?'

'I do, yes,' Dora said. 'But, Cal, I've never given William any reason to think that I—' She halted. Her eyes glowed in the darkness. 'This is hard.'

I felt a circle tightening around us, drawing us together.

'What should I do, Cal?' she asked. 'He's getting better. I wouldn't want to do anything that might . . .'

'You don't love him, do you?'

'No.'

A fire blazed in me. 'And never can?'

'Never.'

With a confidence I had never felt in my life, a confidence like my mother's, swift and sure, I took Dora's arm and led her toward the bay. We said nothing until we reached the water's edge.

'I don't want to hurt him, Cal,' Dora said.

'I know you don't.'

'I don't know what to do.'

'Maybe there's nothing you can do.'

'I didn't mean for William to—'

'You can't help the fact that you don't love him, Dora. You can't choose who you love. Neither can Billy. He can't help it if he fell in love with you.' I faced her squarely, threw the die, and held my breath. 'Neither can I.'

She looked at me as no woman ever had. 'Cal.'

'It's true.'

Her eyes glistened, and I knew.

'Dora,' I whispered.

A wave rushed me forward. I drew her into my arms.

It was a kiss such as I had never known before, and while it lasted I felt our bodies flow seamlessly one into the other, a stillness all around us, perfect and unbroken, with nothing but the sway of the sea grass and the distant crash of a rushing wave to suggest that anything at all existed beyond or outside the circle of our arms. And I thought, this is what it must surely have been like, the first kiss that ever was, with nothing fixed in all the spinning world but love, all else a maelstrom and a chaos, our only hope, this utter and complete surrender.

When she spoke, her voice was barely audible above the wind in the reeds, but in its very quietness bore a chilling message.

'William.'

'I know.'

'We can't do this, Cal.'

I held her tightly. 'We can do anything.'

'He's your brother.'

'I don't care.'

'William,' she repeated, this time emphatically. 'William.'

I stopped her with a kiss. We sank down onto the

sand, my body pressed against hers, feeling her need as fiercely as my own, a sense of devouring and being devoured at the same time.

Finally, she pushed me away. 'No,' she breathed. 'I can't.' She started to rise, but I grabbed her hand. 'We have to find a way.'

She pulled her hand from my grasp and got to her feet. I expected her to rush off into the night, like all those fevered heroines so beloved by my mother. But she stood motionless, a curious wonder in her eyes that love had come to her by such an unexpected route. 'I never thought that anything like this could . . .'

I started to rise.

She lifted her hand to stop me. 'Tomorrow,' she said, then turned and strode away.

A high rapture swept over me.

And I thought, *She's mine.*

I was still floating in the aftermath of that wild happiness when I arrived at Billy's house the next morning.

He was sitting up in bed when I entered his room, still wearing the clothes he'd worn the night before. One of the ledger books lay open in his lap, others were scattered here and there about the room, pages marked or dog-eared. He looked like a student in the midst of final examinations, the same drawn and weary look in his eyes.

'Something's going on, Cal,' he said.

'What are you talking about?'

'Something strange at the *Sentinel*. With the books. Money is missing.'

'You can't be serious.'

He closed the ledger. 'It's true. For the last six

months. More and more each month. From petty cash. Taken.'

I stared at him, amazed that even in his delusion he could think that anyone at the *Sentinel* would steal from him. 'Billy, listen to me,' I said slowly, deliberately. 'You can't really believe that someone at the *Sentinel* would—'

He waved his hand over the pile of ledgers. 'Check them yourself,' he said.

I stepped toward the bed. 'No, I'll let Dora check them.'

Something ignited behind his eyes. 'Dora?'

'Isn't that who you'd want to check them?'

'Why Dora?'

'Well, she writes the checks, doesn't she?'

'How did you know that? I didn't tell you that.'

I stared at him silently.

'Did Dora tell you?' he demanded.

'Why, was it a secret?'

'Did Dora tell you?' he repeated evenly.

'No, she didn't.'

'Who did?'

'Henry.'

'What did he say?'

I didn't want to give my brother the slightest hint as to Henry's own doubts about Dora. 'Nothing. Just that she was writing checks. That you'd given her the—'

He seemed genuinely pained by what he next said. 'You're lying, Cal.'

'Why would I lie?'

He looked at me desperately. 'I have to trust you, Cal.'

'You can, Billy.'

'I have to trust—' He stopped, looked at me brokenly, as if, for all his wounds, this latest was the deepest yet. 'What if she's a thief?'

I faked a laugh but heard my own desperate fear within it. 'Don't be ridiculous.'

He lifted his arms, placed the palms of his hands against the sides of his head, pressed them against his skull. 'I have to trust . . . someone.'

I rushed over to him, drew his arms down to his sides.

'It couldn't be Dora,' I said emphatically. 'For God's sake, Billy, look at the way she lives. What would she do with money?'

He seemed captured in a cloud of dark confusion. 'Use it to go away. Maybe that's it. To go away with . . .' His eyes widened. 'With someone else.'

'Someone else?'

'Another man.'

I felt my arms around her body. 'What makes you think there's another man?'

He stared at me intently. 'There couldn't be another man, could there, Cal? There couldn't be someone else.'

I knew that he was waiting for me to assure him that in all the world there was no one else for Dora but himself. But I felt her lips on mine, her body in my arms, I couldn't do it.

'Billy, you . . .'

It was then I saw the question rise like a black cloud in his mind: *Is it you?*

My eyes cut away from him, then back. 'I'm sure there's some mistake, Billy,' I said. 'I'll go over the books myself. I'll prove it to you. Nothing's missing. Nothing at all.'

He remained mute as I gathered up the books, but his

eyes never left me, nor ever stopped repeating their terrible question: *Is it you?*

'Everything's fine, believe me,' I told him as I heaved the box into my arms.

His gaze followed me across the room, then down the stairs, as it seemed to me, and out into the yard, forever at my back, silent, staring, and which, weeks later, as I made my way toward Tom Shay's mountain home, I could feel behind me still.

Chapter Twenty-three

The road to Tom Shay's cabin wound through the mountains along a sheer, rocky ledge. A wall of granite rose on my right, while at the left, I could see a rapidly flowing stream that swirled white and foamy around gray stones. From time to time, a curl of smoke snaked up from a mountain cabin, but for the nearly sixty miles I drove among the mountains that day, following Hedda Locke's vague directions, I never saw a single human being, nor so much as a cat or dog.

And so it seemed to me that Shay had done what any father would, given the circumstances. He'd summoned his daughter into the mountains, away from the desert with its nightmarish associations, the bite of the metal blade as it raked her back. So deep into the mountains that as the road grew more narrow, it seemed to form a prison around me.

As I drove, I felt that I was moving toward the end of it, found myself returning to my brother's final days, letting the pieces fall into place, everything that had occurred from the time I'd left his house, bound for the *Sentinel*, the box of ledgers cradled in my arms, until three days later, when I'd entered Dora's cottage, found him waiting for me there.

Henry Mason turned toward me as I came through

the door of the newspaper office, his eyes shining anxiously.

'Well, was everything to William's satisfaction?' he asked.

I lowered the box of ledgers to his desk. 'Not exactly.'

He looked at me, alarmed.

'Just a few small things,' I said.

I couldn't bring myself to repeat my brother's suspicions, implicate Dora, confirm Henry's own grave doubts. His words returned to me, spoken as we'd sat in Ollie's Barber Shop, *strange, unstable*, Dora already the subject of a deep unease.

And so I hid behind a lie. 'He just asked me to go over the books myself at some point. To check a few things out. Nothing important.'

I'd hoped to give no further explanation, but Henry would not let me off so easily.

'So there were problems,' he said matter-of-factly.

'A few small things,' I repeated, still unwilling to go into detail, convinced that it was an illusion, something that existed only in my brother's tormented mind, that Dora, no matter whatever else she might be, whatever else her past might reveal, could not be a thief.

But I knew Henry wouldn't stop gnawing at it until he got a morsel. 'There might be some money that's unaccounted for,' I told him.

'Since when?'

'During the last six months or so.'

'The last six months?'

'Yes.'

I could see his mind working meticulously, sorting through the vague references I'd given him, offering, then dismissing, various possibilities.

'At the moment, I can't even be sure that a single dime is missing, Henry,' I said quickly, like a man covering his footprints on the forest floor.

Henry looked aghast. 'This is hard to believe, Cal.'

In order to protect Dora, I shifted the blame to my brother.

'I know it is, but I wouldn't get too upset about it. Billy has been a little off base lately. In his thinking, I mean. Since the accident.'

Henry seemed barely able to get his breath, a pallor descending upon him, his breathing suddenly more labored. 'But surely William doesn't think that anyone here at the *Sentinel* would—'

'No, of course not,' I assured him. 'Not at all.'

Despite my effort, I saw the dreadful thought surface.

'Six months,' Henry said thoughtfully. 'Wasn't that about the time when Dora—' He stopped, stared at me wonderingly. 'Could it be Dora?' he asked.

I leaped to stamp out any such speculation. 'Look, Henry, this is probably all just a big mistake. I want you to promise me that you'll keep it to yourself until I've straightened it out.'

Henry's eyes narrowed into tiny slits. 'Dora. My God.'

'She's not a thief, Henry,' I said sharply. 'She absolutely is not. And I don't want the question raised. Do you understand me? I don't even want the question raised.'

He nodded reluctantly. 'All right, Cal,' he said.

'This stays between us. Everything. Until I've had time to sort it out.'

Henry stepped back, a small, docile animal edging

away from a larger, far more threatening one. 'What-ever you say, Cal.'

'I'll talk to you after I've had a chance to go over the books,' I told him.

'Of course,' Henry said. 'However you want to do it.'

'Believe me, Henry, there's nothing to any of this. Nothing at all. The whole thing is just a mistake. It'll all go away.'

'I'm sure it will,' Henry said, all but trembling before me now.

But it didn't go away. And for the rest of the day, each time I tried to push it from my brain, my brother's face would swim into my mind, utterly aggrieved that he'd stumbled upon something dark and terrible in Dora, a dishonesty he had not guessed, all her innocence nothing more than a clever ruse.

That would have been bad enough. But I knew that Billy had glimpsed something even darker than Dora's fraud. Over and over, I heard him say, *Another man*, then saw the question in his eyes: *Is it you?* Far more than the missing money, or even the possibility that Dora, for reasons still unfathomable to me, might have embezzled it, his question circled incessantly in my mind. For although my brother might be wrong about the books, he had incontestably been right about me.

Is it you?

It had not been a question at all. It had been an indictment, based on evidence that only Billy could have seen, some exchange of word or look between Dora and myself. He had sensed betrayal, I felt sure, sensed that something more than money had been stolen from him.

Repeatedly, incessantly, I relived the kiss Dora and I had shared by the bay, the look in her eyes as I'd drawn her into my arms. My brother could not have seen any of this, nor heard a single word of what had been said beforehand. And yet I could not escape a grim conclusion: *He knows.*

And so, almost as a way of distracting myself from the disturbing force I felt gathering within and around me, I returned to the *Sentinel* late that night, when I knew no one would be there.

Henry had returned the ledgers to their place on the shelf, and one by one, seated at Billy's desk, my face no doubt pale and ghostly in the yellow light of the lamp, I read through the endless lines of figures, the evidence building one insignificant discrepancy at a time, a few dollars removed from petty cash, or withdrawn to pay a nonexistent bill, and always fraudulently recorded in the distinctly fractured script that gave no room for doubt that the recording hand was Dora's.

It was past midnight when I finished, a faint light rising at the horizon beyond the windows. I returned the books to their place atop the wooden filing cabinet, then strode out into the early morning mist and made my way to the seawall, where, for a long time, I peered toward MacAndrews Island, trying to reason it all out, find some clue as to why she'd done it.

I knew that it had been my brother's boyish trust that had made this possible, along with the fact he was unlikely ever to go over the accounting books with sufficient thoroughness to notice anything amiss. Dora would have known that about him, of course, and so she could have felt quite certain that she'd never be found out. Had a small gear not broken on an old machine, sent him off to Portland, where he'd swerved into a ditch and dislodged something in his mind, I had no doubt that he would never have come across the slightest hint of missing funds.

But what struck me most about the discovery, during that long night, was how little I cared that Dora was a thief. I even tried to convince myself that her reasons were pure. I imagined her handing the money over, bill by crisp new bill, to the men who lived in the hobo village outside of town, an angel of mercy, they would call her, sent to help them get back on their feet. It was pure fantasy, of course, but I was now captured in a world of fantasy, feeling nothing so powerfully as the memory of her lips on mine, the searing pleasure of her body in my arms. I resolved that I would do whatever I had to do in order to feel that happiness again. I gazed across the bay, dead-eyed and silent, at the great hump of MacAndrews Island, imagined Dora standing atop its black cliffs, and felt my love for her crash over me in a boiling wave, heard its steamy whisper pronounce a single word, *Anything.*

She opened the door tentatively. 'You shouldn't have come here.'

'I had to.'

'It's past midnight. I'm not dressed.'

'I have to talk to you, Dora.'

'Just a minute.'

The door closed. I lingered on the porch, motionless in the utter blackness, until it swung open.

'All right,' she told me.

She stepped back, watched me come into the room, her gaze following me as I strode to the small fireplace, then turned to face her.

She was wearing a long, dark robe, her feet barely

visible below its hem. Her hair, long and in disarray, shimmered in the firelight, filaments of gold.

'I can't stop thinking about you,' I said. 'On the beach. The way we . . .' I felt everything within me grow fierce and bold, as if suddenly enamored by a single, stirring truth. 'I can't let you go, Dora.'

She shook her head gently. 'Cal, please, there's something you don't know.'

I saw her script in the ledger books. 'It doesn't matter, Dora.' I swept forward, drew her into my arms, felt her body grow taut. 'I don't care what you've done. Nothing matters to me but you.'

She eased herself out of my embrace. 'I can't, Cal.'

'Why not?'

She seemed unable to answer, so I provided an answer of my own.

'I know you don't want to hurt Billy,' I said.

She looked at me regretfully. 'I already have.'

'You can't help who you fall in love with.'

She said nothing, and so I made the only demand that mattered to me. 'Tell me you love me.'

She touched my face. 'I do.'

'Then?'

She drew her hand away. 'I can't, Cal.'

'You can do whatever you want.'

'No,' Dora said.

'I won't let him stand in the way.'

Her eyes flared, and I saw a terrible resolve rise in her. She walked to the fireplace and stood beside it, rigid now, suddenly more stone than flesh. 'You'd better go, Cal.'

'I won't give you up. I'll do anything, but I won't give you up.'

'You don't care who you hurt?'

'No.'

I moved toward her again, but she stepped aside and quickly opened the door.

'Please go,' she said.

'I'll do anything,' I repeated as I stepped outside. 'Remember that.'

'Good-bye, Cal,' she said in a tone that sounded so final, I whirled around, determined to appeal it.

But the door was already closed.

Chapter Twenty-four

And you never saw Dora again?

It was Hap Ferguson's voice, sounding urgently in my mind as I drove the final miles toward Tom Shay's cabin. He'd called me in the day following my brother's funeral. Later, as we'd talked in his office, he'd sometimes scribbled notes into the same small pad in which he'd once written Dora's name.

And you never saw Dora again?

No, never again.

And during that last meeting, Miss March didn't say anything about leaving Port Alma?

No.

You only talked about business?

Yes.

The fact that she might need to take over for William?

That's all we talked about.

Where did you go after you left her house?

I walked home.

I heard my footsteps in the autumn leaves, moving along the walkway, headed home.

Straight home?

Yes.

Straight home until I noticed the light burning in my mother's room.

So you didn't see William at all that night?

No.

The door to Emma's room was closed, as I saw when I stepped into the shadowy foyer, but Billy had left the door of our mother's room ajar. I could see them in the light, my mother in her bed, Billy in a chair beside it. He was hunched forward, his hair wild and unruly, his face buried in his hands. My mother watched him silently, her expression so grave that I knew he'd told her everything, poured out all his love for Dora, what he knew of her and didn't know, his brightest hope, his darkest dread, then sunk his face in his hands, and waited for The Great Example to point the way.

For a time, she remained silent, her eyes very still, turning the question over in her mind, trying to decide what her son should do, follow his heart no matter how perilous and uncertain the route, or choose the unimpassioned path, leave his one true love behind. Then, with great effort she lifted her hand, drew the gold band her own mother had given her years before from her finger, and gave it to my brother, her head high, determined, as certain as she had ever been that the heart knew best.

'For Dora,' she said.

Billy leaned forward, kissed her cheek, and took the ring from her hand. He grasped the cane he'd propped against her bed and brought himself to his feet, the issue now settled for all time.

By the time he turned back toward the door, I was gone.

What did you do after you got home?
Nothing.
And you stayed there the rest of the night?
Yes.

And the next morning?

I went to see my brother.

All that night and the following morning, I'd relived the scene I'd witnessed in my mother's chamber the evening before. I had no doubt that Billy would do exactly as she advised. He would go with his heart, rely upon his deepest gift, the trust he had in life, the deep and all-surpassing nature of his love. I also knew that once he'd confronted Dora, she would have no choice but leave Port Alma. Nothing I might say or do would be able to dissuade her after that. And so my only question as I drove toward my brother's house that morning was what I could do to stop him, and in doing that, buy the time I needed to convince Dora that we could be together, even if we had to leave Port Alma. I could hear myself urging her to do just that, assuring her that in time Billy would get over it, forgive us both, welcome us back into his life again, my voice no longer a lawyer's voice as I said these things, no longer calm, reasoned, but charged with an ardent passion.

Were you going to William's for any particular reason?

No.

Even as I recalled the lies I'd told Hap that day, all I'd concealed from him, I still couldn't fathom how it had all happened, the whole tortured story that had led me to the mountain road I now drove down, my life reduced to a single purpose: *Find her.*

I knew I was closing in upon her, the road narrowing steadily, drawing toward the dead end Hedda Locke had described, Tom Shay's mountain refuge only a few short miles away. But with each mile, I could feel an inescapable desperation building in me, a ravenous hunger to recall everything that had happened, so that I could fit it neatly into whatever Dora might later tell me, and thus bring it into conformity with my own sense of things, reach, at last, the center of the web I dangled in.

So you just decided to drop by William's house?

Yes.

And that was on Saturday?

Yes.

The day he died.

Yes.

Did you mention to William that you'd seen Dora the night before?

Hap's face appeared again, his eyes closing slowly as he leaned back in his chair, tugged gently at his right ear.

No.

Why not?

He was in a strange mood. I didn't want to disturb him.

What sort of mood?

He seemed . . . elated.

Elated? Why?

Because he was himself again, I suppose.

How did he look?

Like our mother. That same look in his face.

What do you mean?

Completely self-assured.

A door opened, just as it had that afternoon, and I saw Billy sitting upright beside the fire, his gaze no longer puzzled. All doubt and all confusion had fled. No man before or since ever looked more reborn.

'I'm glad you came by, Cal,' he said, his voice quite calm. 'I wanted to tell you that I made a mistake.'

'Mistake?'

'About the money. There's nothing missing. Not a penny.' He grasped his cane and drew himself to his feet in a single graceful sweep. 'So you don't have to go over the books. They're perfectly in order.'

There'd been no mistake, of course. Billy had simply decided to blind himself permanently to whatever darkness he'd glimpsed in Dora, no doubt realizing what we all must realize in the end, that it is only by choosing not to see that we can love at all.

He walked to the window, parted the curtains. 'You haven't spoken to her, have you?'

'To Dora? About the ledgers? No, I haven't.'

'I don't mean the ledgers.'

'What, then?'

He released the curtains but did not face me. 'About me,' he said softly.

I felt her lips touch mine, heard again our fervent whispers. 'I haven't talked to Dora at all,' I lied.

He turned to face me. 'Good. Because I've decided to do it myself. Tell her how I feel.' His voice took on a fierce certainty. 'Without her, I wouldn't have made it through, Cal. I've been thinking about all she did for me. While I was hurt, sick, whatever you want to call it. Anyway, it came clear all of a sudden. What love really is.' His eyes shone brightly, a knight again, sword at the ready. 'It's sacrifice, Cal. It's how much you're willing to sacrifice what you want for what someone else needs. That's what I feel for Dora. That's how I know I have to do it. Offer myself. Everything. Now.'

I started to speak, tell him the awful truth, that it was all an illusion, that Dora did not love him, never could. But he raised his hand to silence me.

'I know you don't believe any of this, Cal. You never have. But it doesn't matter. It's just between Dora and me now.'

I heard my question, *Do you love him?*

Then her answer, *No.*

Again, I started to speak, but again my brother stopped me.

'I've made up my mind, Cal.' His eyes sparkled with anticipation. 'But first I want to show her how much better I am. That I can drive, walk, that I'm almost like new.' He tossed the cane aside, wobbling slightly, his arms outstretched.

I reached for him. 'Be careful.'

He waved me away. 'Watch,' he commanded. Then he turned and walked from one side of the room to the other, an arduous, painful journey carried out by love and will alone. 'Pretty good, huh?' he asked breathlessly as he lowered himself into a chair.

'Very good,' I replied, my voice oddly brittle.

He seemed to rise on a wave of victory. 'Dora saved me, Cal. I was drowning. I could feel it. I couldn't breathe. Something in my mind couldn't breathe. But she saved me.'

He struggled to his feet again. 'I need a favor, Cal. A big favor.'

The word came from me emptily. 'Anything,' I said.

He wanted you to drive him out to Fox Creek?

Yes.

And you did that?

Yes, I did.

Why didn't he drive himself? His car had been repaired by then, hadn't it?

Yes, it had. But he wanted me to go with him. We'd done it many times before. Gone to Fox Creek together.

Why did he want to go to Fox Creek in particular?

Because he'd picked it.

Picked it for what?

Picked it as the place he intended to bring Dora. The place where he intended to ask her to marry him. He was going to bring her there, walk along the creek, the way our father had done with our mother. He wanted to practice that walk. So he wouldn't stumble.

And he needed you to help him?

Yes.

It was just after ten in the morning when we arrived at Fox Creek. Billy had managed to drive us there himself, hunched behind the wheel of my car. He'd placed his cane in the backseat, but he didn't reach for it when we arrived. Instead, he pulled himself from the car without its aid, then stood, clearly pleased with himself, looking first at our mother's abandoned cottage, then toward the water.

'That's the place to do it. Don't you think so, Cal?'

'I suppose,' I answered dryly.

He looked at me with a brother's care. 'Are you all right?'

'I'm fine.'

'You're very quiet.'

'I get that way sometimes.'

'Anything wrong?'

'No.'

He glanced back toward the cottage, briefly lost in thought, then returned his attention to me and said,

'Two children. I'd like us to have two children. Dora and me. Two boys. Like us, Cal. Brothers.'

With that, he headed toward the coursing stream of Fox Creek, shuffling slowly, but with ever-increasing confidence, across the cool, leaf-strewn ground.

I followed behind him, watching as he struggled forward, a gusty wind whipping around, but not in the least deterring Billy from the goal he had in mind. He was going for the bridge that arched over the creek, and as I moved silently behind him, my hands deep in my coat pockets, my head bent against the wind, I knew that it was precisely at that spot he intended to pour out his heart to Dora, ask her to marry him as our father had once asked our mother.

He reached the bridge, then mounted it far more easily than I had expected. As he grasped the wooden railing and stared out over the swirling water, he seemed incontestably renewed and invigorated, a figure strong and resolute, thrillingly bold, ennobled by romance.

'She won't say no to me, Cal,' he declared.

I said nothing, but simply held my place at the end of the bridge, leaning against its weaving, unsteady rail.

'Come up here,' he said, almost playfully. 'Stand with me. Like when we were boys.'

I hesitated, but he waved again.

'Stand with me, Cal,' he repeated. 'My best man.'

The old timbers creaked as I reluctantly mounted the bridge, then stood, just behind my brother, the two of us poised over the dark current, watching a vortex of sodden leaves swirl madly beneath us.

'I'll never let her go,' he said. 'I'll never give up. No matter what she says tomorrow.'

A blast of wind struck suddenly, and Billy staggered

forward, as if pushed from behind, the wind pressing him against the old wooden railing which, as I noticed, yielded dangerously to his weight, so that it seemed to make a slow, deliberate bow toward the black water, urging him into its turbulent depths.

'Good God,' he said with a quick, nervous laugh as he straightened himself. He let go of the rail, grabbed my hand, held it tightly. 'I thought I was going into the drink.'

A second gust battered us, but by then he'd regained his footing. He stepped away from the railing, lifted his face toward the clouds. 'They say a storm's coming in this afternoon. Could be rain. Could be snow.'

I seized a final opportunity. 'Either way, you might have to wait until it's over to bring Dora out here,' I told him.

Billy heaved himself forward, now moving off the bridge with surprising speed and agility. 'No. I'm not going to wait. I've waited long enough.' He'd already returned to the car and pulled himself behind the wheel when he added, 'No matter what, Cal, I'm going to do it tomorrow.'

We drove back to Port Alma, and now, elated with how well he'd maneuvered himself during the previous hour, Billy refused to allow me to accompany him into the house.

'I don't think I'm going to be needing all that much help anymore,' he said confidently. He smiled. 'Thanks for everything you've done,' he added. 'I know I've been pretty difficult lately.'

I didn't bother waiting until he got to the door, but simply moved behind the wheel and drove away. In the rearview mirror, I could see him struggling up the walkway, the wind whipping at his coat. At the bottom of the stairs, he paused and drew in a long, restorative breath. Then, with that courage he had always shown toward life, he bore himself upward once again.

So that's all you know about William's last day?

Yes.

You didn't see him again until several hours later?

When I found him.

Already dead.

In my memory, I saw my brother's eyes peer into mine, heard his anguished question once again: *Cal?*

Cal? He was already dead when you found him?

Yes. Already dead.

I remembered that with my final answer, Hap's face had taken on a deep sympathy for what I'd been through, the deep, enduring nature of my loss.

The Shay house was little different from the few others I'd passed on my way to it, a log mountain cabin with a roof of corrugated tin. A stone well stood near the middle of the yard, covered with a sheet of plywood, a wooden bucket dangling from a length of thick gray rope. To the left, there was a small stable and corral, both apparently empty, and a sagging storage shed. A battered saddle had been flung over one of the fence rails, along with a pair of reins and a bridle.

The air was crisp and clean, but I could feel only the heaviness of things, the weariness of my long search, all that had conspired to bring me so far from home.

I walked toward the house, then stopped as the door suddenly opened and a man stepped onto the porch. He wore a flannel shirt and dark blue pants. His boots were dusty but not caked with mud, and I could see where he'd scraped them against the steps before going inside. A long mane of gleaming white hair hung about his shoulders. It gave him an even more formidable and commanding look, like a patriarch in some Old Testament story.

'Can I help you, mister?' he said.

'My name's Chase.' Dora's face rose in my mind, cupped in my hands. 'I've come to see your daughter.'

'My daughter?' He looked at me sternly.

'Catherine,' I said. 'Catherine Shay.'

He remained silent, wary, one animal watching another approach his burrow. 'Catherine isn't seeing people,' he said.

'She'll see me,' I told him.

He stepped to the edge of the porch, tall, powerful, ready to do anything to protect his daughter. 'Why? Is Catherine expecting you?'

I couldn't be sure. Perhaps, even as she'd fled, Dora had known I would follow her, track her down. And so I said, 'I don't know. Maybe she is.'

'Why do you want to see her?' Shay asked.

How could I answer such a question? Instead, I relied on my usual device, put on my professional disguise. 'I'm from the district attorney's office,' I said.

Shay seemed suddenly deflated. He looked at me resignedly, as if he'd been expecting such a visit. I thought of Sheriff Vernon's remark: *She's had some run-ins with the law.*

'What did she do?' Shay asked. 'Did she steal something?'

I didn't answer, merely looked at him steadily.

'Whatever it is, I'll pay it,' he assured me. 'Every cent. I always have. You can ask anyone. I've always made good on whatever she did.' He stepped off the porch, coming toward me slowly, now oddly at my command, asking that I go gently on his daughter. 'She's not responsible, Mr Chase. It started after what happened to her.' He fell silent, unwilling to go further, to describe once again a young girl crouched in the darkness, watching a beam of yellow light crawl toward her, the face that had peered at her from behind that light, then bent forward, knife in hand.

'Do you know what happened to her?' he asked.

'Yes.'

'Well, that's when it started,' Shay said. 'People react this way sometimes. That's what the doctors told me. Something happens to them and they start doing things they'd never done before. Bad things. Stealing and—'

'It's not about money,' I told him.

'What, then? What is it about?'

Suddenly all the weeks that had passed since the moment of my brother's death vanished. I felt my foot press down upon the accelerator, heard the rhythmic sweep of the windshield wipers, the mad beating of the rain as I raced toward Dora's house, so desperate and driven that everything seemed to blur around me, the town in which I had been born, the hills, the sea, all of it dissolving into an insubstantial haze, my only thought, on that last day, to get to Dora before Billy did, claim her for myself.

'What did Catherine do?' Shay asked.

Her cottage swung into view, and there it was, sitting in the flooded driveway, Billy's car, lashed by wind, leaves scattered across the roof and hood. He'd acted impulsively, as I realized instantly, unable to wait until the next day, or for the weather to clear, for Fox Creek and the perfect place to speak to her. He'd determined to win her then, at that very moment. I imagined him before her, making his case, so pure and noble at that moment in his life that he could hardly be rejected, a knight upon bent knee before his lady, awaiting the slow fall of her white handkerchief.

'What did Catherine do that you've come all this way?'

The door had creaked open as I'd stepped inside the cottage, a dim light washing over everything, so that I'd seen nothing, heard only the rain pounding everywhere, and so had called her name, *Dora*.

'She ran away,' I told Shay. I saw her rushing through the undergrowth, toward the road where Henry Mason would ultimately see her, drenched and trembling, offer her a lift, take her to the bus station in Port Alma.

Shay looked at me demandingly. 'What's this about?'

'A murder,' I said.

The gravity of the word seemed to strike him like a stone. 'A murder? Catherine couldn't have been involved in a murder.'

A blade glinted in my mind. My voice turned steely. 'Let her tell me that.'

He nodded firmly, with a father's faith that his daughter was free of guilt, couldn't possibly have done whatever she was charged with, love like a blindfold wrapped around the eyes. 'All right,' he said. 'I will.'

I followed him around the house to where I saw her sitting on a gray stone, facing the mountain lake that stretched before her, mirroring the sky.

'Catherine,' Shay called loudly as we moved toward her across a carpet of thick green grass.

She stirred, began to turn, her long, blond hair shimmering in the sunlight.

'She still has awful nightmares,' Shay told me as we closed in upon her. 'Not about the man though. Always about that girl. The one who held her down.'

I could see Catherine's face now, the quizzical look she offered me, the utter lack of recognition, staring at a man who walked beside her father, a man she'd never seen before.

'It's the green eyes she remembers,' Shay added. 'How dead they looked.'

I stopped, saw those eyes in the shadows of her cottage, then felt the knife slide between my own ribs, not my brother's.

'Sometimes I think it was that girl Catherine was running from more than she was running from Cash.'

I heard Dora's voice sound in my mind, *There's something you don't know,* then whispered her true name at last, *Irene.*

Chapter Twenty-five

In the newspaper photograph, her long, stringy hair obscured her face. And yet, looking closely, I could see Dora as if in pentimento below the starved and savage visage of Judith Irene Dement. The caption below the picture had given the stark facts: *Teenager charged in Dayton family murders*.

'Irene was thirteen,' Tom Shay said as he drew the picture from my hand. 'Not much more than a kid herself.' He returned the photo to the grim scrapbook he'd maintained through the years. 'They really didn't know what to do with her. Too young for prison, but they couldn't just let her go.' He closed he scrapbook. 'So they gave her to the nuns.'

'The nuns?'

'The Sisters of Charity,' Shay replied. 'They have a home for girls over near Lobo City. They said they'd take Irene in, keep her with them until she'd served her sentence. Fifteen years, that's what the jury gave her. Three people dead.' He glanced over to where Catherine sat in the far corner of the cabin, staring blankly out the window. 'And another half dead. And all Irene got was fifteen years. In a convent, can you believe it? Not even a prison.'

In all the time since Dora's arrival in Port Alma, there'd been but one real clue. *I think I know your secret.* She'd looked at me with unmistakable dread until I'd added only, *You're a Catholic.* It was the sole thing I'd gotten right about her, the one truth I'd gathered from the cloud that surrounded and concealed her.

Shay returned the scrapbook to the drawer of his desk, locked it. 'It's good for you though, I guess.'

'What do you mean?'

'As far as finding her is concerned. Because if anybody knows where Irene Dement is, it would be the Sisters.'

He accompanied me to my car a few minutes later, Catherine following idly behind us, watching vacantly as I sat behind the wheel, saying nothing, standing motionless and forever damaged as I pulled away.

It was only fifty miles back along the winding mountain road that had taken me to Catherine Shay, then into the desert once again, through Lobo City, past the little thrift shop the nuns maintained on its dusty main street, then along a narrow gravel road, and into a circular drive, the high oak doors of the Sisters of Charity Home for Girls looming before me.

They opened at my first knock. A tiny woman peered at me, dressed in full habit. 'I'm Sister Colleen,' she said. 'May I help you?'

'My name's Calvin Chase. I'm looking for Irene Dement.'

Sister Colleen seemed surprised that given my bedraggled state I hadn't asked for work or food. 'May I tell Mother Superior why you're looking for Irene, Mr Chase?'

I managed an official pose. 'It's a legal matter.'

Sister Colleen's eyes darkened. 'I see.' She stepped back from the door. 'Follow me, please.'

I trailed behind her, first into a simple vestibule, then along an unadorned corridor, and finally through a thick doorway and down an arched colonnade. A sandy garden had been planted at the end of it, ablaze in flowering cacti and desert roses.

'Wait here, please,' Sister Colleen told me, indicating a stone bench, then disappeared down one of the walkways.

I sat alone, letting my gaze drift along the colonnade, following the strangely restful rise and fall of the arches, gentle as lapping waves, remembering what Dora had once said she wanted most in life, *Peace*, trying to imagine how, given a life on the run, her murderous past, she'd ever expected to attain it. Or perhaps she'd never wanted anything of the kind, the sentiment entirely false, merely part of an elaborate disguise.

After a moment, I heard footsteps, turned, and saw a figure moving down one of the archways, an elderly woman dressed in full habit, a rosary hanging from the belt at her waist.

'Mr Chase,' she said when she reached me.

I nodded.

'I'm Mother Pauline.' She sat down beside me, folded her hands together, and lowered them into her lap. 'I understand that you've come about Irene Dement.'

'When *I* knew her, her name was Dora March.'

The false name did not seem to surprise her.

'She never mentioned the Daytons, of course,' I added.

Mother Pauline's fingers touched the rosary. 'People do evil things, Mr Chase.'

I saw my brother in his bloody ruin. 'Yes, they do.'

'They also have evil things done to them,' Mother Pauline said. 'I'm speaking of Irene now. Of what was done to her.'

I heard my dead brother's voice. *Something happened to her, Cal. Something happened to Dora.*

'She didn't go to the Dayton ranch that night because she wanted to, Mr Chase,' Mother Pauline said. 'She'd been abandoned. Years before. By her father. Left in the desert with nothing to eat but a few scraps. When that was gone, she started foraging. Like an animal. Eating anything she could find. She was only eight years old.'

She appeared to me as a little girl, peering out at the desert waste, clothed in a tattered dress, left to live like the wild child whose name she'd later taken.

'So you can imagine how she felt when she saw a man coming out of the desert,' Mother Pauline added. 'How relieved she must have been. Someone to help her, take care of her, maybe even love her.'

Dora's warning sounded in my mind, *Be careful, Cal. Of needing love too much.*'

'Adrian Cash,' Mother Pauline said.

In one of the photographs from Tom Shay's scrapbook, he'd appeared tall, thin, and lanky, insanity like a fire leaping in his eyes.

'Cash had been living in the mountains,' Mother Pauline went on. 'He told Irene that a voice had told him where she was, that it was up to him to take care of her. They lived together for five years, and at first, he didn't hurt her.' She drew in a taut breath. 'Then the voice spoke again. Evidently, it told him that children had to be chastised. After that, he did terrible things to Irene. To purify her, he said.'

The bedroom door opened on a chair stacked with pillows, a bed with bare springs.

'Terrible things,' Mother Pauline murmured again.

Her red robe dropped away, revealing a crisscross of white scars.

'She was thirteen when Cash decided he'd had enough of the desert,' Mother Pauline continued. 'So they simply walked out of it. It took them two days. They weren't looking for the Dayton ranch. It was just the first place they came upon.'

The lights of the Dayton ranch flickered in my mind, Cash slowing down as he approached it, pushing Irene ahead of him, *Tell them you're hungry. Ask for food.*

'You already know what happened once they got there,' Mother Pauline said.

I saw Catherine Shay pressed upon the wooden floor, a man and a teenage girl peering down at her, Irene Dement with dead green eyes, following Adrian Cash's commands, *Hold her down, Pull up her blouse.*

'But do you know what Irene said to Catherine Shay?' Mother Pauline asked.

'Said?'

'Just before Cash cut her, Irene leaned over and whispered into Catherine's ear. "It won't hurt." That's what she said.' Mother Pauline smiled quietly. 'She had no malice in her heart, Mr Chase. That was why she flourished here.'

I glanced about the garden, imagined how, if Dora had remained a continent away from the rocky cliffs of Maine, I would still be with my whores and my brother would still be dreaming of his one true love.

'When did she leave?' I asked.

'Just over a year ago,' Mother Pauline answered. She

watched me a moment, as if trying to determine some issue in her mind. Then she said, 'She loved you both, you know.' She looked at me pointedly. 'You and your brother, William.'

I stared at her, astonished. 'You've talked to her since . . .'

'Yes.'

'Do you know where she is?'

Mother Pauline rose, nodded toward the archway to my right. 'There,' she said, then turned and walked away.

She stood beneath the archway, clothed in a plain white dress, her blond hair cut short, a pair of gold-rimmed glasses cradled in her hand.

'Hello, Cal,' she said, then stepped out of the shadows and came toward me.

My lips parted silently as I watched her move down the colonnade until she reached me.

'I didn't want to leave Port Alma the way I did, Cal,' she said. She sat down beside me. 'Without speaking to you. I mean, face-to-face.' For a moment she seemed at a loss as to where she should begin. 'But I was afraid.'

'Of what?'

'Everything,' she said.

'Me?'

'You, yes. And William.' She shook her head. 'But myself more than anyone.'

'What happened, Dora?'

The question seemed to release a tide in her. 'I couldn't think of any way out, Cal. It's as simple as that. I didn't want to hurt anyone. Not you or William. I couldn't be with either one of you. All I could do was leave.'

I saw the golden ring on the floor of her cottage, the blood-drenched roses, imagined Billy flinging them to the ground in a sudden surge of bitter disappointment. 'He asked you to marry him.'

'He was going to. That's why I couldn't face him.'

'Face him? You didn't see William at all the day you left?'

'No,' she answered. 'The night before, he'd told me that he wanted us to go to Fox Creek together in a day or so. Then suddenly he said, "Tomorrow. I'll come for you tomorrow." I knew then that he was going to— And I couldn't, Cal. Like I said in the letter, I just—'

'What letter?'

'The one I left.'

Her empty cottage swam into my mind. 'Where did you leave this letter?'

'With Mr Mason,' Dora said. 'I saw him in the office when I passed by on the way to the bus station.'

'Henry was in the office on a Sunday afternoon?'

'Yes, he was. He was going over the ledgers.'

A dark shape gathered in my mind.

'Did you tell him you were leaving Port Alma?' I asked.

'Yes,' Dora said. 'And that William would be going over to my house that afternoon. That's when I gave him the letter. So that he could give it to William.'

I saw Henry Mason's hand reach for Dora's letter, hold it silently as she turned, made her way toward the door.

'It was raining,' she added. 'He offered to take me to the station.'

'Did you tell Henry what was in the letter?' I asked.

'No.' She looked at me, puzzled. 'He never gave William my letter?'

'No,' I answered quietly, the shape rising now, dark and sinister, like something from the murky depths. 'No, he never did.'

At that instant, it broke the surface. I saw Henry in his car, watching through the rain-black trees as Billy arrived at Dora's cottage with roses and the ring, knowing that she was already gone and that, without the letter she had left with him, my brother would never know why or where she'd gone, nor have any way to find her. By then he'd no doubt composed a lie he thought Billy surely would believe, that Dora had betrayed him, stolen from him, fled from him, that she had never, ever loved him, a tale to which Billy could have responded only with the words Betty Gaines had heard as she'd passed Dora's house.

> *Don't say that,*
> *I don't believe it.*
> *It's not true.*

Then the moment of shattering recognition.

> *It's you!*

I could feel the anguish that must have broken over my brother, then the rage that seized him, drove him forward, fierce and wrathful, Henry, stricken that his plan could have gone so desperately awry, now stumbling backward, through the kitchen, hands flailing, finding in their panicked flight a long kitchen knife, breathless, wheezing, begging my brother to please, please, believe him, determined to do what must be done if he did not.

'Billy,' I said, now lost in memory, rushing toward Dora's cottage, driving through the rain, listening to the heavy thump of the windshield wipers, loud and rhythmic, as if the car itself had sprung to life, its metal heart beating as urgently as mine.

Dora's voice was very soft. 'I never meant to hurt him, Cal. And I couldn't let you hurt him either.'

The door swung open, and he was there, sprawled on his back, a swath of blood across his white shirt, one hand rising toward me, weak and trembling, his eyes beseeching me as he labored to speak.

'Leaving was the only thing I could do,' Dora said.

I saw a wink of gold in the light, the ring lying at the edge of a scarlet pool, a bloody knife flung a few inches away. His voice sounded in the stillness, faint and deathly, but loud enough for me to hear the faith it carried, the sure and certain knowledge that I had come to save him: *Cal.*

'I loved William,' Dora said. 'I hope he knows that.'

He lifted his arms toward me, expecting me to rush to his aid, but I stood, frozen, staring down at him, listening to the rattle of his breath, the single word that managed to rise above it: *Cal.*

'But I couldn't love him in *that* way.'

He stared at me wonderingly, baffled that I remained in place, towering above him, putting all that agonized confusion into a question carried on my name: *Cal?*

I looked at him with cold, dead eyes, no longer my brother Billy, but only a sack of breath whose breathing blocked my way to Dora. In a single shuddering instant, I felt all my passion surge in a mute and blackened prayer: *Die, William. Die!*

It was an instant, nothing more, a single, explosive

second, followed by a terrible seizure of recognition and self-loathing. 'Dear God,' I cried, dropped to my knees, gathered my brother into my arms, rushed him to the car, and raced to Doc Bradshaw's office, calling to him again and again, my voice like a lifeline flung to him across the engulfing waters, *Billy, hold on, please, hold on,* watching helplessly as he sank, *Billy, please, Billy,* deeper and deeper, drowning in his own lungs, *Billy, Billy,* until a final bubble of blood burst on his lips, carrying the name of the one he'd dreamed of all his life, *Dora.*

'You have to tell William that I loved him,' she said. *Billy . . .*

I looked at her softly. 'I will.'

'But, Cal, never tell him . . .'

. . . please . . .

'. . . about you.'

'No,' I said. 'No, I never will.'

. . . forgive me.

She rose, a curious relief lifting her, pleased that we'd come through this final meeting with what she took for grace. 'Come,' she said. 'Come with me. I want to show you something.'

She led me to the garden, then along its quiet lanes, pointing out the desert plants that grew there, how little they required, sunlight, a taste of rain. She would remain with the Sisters for another few weeks, she said, then move to some other place, where she hoped to serve in some way, 'be of use at last,' as she phrased it.

Finally, at the end of the day, as we stood beside my car, she drew the small porcelain figure she'd taken from Ed Dillard's house from her pocket, a young girl with long, blond hair, placed it in my hand, and folded my fingers around it. 'For you,' she said. 'Good-bye, Cal.'

'Good-bye, Dora.'

She stood in the drive as I pulled away. In the mirror, I saw her lift her hand in a last farewell, then grow small, a point of light, and finally disappear.

Had my soul been made of bone, I would have heard it crack.

Chapter Twenty-six

Henry Mason's long illness had overwhelmed him by the time I got back to Port Alma. He'd died in Portland Hospital, though not before penning a full confession of what he'd done, Dora's letter to Billy folded inside it.

'Henry wanted you to see these,' Hap said when he showed both to me.

In his letter, Henry described in an oddly formal language how he'd carefully copied Dora's script, writing fraudulent entries in the ledgers, never expecting the books to be checked. 'I was, of course, aware,' he wrote, 'that even should William review the books, he would never accuse Miss March of stealing from him. For it was common knowledge, often spoken of by the staff, that he was in love with her.'

The money had been for his retarded daughter Lois, Henry added. He'd stolen it because he was dying and needed to provide for her. 'It remains my hope,' he wrote, 'that some provision can be made for Lois, as she cannot, in my absence, provide for herself.'

As to Billy's death, it had occurred somewhat differently than I'd imagined it on the afternoon I'd sat with Dora in the convent garden. I'd been right that Henry had accused Dora of embezzlement, and right that Billy had seen through the ruse. But I'd been wrong about my brother's reaction. For rather than flying into a rage, he'd simply demanded to know where Dora was, what Henry had said or done to send her fleeing from Port Alma. Henry had attempted to leave, rushed through the kitchen, Billy in pursuit. It was there, according to Henry, that Billy tripped suddenly, a shattered leg giving way, and tumbled forward, knocking the kitchen knife from the table, then falling upon it with all his weight. 'On my soul, I swear that I did not murder William Chase,' Mason wrote. 'My crime was that I left him, knowing that without my assistance his wound would prove fatal.'

'So now we know what happened,' Hap said. He waited for my response. When I offered none, he said, 'Cal, what would you think about coming back to work for me?'

I shook my head.

'What do you plan to do?'

'I don't know,' I said.

He gave me one of his cautionary looks. 'Well, you know it's not good for a man to . . . Hell, I guess you know what's good for you.'

I knew only what was no longer good for me, prosecuting men and women whose suffering I knew nothing of, spending Saturday nights in Royston. Needing love too much.

'I'd better be going,' I said.

Hap looked at me sadly. 'How are your parents, Cal?'

'Dying,' I answered.

For the next three months I did all that was required to sustain them both.

Often, when I sat in the evening with my father, a silence would fall between us, but there were other times when we went over things, remembering what we could bear to remember, holding the rest inside. He remained stoical to the last, refusing all pity or self-pity. 'Better to die like Socrates,' he said, the last of his classical references. 'Remembering that you owe someone a chicken.'

He died the following spring.

I moved in with my mother a few days later.

During that long, sweltering summer, I fed and dressed her, kept her clean and as comfortable as I could.

In the evenings I would read to her as Billy had, though she made it clear that she could no longer bear the romantic poetry that had, until then, served as her guide through life.

As the airless summer days passed, she grew steadily weaker. She lost interest in the play of nature outside her window, the flight of birds in the overhanging sky, her eyes often fixed instead upon the copy of the *Sentinel* she kept on the table beside her bed, the one that carried Billy's obituary.

Then, one evening, as I was about to put out the light, she groaned, and I saw something dark gather in her eyes, as if, after a long meditation, she had reached a grim conclusion.

'What is it, Mother?' I asked.

She started to speak, then stopped, her mind turned inward.

'You can tell me.'

She looked at me brokenly, her face the shattered bust of the once-proud woman she had been. 'I murdered my son.'

'No,' I said. 'No, you didn't.'

Her voice shook with grief and regret. 'Snakes, Cal. He was just a little boy, and I put snakes in his head.'

'Mother, please.'

'Snakes.'

She slumped backward, and in that movement I saw the great wall of her self-assurance crumble into dust, the vast confidence she'd once had in her view of life, and remembered what Billy had said so many years before, that without it, she would surely die.

I bolted forward. 'You taught Billy how to love,' I told her desperately. 'And he did it well, Mother. To the very end.'

She seemed not to hear me, lifted her hand, and began to make the sign of the cross. '*Mea culpa.*'

'Don't.'

Her hand crossed her breast. '*Mea culpa.*'

'Stop it, please.'

'*Mea maxima culpa.*'

I snatched her hand from the dark air, held it to my chest. 'You never stopped loving him. Never. Not for a second. Not for the briefest . . .' My head dropped forward, heavy as a stone. 'But I . . . I . . .'

A silence settled upon us. Then, after a time, I felt her fingers in my hair.

'Cal?'

I looked up.

She watched me softly for a moment, then reached for the copy of the *Sentinel* that lay on the table beside her bed and lifted it toward me.

'What?' I asked.

She said nothing, only continued to hold the paper tremblingly in the air between us.

Then I knew.

'I can't take over the paper,' I told her. 'You said it yourself. Years ago. That I didn't have the heart for it.'

She gazed at me more tenderly than she ever had. Her voice was barely a whisper. 'Now you do,' she said.

She died the next morning. I buried her amid a flurry of red leaves.

A few weeks later, I started the paper up again, honoring what had seemed to me the last wish of a great example.

I rehired the old staff, then added Lois Mason, Henry's daughter, to it, teaching her to sweep and clean, greet whoever stepped up to the front desk with her childlike smile.

And each Sunday, I visited their graves. To my mother, I brought mountain laurel. To my father, ivy. To Billy, always a single bloodred rose.

Spring came early the next year, melting the snow first from the cliffs of MacAndrews Island, then from the lip of the seawall, finally from the earthen mounds beneath which, in endless night, my brother Billy slept.

'You're Cal Chase.'

I looked up from the rose I'd just placed upon his grave.

'You came by my house in Royston,' she said. She offered her hand. 'Rachel Bass.' She pointed to a small stone memorial. 'My husband. I always come here on the anniversary.'

'Of his death?'

She shook her head. 'Of his life. I come once a year. On his birthday.'

'I come every Sunday.'

Her eyes touched the rose. 'You must have loved your brother very much.'

A wave of grief washed over me. 'I can't get over it,' I admitted.

She gazed at me softly. 'Maybe you're not meant to, Cal,' she said.

Then she took my arm, and together we made our way down the hill, talking quietly as we passed beneath the old iron gate, then moved on beyond it, through the reeds, and over the pebbled ground, to where the gulls dove and circled, crying distantly in the cold blue air, and the sea swept out forever.

All Orion/Phoenix titles are available at your local bookshop or from the following address:

> Mail Order Department
> Littlehampton Book Services
> FREEPOST BR535
> Worthing, West Sussex, BN13 3BR
> *telephone* 01903 828503, *facsimile* 01903 828802
> *e-mail* MailOrders@lbsltd.co.uk
> (Please ensure that you include full postal address details)

Payment can be made either by credit/debit card (Visa, Mastercard, Access and Switch accepted) or by sending a £ Sterling cheque or postal order made payable to *Littlehampton Book Services*.
DO NOT SEND CASH OR CURRENCY.

Please add the following to cover postage and packing

UK and BFPO:
£1.50 for the first book, and 50p for each additional book to a maximum of £3.50

Overseas and Eire:
£2.50 for the first book plus £1.00 for the second book and 50p for each additional book ordered

---

BLOCK CAPITALS PLEASE

name of cardholder _____   *delivery address*
_____   *(if different from cardholder)*
address of cardholder _____   _____
_____   _____
_____   _____
_____   _____
postcode _____   *postcode* _____

☐ I enclose my remittance for £_____

☐ please debit my Mastercard/Visa/Access/Switch (delete as appropriate)

card number ☐☐☐☐ ☐☐☐☐ ☐☐☐☐ ☐☐☐☐

expiry date ☐☐☐☐   Switch issue no. ☐☐

signature _____

prices and availability are subject to change without notice